Running Homeless

RUNNING HOMELESS

AL LAMANDA

FIVE STAR
A part of Gale, Cengage Learning

GALE
CENGAGE Learning™

Detroit • New York • San Francisco • New Haven, Conn • Waterville, Maine • London

GALE
CENGAGE Learning˜

LIBRARY OF CONGRESS CATALOGING-IN-PUBLICATION DATA

Lamanda, Al.
 Running homeless / Al Lamanda. — 1st ed.
 p. cm.
 ISBN-13: 978-1-4328-2538-6 (hardcover)
 ISBN-10: 1-4328-2538-0 (hardcover)
 1. Amnesia—Fiction. 2. Identity theft—Fiction. 3. Government investigators—Fiction. 4. Psychological fiction. I. Title.
 PS3612.A5433R86 2011
 813'.6—dc22   2011013173

First Edition. First Printing: July 2011.
Published in 2011 in conjunction with Tekno Books and Ed Gorman.

b19686298

For Ethan and Lois.

ONE

Bone-dry heat rose off the desert floor to slap you in the face. Even at night, the heat was oppressive. Breathing was difficult, as if trying to suck air through a thick wool blanket. He took shallow breaths, which had a calming effect on his mind and body. Sweat, which should have been pouring off his skin, wasn't flowing. That's how you got into trouble in the desert. Sweat evaporates on contact with the air, creating the illusion that the body isn't losing fluids. If you don't drink enough water to replenish those lost fluids, heatstroke overtakes you, bakes the brain, and death soon follows.

From his perch behind the wire fence that surrounded the small, private airport, he took several sips of water from a quart bottle hung on his belt. He wanted to smoke, but resisted the urge. At night, even the tiny flame of a match could be seen for hundreds of yards. He settled for a stick of spearmint gum instead. As he chewed, he looked at the massive stainless-steel Rolex on his wrist. It was painted black to prevent reflecting light at night. The time was twelve-forty A.M. If the plane were on time, it would land in twenty minutes. If it were on time. Flying at night was a difficult enough task; flying a small aircraft under the radar on a moonless night had to be particularly trying for even a highly skilled pilot.

He picked up the night-vision binoculars, turned on the power and used them to scan the immediate area surrounding the airport office. Harnessing a minuscule amount of light, the binoculars allowed him to see in near-total darkness, although with a green tint. He remembered from somewhere that the color green is the easiest color for the human eye to see in darkness. With or without the binoculars, he knew that the human eye was sensitive to movement at night. That was why you could see a mouse scurrying across the floor in a dark room. If the mouse stood still in the shadows, chances are you would never see it.

However, mice were not on his menu tonight. Humans were. Specifically, men. If the intel was correct, six of them. Four arriving in the plane, two on the ground, probably inside the office right now, drinking coffee.

He scanned the area around the office, the hangar, and the runway, but saw no movement. He trained the binoculars on the office windows, but if the men were inside, they stayed away from the windows. That was smart. That's what he would have done. Minimizing the risk until the last possible moment enhanced the chance for success. Exposure, even brief, reduces the success ratio. You never know who might be watching. Waiting. Planning an ambush.

He glanced at his watch again. Seventeen minutes to the hour. If the plane were on time, in a few minutes he should hear the faint sound of the engines. He heard a noise and used the binoculars to trace it to the source. A hangar door was opening. A man stepped out, visible in faint outline. The man was smoking a cigarette. He could see the red ember glow brightly as the man inhaled.

The man was confident he wasn't at risk. That was a serious mistake. Knowing that risk was always present, was always just around the next corner, separated the amateur from the professional and the living from the dead.

At least in this line of work.

His line of work.

He concentrated on seeing the man's face in the binoculars. The man was about forty, with thick, heavy features, a strong chin and receding hairline. The man inhaled on the cigarette again and the end glowed bright red.

He lowered the binoculars and focused his eyes on the tiny red dot in the dark. If he had a high-powered rifle with a good scope, he could have put one right through the center of the man's skull.

He stared at the red dot, fascinated by the tiny spark of light against a backdrop of black.

She said, "How do you feel tonight, John?" Her voice was soothing, a constant like an old friend.

He was in the serving line at the mission in San Diego. Holding a tray of hot food, he looked at her from where she stood opposite the counter. "Fine," he said.

"That's good," she said. "Don't forget, you have a doctor's appointment at four."

"Am I sick?" he said, more a question than a concern.

She smiled. "No, John, you're not sick. It's just your yearly physical. We need to keep you in the pink if you're to keep helping out around here."

He nodded. "That reminds me. We need at least eight more bundles of shingles for the west roof. I'll be out by tonight."

"Write down what you need and I'll see to it that it gets delivered," she said.

He nodded and walked away to an empty table by the window where he could look out while he ate. As usual, the sun shone brightly and the temperature stayed right around eighty degrees, although the breeze coming off the ocean kept things comfortable while on the roof.

Outside the window, some men from the mission hung around after eating lunch. Their clothes were seedy, as were their hair and beards. Not that his own clothes weren't just as used, but he laundered them regularly in the mission laundromat and did his best not to rip or wear them out. If something happened to be torn, he repaired it with a sewing kit stored under his bed. He shaved often, three or four times per week. He wore his graying hair short in almost a crew cut, not to be fashionable but because it was easier to deal with in the heat.

Spending so much time shirtless on the roof lately had tanned his skin and given his face a hardened, leathery appearance. It made him look mean and angry, he thought, although neither was true. He didn't feel mean at all, though he tended to stay aloof and he could be perceived that way by others living in the mission. Angry wasn't even on the table. How could he be angry about anything when he couldn't remember a single thing about his life?

Amnesia, they said. Caused by blunt force trauma, they said. He may or may not regain partial or full memory, they said. In the meantime, he didn't know one damn thing about his life. Not who he was, how he lost his memory, if he had a family or how he arrived at the mission. Just what they told him, which wasn't much. That he was taken by ambulance from San Diego General to the mission after a month's stay a year ago. How he arrived at SDG, neither he nor anybody else had a clue.

She was suddenly at his table. A small notepad and pen were in her hands. "You said eight bundles of shingles?" she said.

"That should finish off the west roof," he said. "I won't know about the south roof until I get up there."

She nodded and scribbled on the pad. "Anything else?" He watched her write. She had beautiful hands, sensual fingers. He'd read or heard somewhere that you could tell a great deal about a woman from her hands. What that was, he had no idea.

"Maybe another dozen boxes of nails for the roofing gun," he said. "And knee pads, the kind made for roofers. It's rough on the knees up there."

She made another note. He watched her write on the pad. She was a striking-looking woman of thirty-five or six, with shoulder-length *dark hair and piercing, coal-black eyes. The tip of her tongue poked out between her full lips as she moved the pen along the paper. It was very sensual to watch.*

"I'll take care of this today," she said. "Just don't forget your doctor's appointment."

"Four o'clock," he said. "I won't forget, Julie."

She smiled at him.

He suddenly became aware that the red ember of the cigarette was no longer visible. He scanned the area with the binoculars, but the man was gone. Probably returned to the office. He glanced at his watch. Twelve minutes to one. As he removed the wrapper from another stick of gum, he heard the faint sound of a plane engine. He scanned the dark skies, but was unable to pick it up just yet. Judging from the sound, he figured it was ten minutes from its runway approach.

Then, suddenly, the runway lights came on and the landing strip was a beacon in the dark, deserted desert canyons. He didn't look at the lights because they would ruin his night vision, and it would take a good half hour to get it back. Instead, he focused on the airport office. A light had come on and he could see the outline of two men at the window. They, like him, were waiting for the plane to land.

But for altogether different reasons.

James Farris read all the reports several times before making the decision to call in his second-in-command, Ben Freeman. At sixty-two years of age, Farris had grown cautious about who he delegated assignments to. With just ten months to his retirement, Farris had spent the past year grooming Freeman as heir to his throne, so Freeman drew assignments only when classified a Level Five priority, which this one was.

Farris picked up a file, opened it and glanced at the contents one more time. Behind him, bright sunlight shone through the window that faced the Washington Monument. In another hour, he would close the drapes or bake from the heat. Even with the AC on high, that sun on your neck baked the skin raw.

He closed the file and made a small notation in the top right-hand corner. The notation was in code, a code that only he and Freeman could decipher. When Freeman took Farris' chair, he would create his own personal code, but for now, Farris' code was the word of the day.

Ten more months and his life's work would come to fruition. His pension, though substantial, would come from some obscure government agency no one had heard of or would question, not even Congress. He had stocks, bonds, investments and a personal 401(k) in excess of a million, more than enough to make his retirement years comfortable. The thing was, he wanted to go out on top with one more major assignment under his already impressive belt. The fighter's mentality, he supposed. More likely, his ego.

The file on his desk was just such an assignment.

Ben Freeman arrived exactly on time. Farris expected no less. At forty-six, Freeman stood six foot two and had the wide build of a well-conditioned athlete. The only concession to Freeman's age that Farris could see was a slight graying of his thick, dark hair around the ears.

Freeman took the chair opposite the desk. Farris said, "I'll come right to the point on this one, Ben. Extreme prejudice is called for, nothing less. Understood?"

"What's the mission?" Freeman said quietly.

Farris spoke freely. His office was above reproach, above eavesdropping and the usual Washington leaks and bullshit. "The government of an unnamed country in South America finances its military through drug trafficking into the States. DEA has been working in conjunction with the FBI and Homeland Security to shut this operation down. Twice a month, a plane delivers shipments of cocaine and heroin to a private airport in New Mexico that operates as a training

school. *Two men own the school and are the contacts for the cartel
that makes the delivery. Make it known that the operation is closed
and that any additional activity by this government on American
soil will not be tolerated.*"

"*Extreme prejudice,*" Freeman said.

"*Yes.*"

"*Timeline?*"

"*The next shipment is in exactly two weeks.*"

Freeman nodded, then said, "*I've used John Tibbets twice since his
relocation to San Diego. I think he can handle this job.*"

"*Alone?*"

"*An extraction team to shut him down, but otherwise, yes, alone.*"

"*He's still that good?*"

"*He's aging like fine wine, James,*" Freeman said. "*Plus, if
something should go wrong, it's the mad ravings of a homeless
amnesia victim.*"

"*But, nothing will go wrong.*"

"*No.*"

"*Contact Doctor Monroe and have him begin prep work on Tibbets immediately,*" Farris said.

"*Should I go along as part of the extraction team?*" Freeman said.

"*I don't think that's necessary,*" Farris said. "*You're not a field
agent anymore and besides, if the extraction team is good, you won't
be needed.*"

Freeman nodded. "*I'll give Monroe a call right away.*"

The twin-engine propeller plane came in low against the
backdrop of dark sky. The man at the controls knew what he
was doing. He brought her in at an airspeed of about sixty-five
knots and touched down on the runway with the lightness of a
feather hitting ground.

The time was three minutes past one A.M. He removed the
wire cutters from his belt and snipped a hole in the fence large

enough for him to fit through. By the time he was on the other side, the plane had rolled to a stop in front of the hangar doors.

He removed the twin, blued Ruger .22-caliber pistols from the small of his back, inserted twenty-round magazines into each and racked the slide. On the end of each pistol, he secured a four-inch-long black silencer. Always assemble your gear last so you're positive you didn't overlook something.

Men were emerging from the plane.

He started walking toward them. He was in no particular hurry and moved with the grace and fluidity of a cat in its prime about to undertake a hunt.

Two men emerged from the office to meet the men coming off the plane.

The Ruger pistols felt like extensions of his hands, like they were a part of his flesh and blood and bones.

Four men had exited the plane now, upping the total to six men in all.

He closed the gap to five hundred feet. He was walking from shadow into light, and even if they'd had time to allow their eyes to adjust, he would be difficult to see. They were shaking hands, distracted by each other's company.

He closed the gap to three hundred feet, then two hundred.

They turned and started walking toward the office.

The gap closed to one hundred feet, then fifty.

One of the men from the plane must have sensed something, because he slowly turned and peered into the shadows. He appeared confused and he died with that look on his face as he took two shots to the head. The silenced Ruger pistols produced little more than a cough, but the man's violent reaction as he fell caused the remaining five men to turn around.

One man screamed when bits of skull and blood splattered onto his shoulders. Two rounds in the face silenced him.

The other four, confused, but frightened into action, started to run for cover. He was close now, just ten or twelve feet from them, and it became target practice. He shot the third man twice in the head. The fourth man threw himself to the ground, but he shot him once in the neck and once more in the face, and he was dead before he landed.

The remaining two men put their hands above their heads. He put two shots between the eyes of the fifth man. As the sixth man started to cry and beg for his life, he shot him point-blank in the head.

Set back off the road around the perimeter of the airport, Freeman's crew of six agents watched the scene unfold outside the hangar on a closed-circuit television monitor. Earlier, an agent had installed a mini camera on the fence that was equipped with night-vision capabilities.

As the plane landed, Tibbets emerged from the shadows and used the cutters to penetrate the fence. They watched as he made his way toward the six men.

"He's getting ready to rock and roll," an agent commented.

"Is this guy as good as Ben said he is?" another agent said.

"I don't know," the first agent said. "We'll find out soon enough."

They watched the monitor with intense curiosity, anxious to see what would happen. Their curiosity quickly turned to silent awe as he went about the task of assassination with the skill and timing of a master surgeon. In less than eight seconds, all six men were dead.

The agent closest to the monitor said, "Holy motherfucking shit."

The leader of the four-man extraction team said, "Give him a second to reprocess and shut down, then we'll move out."

He looked at the six dead men at his feet. Six men, twelve bullets, less than eight seconds. He tucked the Ruger pistols into the waistband of his pants, then reached into a pocket of his light windbreaker for his cigarettes. He cupped his hands to hide the tiny flame of the match, then took a long, satisfying puff.

With his right foot, he turned over a body to look at the man's face. The dead man had the thick features and skin color of a South American, but of which country there was no way to know by looking at him.

Suddenly, the Rolex on his wrist started to beep. He didn't remember setting the alarm. He raised his wrist and looked at the massive watch. He wanted to shut the alarm off, but he hesitated. He found himself staring at the black face of the Rolex, transfixed by some unknown force that tugged at him.

Shirtless, John sat on Doctor Monroe's examination table while the doctor listened to his heart with a stethoscope. In the corner of the room, Ben Freeman waited until Monroe completed the physical, then said, "So how is he?"

"Remarkably fit," Monroe said.

"I can see that," Freeman said. "I meant up here." He tapped his forehead with a finger.

Monroe smiled and turned to John. "John, how do you feel?"

"Fine," John said.

"Are you ready for your mission?" Monroe said.

"Yes."

"And what is your mission?"

"To terminate a drug cartel with extreme prejudice."

"Extreme?"

"Yes," John said. "Extreme."

"How do we turn him off when the mission is completed?" Freeman said.

"Preprogrammed suggestion," Monroe said. He removed a heavy,

black Rolex watch from the pocket of his white lab coat and held it up for John to see. "John, when you hear the alarm on this watch sound, what will you do?"

John looked at the watch. "Wait."

"For what?" Monroe said.

"The extraction team to take me home," John said.

Freeman looked at Monroe. "I don't know how you do it," he said.

"It isn't that difficult when you work with the same subject over a period of years," Monroe said. "There's a comfort level."

"Can I take him?" Freeman said.

"Yes."

"And he'll answer to me just like the other times?" Freeman said.

"Tell him something," Monroe said.

Freeman looked at John. "Put your shirt on, John. We have to leave now."

John stood up from the examination table and reached for his shirt. At six foot two inches tall, Freeman wasn't used to looking up at people, but damned if John didn't tower over him. Even in middle age, John Tibbets was no one to mess with. Freeman knew that only too well.

"I need him back in one week," Monroe said. "After that, the posthypnotic suggestions weaken and he'll be more difficult to control."

"I know," Freeman said. "Not to worry."

"But I do, Ben," Monroe said. "Like a father sending his son off to war."

The four men that made up the extraction team cautiously exited the van and made their way down to the airport. They were dressed all in black, including Kevlar vests, and carried M16 rifles slung over their right shoulders and nine-millimeter pistols in holsters on their belts. They were experienced, highly trained men, ex-military handpicked by Ben Freeman for their suitability.

They reached the hole in the fence and silently passed through it. The team leader spotted Tibbets by the hangar and motioned with his right hand, giving a point-look signal. John appeared to be doing exactly what Freeman had said he would do upon hearing his watch alarm sound. Stand and wait.

The team leader led his men closer to their target.

Two

Inside the van, Johnson and Becker—the remaining two members of the extraction team—watched the monitor closely. The four-man approach team made their way toward John, slowly and carefully, staying in the shadows to avoid detection.

"Go to Tibbets," Johnson said. "Freeman wants complete surveillance video for the archives."

Becker used a remote control to pan the tiny camera and zoom in on John, who stood waiting beside the hangar door.

"He's just standing there," Johnson said.

"That's what he's supposed to do."

"Wait," Johnson said. "It looks like he's moving."

"Zoom in," Becker said.

Something made him take another look at his watch. Only eight minutes had passed since he first entered the airport through the hole in the fence. The alarm hadn't sounded again, yet his attention was drawn to the watch. He wondered why. He knew he was supposed to wait for the extraction team, yet he couldn't stop looking at the damned watch.

Beads of sweat formed on his forehead. A bead trickled down into his eye and he wiped the eye with a finger.

Something was wrong. He could feel it, sense it.

Something.

What?

★ ★ ★ ★ ★

Inside the van, Becker and Johnson continued to watch the monitor. Becker zoomed in on John's face, which appeared green in night vision. "He seems okay," he said.

"Yeah, yeah, I guess so," Johnson said.

"Should we call in the FBI?"

"Wait until he's in the van. That's what Freeman said."

"Sure."

They continued to watch the monitor. The four-man team came into view behind John and stopped twenty feet from him. For a few seconds nobody moved. Then the team leader stepped forward. He moved silently, gracefully toward John, and John turned to look at him.

"Looks good, looks good," Becker said by remote to the team leader.

Suddenly John reached behind his back and pulled his pistols. It happened so fast, they almost missed it. In the blink of an eye, John shot the team leader twice in the head. As the man fell backward, the remaining three team members slung their M16 rifles from their shoulders.

"Oh my God, oh my God," Becker cried.

John turned and fired six more shots at the remaining three men, putting two into each of their skulls.

Johnson said, "Jesus Christ, he's killed the extraction team."

He looked at the four men dressed in black. They were dead, like the other six. Had the six killed the extraction team? Is that why they were here, to kill him next?

He didn't plan to stick around and find out. He turned to run, paused and turned back around. Instinct drove his next move as he went through the pockets of the ten corpses and removed all of their cash. One man had a four-inch serrated folding knife, and he took that along with the money.

Scanning the immediate area and the shadows for movement, he was satisfied he was alone and walked toward the exit gate of the airport.

Inside the van, both men panicked.

"Jesus mother of God, he killed them," Becker said. "He fucking killed them."

"Shut up," Johnson shouted. "Shut the fuck up."

"Where is he? Do you see him? Where is he?"

"Gone."

"Gone? How could he be gone? Gone where?"

Johnson turned to look at Becker. "You want to go after him, see if you can talk him down?"

At his home in Virginia just across the Potomac, Freeman was killing time watching *True Grit* on the Classics Film Channel. A creature of habit, he knew he would never be able to sleep while a mission was in progress until the call came in with the final results. Like a doctor who knew his patient would live, but wanted to see test results just the same.

Not that he was overly concerned, just cautious. He'd handpicked top men for the mission—but John Tibbets, even controlled by drugs and brainwashing, was in a completely different league than the average field agent.

He wanted a beer, but settled for coffee and a cigarette. His mind must have wandered, because the movie had started with a young Kim Darby burying her father, who was murdered by a hired hand—played by an unknown at the time named Robert Duvall. When he zoned back in, John Wayne, the one-eyed marshal, was kicking an outlaw in the ass.

He looked at his watch. Twenty minutes had passed. He sipped his coffee. It was cold. He went to the kitchen to dump it and fill the cup with fresh brew, then returned to the sofa to smoke another cigarette.

He watched some more of the movie. Right when Glenn Campbell was about to spank Kim Darby at the dinner table, Freeman's landline phone rang. The number was unlisted. In fact, the number didn't exist in any phone company records. It was routed. Although the number had a DC area code, his phone in Virginia received the incoming call.

He answered on the second ring. "Freeman."

"Ben, it's Johnson. I'm in the van," the man on the other end said.

Freeman knew something had gone wrong by the tone in Johnson's voice. "I'm listening."

"He's . . . he's gone," Johnson said. "I mean Tibbets."

"I know who you mean, you fucking idiot," Freeman said. "Tell me what happened that made him gone."

"He took out the targets like clockwork," Johnson said. "It was over in seconds."

Freeman could visualize John going about his work with the precision of open-heart surgery. A killing machine. "And then?" Freeman said.

"The team went to retrieve him and . . . he turned on them," Johnson said. "It happened so fast, I could hardly believe what I was watching."

"Dead?" Freeman said.

"Sir?"

"The extraction team, did he kill them?"

"Yes."

"And?"

"Sir?"

"Did you pursue him, Johnson?" Freeman said, feeling his patience wane. "Did you leave the van and pursue Tibbets?"

"No, sir," Johnson said. "We're support techs, not field agents. He would have just killed us, too."

22

Freeman sighed and lit a fresh cigarette off the spent one. "His watch is a GPS unit, Johnson. I'm sending you a feed. Follow him from a safe distance until a backup crew arrives. Understood?"

"Yes, sir," Johnson said.

"And Johnson, don't let him see you."

"Yes, sir," Johnson said again.

Freeman severed the call and immediately dialed the routed number for Farris. The man was sound asleep, but woke up as if struck by a bolt of lightning when Freeman told him the situation.

"Meet me in my office immediately," Farris said. "Monroe is staying at the downtown Marriott. Pick him up on the way in."

Johnson stared at the GPS unit in the dashboard of the van. Becker sat next to him and gently rocked back and forth in his seat.

"Would you stop that fucking rocking," Johnson snapped.

"This is taking too long," Becker said. "The GPS should have . . ."

The GPS unit suddenly activated. A map of the airport, land and surrounding roads appeared on the screen. A blip indicating Tibbets' watch moved along the main road outside the airport gate.

"That's him," Becker said.

"Really?" Johnson said. "Ya don't say."

"How do you want to play this?"

"Freeman said to follow him, but not get too close."

"How close is not too close?" Becker said.

"How far can he shoot?"

John walked along the road, not knowing where it led, but every road—even one as desolate as this one—led somewhere, and somewhere was better than where he was. It was too dark to see much of his surroundings. Desert wasteland surrounded the road on each side, but the question in his mind was what desert and where? Arizona, Texas, Nevada, New Mexico, California, it all looked the same in the dark and without a reference point to distinguish one from the other.

The other question was, how far would he have to walk before he reached a town or at the very least, a gas station? He didn't have much water or food, but he could last a few days if it came down to that. He looked at his watch. It was one fifty-nine in the morning, but he wasn't tired in the least. He would walk until he reached a town or until sunrise, whichever came first. If by sunrise he was still on the road, he would find a shady spot for a quick nap.

The watch alarm went off again. He didn't remember setting it for two A.M. and shut it off by pressing the button on the side. The alarm must have been set to remind him of something, but what?

But what?

This was one of the few times in his career that Freeman saw Farris without a suit and tie in his office. Hastily dressed in slacks and pullover shirt, Farris sat behind his desk and looked at Freeman and Monroe through red, sleep-swollen eyes.

In crisis mode, Farris was more direct than usual. "What went wrong?" he said, more to Monroe than Freeman.

"I don't know," Monroe admitted. Wearing a bathrobe over pajamas, he'd barely had time to comb his hair before Freeman pulled him from his hotel room.

"You don't know," Farris said.

"I don't, no," Monroe said with flat honesty.

"Guess," Farris said.

Monroe glanced at Freeman, who sat next to him in a chair.

Freeman was smoking a cigarette and sipping coffee from a deli container. The smoke was bothering Monroe a bit, but he tried to ignore it. "I can't say with any certainty at this point," he said. "But I can speculate that the posthypnotic suggestion didn't have the desired result."

"He killed the entire extraction team in less time that it takes to say it, so I would say it's a fair bet that the posthypnotic suggestion didn't have the desired result," Farris said. "The question is why?"

"I can't say for certain until I have the opportunity to examine him," Monroe answered. "That said, John Tibbets is extremely strong-willed and his mind has been through a great deal of trauma. It's possible something snapped as past met present and they canceled each other out."

"Forget strong-willed," Farris said. "What John Tibbets is most of all, is extremely dangerous. Perhaps the most dangerous man alive, so don't give me 'something snapped.' I need answers and I need them now."

Monroe took his scolding and remained quiet. Farris was not a man to give excuses to, especially on so important a topic.

Farris turned his attention to Freeman. "I stand corrected, Ben," he said. "Your instinct to go along on this one was correct."

"Not important now, James," Freeman said, accepting his bone. "The FBI will be arriving at the airport in thirty minutes. We'll have a great deal of explaining to do concerning the extraction team, but I'm sure they'll cooperate with us because they'll be taking the credit for the raid on the airport. My two field techs are tracking John by GPS, and I'll ask the FBI to pick him up using their information."

"Just like that?" Farris said.

"Nothing is ever just like that when it comes to John Tibbets," Freeman said.

"They will have to be told," Farris said. "We can't have FBI agents go after him without knowing what they're dealing with."

"Agreed," Freeman said.

Softly, Monroe said, "There is something else."

Farris and Freeman looked at him. "Yes," Farris said.

"At two A.M., his watch alarm will sound again," Monroe said. "It will wipe out all memory of what happened at the airport."

"Why did you do that?" Farris said.

"To make him easier to control."

"If in lockdown," Farris said. "Out in the open?"

"Not knowing who he is, what he's done, will only make him that much more dangerous," Monroe said. "Like a caged lion that can't see its attacker."

"Well, that's just fucking great," Freeman said.

"Those FBI agents," Farris said.

Freeman stood up from his chair. "I'm on it, James."

Up ahead, the road curved into a near-hairpin turn. Why there was a need for such a turn in the middle of nowhere was anyone's guess. As he walked into the turn, he paused for a moment to light a cigarette. The night air was still and heavy, and he was perspiring heavily under the windbreaker. He removed the jacket and tied it around his waist, then took a sip from the water bottle and splashed a bit on his face. He was about to move out again when he heard a faint sound behind him, maybe five hundred yards to the west.

He turned to face the noise for maximum exposure to the sound waves. It sounded like the engine of a car approaching at very slow speed. Too slow to be traveling to a destination, just fast enough to be following him.

Why would someone be following him?

John left the road and stood behind the cover of a cactus

tree. After a few seconds, the approaching sound of the car engine seemed to stop in place, as if someone had stepped on the brakes.

There was no question now. Someone was following him.

John tossed the cigarette and stepped on it. Then he pulled one of the Ruger pistols and turned away from the tree.

Inside the van, Becker said, "Stop. Hit the brakes."

Johnson hit the brakes and looked at Becker. "What?"

"The GPS," Becker said. "Look."

The movement they were tracking had stopped several hundred yards ahead of the van. "Maybe he's taking a rest?" Johnson suggested.

"He just suddenly decided to sit down on the road?" Becker said. "And rest?"

"I don't fucking know," Johnson said. "Watch the damn thing and see what he does next."

"It's moving. He's moving," Becker said.

"Backwards," Johnson said.

"Kill the lights," Becker said.

Johnson turned off the headlights. A thick wall of darkness surrounded them. Becker hit the battery switch on the GPS and it came back to life. The blip that was John Tibbets continued making its way toward them.

"He's not going backwards," Johnson said. "He's looking for us."

"Freeman said he wouldn't remember," Becker said. "Why would he be looking for us?"

"I know what Freeman said, but Freeman ain't fucking here and we are," Johnson said. "And this bloodthirsty son of a bitch is stalking us."

"What are you saying?"

"Look at the GPS," Johnson said. "He's a hundred feet in

front of us. I say we turn around before it's too late and wait for the FBI."

"I agree," Becker said. "Go."

Johnson started the engine, made a three-quarter U-turn and hit the gas. He drove a hundred yards in the dark before turning on the lights. Watching the GPS, Becker said, "He stopped."

"What?"

"Tibbets. He stopped."

Johnson slowed the van to a stop and looked at the GPS. "He really is following us, the son of a bitch."

"They should be at the airport by now," Becker said. "Go."

THREE

From twenty feet into the woods, John watched the van make a U-turn and drive away. He stopped walking, and a few seconds later the van slowed to a stop in the middle of the road. If there was any doubt in his mind they were following him, that doubt was now removed.

John walked to the center of the road and watched the van a hundred feet in front of him. It was too dark for whoever was inside to see him, so he gave them something to look at by striking a match and lighting a cigarette.

Johnson had driven twenty feet when the flame of John's match caught his eye in the rearview mirror. He hit the brakes.

"What?" Becker said.

"Turn around. Look," Johnson said.

Both men turned around and looked through the rear windshield. They saw the red ember of John's cigarette as he took a puff on it.

"The son of a bitch is smoking," Becker said. "He knows we're here and he doesn't care if we see him."

"Let's get the hell out of here," Johnson said, and hit the gas.

They never heard the shots, but the rear window shattered. Two bullet holes appeared in the front windshield, spider-webbing the glass.

"Shit, shit, go," Becker cried. "He's shooting at us."

Johnson floored the gas, and the van raced forward as two

29

more shots came flying their way.

John smiled as the van sped away. His aim was dead center between the two men occupying the front seats, so he knew he didn't hit anyone. He wanted to scare them off and he'd succeeded. That told him whoever was in the van wasn't used to being fired upon. They got rattled and took off, the sign of a panicked amateur.

John returned the pistol to the small of his back, turned and walked back into the shadows.

Special Agent in Charge Richard Cone was unhappy. Not because six dead scumbags got what they deserved, but because four government agents who didn't died along with them. Even after twenty years on the job, it still hit home when one of his own went down. It woke you up and made you realize just how vulnerable you were, no matter how well trained or careful. Something, as was the case tonight, could always go wrong.

Cone turned to Johnson and Becker. "You have the event on disc?"

"In the van," Johnson said.

"I want to see it," Cone said.

They entered the van, and Becker found the place and played it on the monitor for Cone. "Holy motherfucking shit," Cone said as he watched John.

"That's what I said," Becker said.

"Who is this guy?"

"We don't know," Johnson said. "We don't have high-enough clearance to know that, just his name."

"Your office said you're tracking him on GPS," Cone said.

Becker glanced at the GPS unit. "He's on foot a few miles down the road."

"Let's go get him," Cone said.

Becker and Johnson exchanged glances.

"What?" Cone said.

"Just us?" Becker said.

"I'll take three of my men if it will make you feel better," Cone said as he looked at the monitor.

"It doesn't," Becker said.

Another vehicle was approaching. John could tell it wasn't the van by the sound of the engine. The van sounded powerful and well tuned. This engine sounded like it was misfiring and out of synch, probably due to fouled sparkplugs and being long overdue for an oil change.

John walked close to the road and took cover behind a tree. As the vehicle came closer, he could see headlights in the distance. He waited until the headlights were fifty feet away, then stepped out onto the road.

The vehicle braked. It was a pickup, at least twenty years old. In the headlights, he could read the license plate. New Mexico.

So that's where he was.

Slowly, with his hands raised, John approached the pickup. "I need a ride. Can you help me?"

An old woman stuck her head out of the driver's-side window. "You damn fool," she shouted. "What the hell's the matter with you?"

"Sorry," John said. "I didn't mean to frighten you."

"I ain't frightened, you damn idiot," the woman shouted. "I got a twelve-gauge double-barrel on the seat that would bring down a grizzly. It's my eyes. They don't work so good as when I was young. Come closer."

John walked closer to the pickup and stopped a few feet from the driver's-side door. "I need a lift," he said. "Can you help me?"

"Car break down?" the old woman said.

"By the airport," John said.

"I passed the airport. I didn't see a car."

"On the road from the airport."

"From the airport? It's closed after ten."

"I know," John said. "I'm passing through and took a wrong turn. I got a flat making a U-turn and don't have a spare. I figure I'll find a motel for the night and hire a tow truck in the morning."

"Town is twelve miles," the old woman said. "Only one motel. You'll have to wake the owner."

"So you'll give me a ride?" John said.

The old woman peered at John, squinting to see him in the dark. "I'll give you a ride, but mind you, I got one hand on my shotgun."

John smiled. "Don't worry. All I want is a ride."

"Get in," the old woman said.

While Johnson drove, Cone and Becker kept a close eye on the GPS unit. "Something's wrong," Cone said.

"How do you mean?" Johnson said.

"Either his watch is malfunctioning or he can run fifty miles an hour," Cone said. "Or, he found someone to give him a ride."

"He's fifteen miles ahead of us," Becker said.

"What's the range on his watch?" Cone said.

"I don't know," Becker admitted. "We don't have . . ."

"High-enough clearance," Cone said.

"Right."

"Close the gap to a couple of miles," Cone said. "Let's see where he's going."

The old woman pulled the pickup into the dark parking lot of a railroad-style motel. There were sixteen units and three parked cars.

"It's off season," the old woman said. "You won't have no trouble getting a room. Just ring the bell until the old fool that owns this place answers the door."

"Can I pay you for the gas?" John said.

"No need," the old woman said. "I pass by on my way home."

"Thanks again," John said and opened his car door.

"He's hard of hearing, so give the bell a good push," the old woman said.

Watching the GPS unit, Cone said, "He's stopped. How far ahead of us is he?"

Becker read the GPS monitor. "Four miles."

Cone turned to look at the three agents in the back of the van. "Nobody leaves the van without a vest. Weapons on single shot unless I direct full automatic fire."

Johnson glanced at Becker. "We need him alive, Agent Cone," Johnson said.

"That's entirely up to him," Cone said.

The first thing John did upon entering the motel room was to remove his windbreaker, shirt, T-shirt and watch and wash up at the bathroom sink. Directly from the tap, he drank his fill of cold water.

He lit a cigarette, removed the two pistols from the waistband of his pants and took a seat in the chair opposite the bed. He knew he was in New Mexico, but that was all he knew. How he'd arrived, or why he was here, he had no clue about. And the guns, why did he have them? He wasn't in law enforcement that he knew of and they certainly weren't police weapons, not silenced .22s like that.

Luckily, the owner of the motel didn't ask for his name or

ID, because he would have been stumped for an answer. He paid the man double for the room and the man gave him the key, no questions asked.

His stomach rumbled. He asked and the motel owner told him there was an all-night gas station a half mile up the road that had snacks. He stood up, put on the T-shirt, shirt and windbreaker, and at the last minute tucked the pistols into the small of his back. He left the room, leaving the light on and the Rolex watch on the nightstand.

Cone looked at the GPS unit. "Are you sure?" he said.

"He hasn't moved in twenty minutes," Becker said. "He has to be at this motel."

Cone looked out the window at the sixteen-unit motel. "Wake the manager," he said. "Find out which room he's in."

"There are only three cars in the lot," Johnson said. He looked at Cone. "My guess is Tibbets is in the room with the light on."

"We need to be sure," Cone said. "How accurate is that thing?"

"Hold on," Becker said. He pushed some program buttons on the GPS and received the strongest signal from the room with the light on. "A hundred percent."

Cone turned to the three agents behind him. "We don't have time to fuck around here. Crash the door, take him alive."

John walked back to the motel with a paper bag full of snacks and drinks. The road was dark, so he'd purchased a small flashlight along with some personal items. As he neared the motel parking lot, he heard a noise and killed the flashlight.

He stopped on the fringe of the parking lot when he saw a van parked in front of his room. Three men were at his door. They had FBI stenciled on the backs of their jackets and they carried automatic rifles.

John moved to the back of the lot and stepped behind some thick trees. Two FBI agents knelt down while the third kicked in John's motel-room door. As the agent smashed it in, the two kneeling agents rushed inside with weapons at the ready. The third agent quickly followed the first two.

John reached into the paper bag for a stick of beef jerky, removed the wrapper and took a bite as he watched the agents rush into his room. They weren't inside very long, just long enough for him to take three bites of the jerky.

A fourth FBI agent stepped out of the van and walked toward John's room to speak with the three agents. One agent held up John's watch. The fourth agent snatched it from him, then returned to the van.

In the van, a furious Cone said, "He set us up, this son of a bitch. He knew we were following him and he led us to his watch, then took off."

"I don't see how that's possible," Johnson said.

"There is no way he knew about the watch," Becker said.

"Then why am I holding it and his room is empty?" Cone said.

"I don't know," Johnson admitted.

Cone pulled his cell phone from his belt and held it out to Johnson. "I want your boss on the phone right now."

"It's four in the morning," Johnson said.

"I can see that by my new Rolex," Cone snapped.

John sipped milk from a plastic pint container as he watched the fourth man step back out of the van and talk on a cell phone. The man's voice was loud and carried on the night air. John could hear almost every word. The man was angry, demanding to know "who is John Tibbets?"

John took another sip of milk and wondered if he was John Tibbets—and if so, what had he done to bring a team of angry FBI agents to his motel room in the middle of the night?

Then the agent with the phone returned to the van. The other three agents joined him and the van drove away.

John came out of the shadows and looked at the open door of his motel room. *What the hell.* He shrugged, went in and closed the door.

Freeman disconnected the speakerphone, then hung up the receiver. He looked at Monroe. "Is that possible, what the FBI said? Could John have known about the watch?"

"I never spoke about it in front of him," Monroe said. "The only way he could know is if one of your men told him or spoke of it where he could overhear."

"Unlikely," Freeman said.

Farris looked at Monroe. "What happens after a week?"

"All suggestions will be erased from his mind," Monroe said. "He'll be a blank slate, so to speak."

"And then?" Farris said.

Monroe sighed before answering. "Little by little, Tibbets will start to regain his memory."

"How little?" Freeman asked.

John slid the back of the chair under the doorknob, then sat on the bed and dumped the contents of the paper bag on the bedspread. He munched another stick of jerky and tried to recall the details of the FBI agent's phone conversation.

The name John Tibbets meant nothing to him. If he was John Tibbets, he had no memory prior to a few hours ago. What he did know was that the FBI doesn't go crashing down doors at four in the morning without good reason.

What had he done to give them that good reason?

36

Maybe after some sleep, his mind would be sharper and he might remember some details prior to arriving on the road.

He ate a few more snacks, set the rest aside for the morning, checked the chair under the doorknob to make sure it was secure, then fell into a deep sleep on top of the covers.

FOUR

Freeman took the private jet from Washington to the very airport in New Mexico where eight hours earlier John Tibbets shot and killed ten men. The airport was smaller than he expected, with just a half dozen single- and double-engine planes used for teaching students on the runways.

And for smuggling drugs into the country.

Special Agent Cone met Freeman in a rental car and they drove to a diner in the small town less than one mile from where John Tibbets slept in his motel room.

Freeman ordered pancakes. Cone went with scrambled eggs and bacon. They both had orange juice, toast with jam and coffee.

"I expect full cooperation between our departments," Freeman said.

"So do I," Cone said. "You can start by telling me what your department does, who this guy is, what he does and why he's on the run."

Freeman sliced into his pancakes. "Do you really need to know that in order to organize a manhunt?"

"You may have missed it," Cone said. "The I in FBI stands for Investigations."

Freeman forked pancakes into his mouth, chewed and washed it down with coffee. "This doesn't leave this table. It's not for your men, just for you."

"Let me be clear," Cone said.

Freeman held up his fork. "No, let me be clear," he said. "If a word of this leaks, I will have you killed. No argument. That's it."

Cone stared at Freeman. "Did I . . . did you just threaten to kill me?"

"No," Freeman said. "What I said is, I would have you killed, not that I would do it myself."

Cone sat back in his chair. "Who are you people?"

"Do you want to hear this or not?" Freeman said.

"Yes."

"Then I have your word."

"Yes."

Freeman sliced into his pancakes and ate another mouthful before speaking. "John Tibbets may be the greatest assassin and sniper this country ever produced."

"Assassin?" Cone said. "You mean a hit man?"

"Would you just listen," Freeman said.

Cone nodded and sipped coffee.

"For many years, John performed certain functions that, if they were known, would prove very embarrassing to our government," Freeman said.

"You mean he killed people," Cone said. "Like a hit man."

"We prefer sanctioned or targeted," Freeman said. "But anyway, for many years John served his country faithfully. He took assignments others wouldn't, went where others couldn't. To him, a job was a job. No fear. No compunction. No distractions. The tougher it was, the better he performed. Anyway, about five years ago, John started operating outside the department, so to speak."

"What does that mean, so to speak?" Cone said.

"When he wasn't working on assignment for us, John supplemented his income by hiring himself out," Freeman said. "Working for sixty-two thousand a year, plus medical and dental, doesn't buy much and he found those willing to pay five hundred thousand, even a million to have someone removed."

"Killed," Cone said, "is what you mean."

"We didn't mind at first," Freeman said. "What's one less drug dealer or mobster in the world, right? Things got hairy when he started loaning himself out on the global market, so we had to shut him down."

"Global?" Cone said. "You mean foreign governments?"

"He never did anything that could be considered traitorous, but things were getting a bit too cloudy, so we felt it best to pull him in," Freeman said.

"And?" Cone said.

"We pulled him in."

"That doesn't tell me how he wound up here."

"You want it all, huh?" Freeman said.

"When I risk my life, I'm funny that way," Cone said.

Freeman smiled as he took another sip of his coffee. He usually didn't have much use for other agencies inside the Beltway, but Cone seemed like the sort of man his department could use on a regular basis, if he could be trusted. "It was an experimental program at first," he said. "About ten years ago. The idea was to give our servicemen a fighting chance against torture. I don't understand most of it, but the idea is to train their minds through hypnosis, drugs and other classified methods to resist torture techniques. What happened is, the man running the program discovered the procedure could be used in reverse. Instead of implanting information, he found he could remove it."

"Remove it? You mean memory?" Cone said. "All of it, or selective?"

Freeman nodded. Cone caught on quickly. "There are other subjects, but John is the prize. We keep him under wraps in a mission in San Diego. New York before that."

"Wait," Cone said. "Are you telling me Tibbets is that Homeless Hero from a year ago? The guy who saved that New York City cop?"

"One and the same," Freeman admitted.

"So you keep him under wraps in a homeless mission and do what?" Cone said. "Reactivate him for certain assignments?"

"So to speak," Freeman said. "The problem is, John was supposed to shut down after he completed this job. He didn't and we don't know why. We'll have to pick him up to find that out."

Cone sipped coffee and thought for a moment. "What aren't you telling me?"

"Our project director tells me that the longer John is in the field, the more he will start to remember," Freeman said. "We have to bring him in before that happens."

" 'We' meaning you and your men, or we as in just you and me?" Cone said.

"Let's start small and see what happens," Freeman said.

Cone nodded, then said, "So how good is he, really?"

"Ever see Rambo?"

"Yeah."

"Like that, only for real."

Cone pushed his plate away and wiped his mouth with a napkin. "I suggest we get started, then."

Palm trees and pink roofs.

The images crept into his sleep and gently took control. Rows of palm trees swaying softly in afternoon breezes blowing off the ocean.

Pink stucco rooftops on ranch-style homes. Block after block of pink roofs and green lawns.

Everywhere you looked.

Palm trees and pink roofs.

John opened his eyes and stared at the low ceiling above his head. It was a drop ceiling composed of square white tiles without lighting. Lamps on the nightstand and a pole lamp with four bulbs by the window took care of that.

There were footprints on the ceiling tiles above the bed. He wondered why someone would go to all the trouble of placing their footprints on the ceiling. It just seemed like such an odd thing to do.

John turned to reach for his pack of cigarettes on the nightstand and lit one. A phone rested on the nightstand next to the lamp, but there was no alarm clock. Without his watch, he had no idea what the time was, but guessed it to be around eleven, maybe a little later.

He stood up and put the television on, tuning to a weather station where he could see the time. It was ten forty-seven. His stomach rumbled. He needed real food, not snacks of jerky and fruit rollups.

John took a hot shower, then dressed in the same clothes he'd worn the day before. Since he'd paid for the room with cash, there was no need to stop by the motel office, so he removed the chair from under the door, closed it and left.

The road he'd walked on the night before was fairly busy in daylight. Several cars, pickups and trucks passed him as he made his way into town. He stopped at the gas station, bought a pack of cigarettes and asked about a place to eat. The man behind the counter told him there was a diner another half mile up the road, nothing fancy, just good simple food.

Fifteen minutes later, John walked into the very diner where Freeman and Cone had eaten breakfast just an hour earlier. Famished, John ordered a double stack of pancakes, bacon, sausage, toast, juice and coffee.

Behind the counter, a wall-mounted television was tuned to a cable news channel. A breaking news story announced that the FBI midnight raid on a South American drug lord was successful. The drug lord, long suspected of using a small training facility airport in southern New Mexico, was shot and killed by FBI agents when he resisted arrest and opened fire.

Every eye in the diner was on the television. Someone said, "Jesus Christ, that's only a mile from here."

John ate some pancakes and wondered why someone, even a drug lord, would be so stupid as to open fire on federal agents on American soil.

The waitress, a plump but pretty woman of about forty-five, stopped by to touch up John's coffee. She looked at the television. "I live less than a mile from that airport and I didn't hear a thing last night," she said.

"In which direction?" John said.

"North of town, not far from the motel," the waitress said.

"I stayed there last night," John said. "I was wondering if there was a place to catch a bus or a train?"

"Not around here, hon," the waitress said. "Best bet is to catch a ride to El Paso. It's closer than Alamogordo."

"Where's that?"

"Further than El Paso," the waitress said.

"How can I . . ."

"Excuse me, hon," the waitress said, and went to the next table to fill several coffee mugs. She returned to John and said, "Now what was that?"

"Where can I catch a cab?" John said.

"Mister, you got a better chance of getting hit by lightning than finding a cab around here," the waitress said.

"Can you . . ."

"Excuse me again, hon," the waitress said, and dashed off to seat some new customers.

John finished his breakfast and was about to wave the waitress over with the check when she reappeared on her own. "Best bet is to find a trucker heading that way," she said. "Offer him gas money."

"How about you?" John said.

"How about me, what?"

"A lift."

"You mean drive you?"

"I'll pay you for your time and gas."

The waitress shook her head. "Mister, I wasn't born yesterday. Many a woman disappeared from this Earth because she gave a stranger a ride."

"A hundred bucks," John said. "For a ride to El Paso."

The waitress squinted at John as she mulled the offer. "That's three days' worth of tips just for a ninety-minute ride."

"I'm just looking for a ride," John said. "That's all."

"You drive," the waitress said. "I'll ride in back and I warn you, I carry mace and a thirty-two revolver in my purse."

"Deal," John said.

"Not quite," the waitress said. "The fee for the use of my car is a hundred and fifty plus gas money. No stops because I need to pick up my daughter at four. Agreed?"

"Agreed," John said.

"I work five to one," the waitress said. "Read the paper and sit tight."

Her name was Gloria and her car, a thirteen-year-old Ford, needed tires, a tune-up, an oil change and a timing belt. John could tell by the sound of the engine exactly what was wrong with it. How he knew, he had no idea, but that wasn't important right now.

Gloria wore her waitress uniform, but had exchanged her shoes for comfortable walking shoes, the kind nurses wear. Her purse, an oversized red bag, sat on the seat next to her. John had no idea if she really did have mace and a gun in it, but he wasn't going to give her a reason to prove it to him.

They drove past the motel, where the manager was talking to two men in the parking lot. Another mile and Gloria told John to turn south on a state road.

"Did you want the bus station or the train?" Gloria said. "I ask because they are on opposite sides of town."

"Trains are faster," John said.

"Train station it is," Gloria said.

Horace Wilton seemed quite annoyed with Freeman and Cone when they appeared in his office and asked to talk to him. "I already told you everything I know last night," he said to Cone.

"Tell me," Freeman said.

"The man showed up around three-thirty in the morning," Wilton said. "Woke me up from a sound sleep asking for a room. Said he would pay me extra for my trouble. I took his money, which was twice the going rate, gave him the key and went back to bed."

"And that was it?" Freeman said. "Nothing else?"

"Nothing else like what?" Wilton said. "We went over this last night."

Freeman sighed. "Which room?"

"I just fixed the lock," Wilton said. "Who's paying for that?"

"Government," Cone said.

"So payment should be right timely," Wilton said. "Well come on, I was just about to clean the room, anyway."

"Two miles down the road is the interstate," Gloria said. "We want to go south. Sign says El Paso."

"Would it bother you if I smoked a cigarette?" John said.

"Only if you don't give me one," Gloria said. "I forgot my pack on the counter at the diner."

John lit two and passed one back to Gloria. "Can I ask you a question?"

"He ran off when my little girl was two, and, no, I never remarried," Gloria said. "And, yes, my feet hurt all the time, and, no, I don't put out for strangers or anybody else."

"Wasn't what I was going to ask, but I appreciate your honesty," John said with a soft smile.

Gloria returned the smile and said, "I use that as an ice breaker. Ask your question."

"Are their many palm trees around here?" John said.

"Palm trees?" Gloria said. "Mister, this is desert country. Only thing we have around here is cactus and sagebrush. Palm trees?"

"It was just a thought," John said. "I must have seen something in a magazine."

"Interstate's coming up," Gloria said.

Cone said, "What the fuck?" the moment he stepped into the motel room.

"What?" Freeman said.

"This room's been slept in," Cone said. "Look at the bed. There's food wrappers in the trash can, cigarette butts in the ashtray, imprints on the spread."

"Wait," Freeman said. "You're saying none of this was here when you came in last night?"

"None of it," Cone said.

Freeman looked at Wilton. "What didn't you tell us?"

"I didn't know you didn't know," Wilton said and picked up a wrapper from the trash can. "Jerky," he said.

"What?" Freeman said.

"Local brand from the gas station," Wilton said. "I remember now. When he checked in, he said he was hungry. I told him to try the gas station down the road. They have a convenience store stays open all night. They stock a local jerky. Five dollars a stick."

Freeman and Cone looked at each other, both thinking the same thing.

"She was a sickly child, my Rose," Gloria said. "The bills piled up and my husband started drinking. He ran off when she was only two. Some men are like that, afraid of responsibility, afraid of growing up. Maybe they're one and the same, I don't know."

"Is she okay now?" John said.

"Yes, but like most kids around here, she gets bored and that leads to trouble," Gloria said. "She's thirteen now. It was easier when she was three."

The entrance to the interstate was on their right, and John took the ramp for the southbound lane.

"You should remarry," John said. "Kids need a father."

"Sure thing," Gloria said. "Just as soon as I get that face lift and boob job I've been saving up for all these years."

"Yeah, that's mine," the man behind the counter at the gas station said of the jerky wrapper Freeman held. "I wasn't here last night, but that's the only brand we carry. It's made local by the . . ."

"Thanks," Freeman said.

Outside the convenience store, Freeman said, "I'll tell you what I think happened. He checked in, then walked here to buy something to eat. I think that's when you and your men went in and found the room empty."

"He came back after we left and spent the night," Cone said.

"Or were still here," Freeman said. "Maybe even watched you go in and waited for you to leave. Figured it was safe after you cleared out."

"Son of a bitch," Cone said.

"He may not have his marbles, but he still has his instincts," Freeman said.

"And this morning, he . . . what? Walked to town looking for something to eat?" Cone said.

Freeman and Cone looked down the road toward the diner.

"We're not far," Gloria said. "Take the next exit and then a right at the stop sign."

"I don't know if I've ever been to Texas before," John said.

"This far north, it's the same as New Mexico," Gloria said.

"I'm not sure if I've ever been there, either."

"You're not sure of a lot, huh."

"I'm sure you're a decent person," John said. "And I'm sure you could find another husband if you really wanted."

"But you're not sure where you're going or where you've been?" Gloria said.

John grinned and lit two more cigarettes. "Is that so strange?" he said and passed a cigarette back to Gloria.

"We care more about who wins *American Idol* than who wins the White House," Gloria said. "As far as I'm concerned, nothing is strange anymore. Slow down, here's the exit."

The owners of the diner were a married couple. Roger and Irene Edgar. Roger spent all his time in the kitchen. Irene waited tables with Gloria and the other girls.

"Yeah, I think I saw the man you're talking about," Irene said. "Left about an hour ago with one of my girls. Gloria."

"Left?" Cone said.

"She said he was stranded and would pay her for a ride to El Paso," Irene said.

"What's in El Paso?" Freeman said.

"Besides the bus and the train station?" Irene said.

★ ★ ★ ★ ★

John parked Gloria's car in the lot adjacent to the train station. A giant billboard advertised Amtrak Across America. He turned in the seat and passed Gloria two hundred and fifty dollars. She took the money and didn't need to count it to know it was more than the agreed upon one-fifty.

"This is more than we said," Gloria said.

"You need an oil change and a timing belt," John said. He opened the car door. "If I'm ever back this way."

"Yeah," Gloria said and watched John exit her car.

FIVE

Cone drove his rental car twenty miles above the speed limit of sixty-five on the two-lane state highway that led to the interstate. Next to him, Freeman smoked and spoke on his cell phone.

"An hour at most," Freeman said. "FBI agents are en route to the train station in El Paso and the bus station, too. If he hasn't caught one of them out of town, we'll pick him up. If he's gone, we'll try to find out where and have men waiting for him. Do me a favor and have Monroe standing by. I'll call back from El Paso."

Freeman disconnected the call, tossed the spent cigarette out the window, shoved the phone into his jacket pocket and pulled out a pack of cigarettes. "Your men going to beat us there?" he said, removing a cigarette from the pack.

"They have a head start," Cone said.

Freeman lit the cigarette with a disposable lighter.

"Listen, Ben, I'm in this all the way until we apprehend him," Cone said.

Freeman blew smoke out his open window, turned his head to look at Cone and said, "Agent Cone . . . no, forget that bullshit. What's your first name?"

"Richard."

"Go by Rick?"

"No, just Richard."

"Well, Richard, I'll lay it out for you," Freeman said. "I'm not here to get you a desk job in Washington. One word of this leaks to the press, to your wife or mother, hell, the weekly rag you pick up for free at the local grocery store, you and all your men will be put down like sick dogs at the vet. Those are the rules, no exceptions. That said, arc you in or out?"

"In."

"Glad to have your help," Freeman said. "Maybe when this is over and done with, we can talk about your transfer."

"My transfer? You mean over to your department?"

"Pay is better and we don't have to read assholes their rights," Freeman said. He pointed to a sign down the road. "Our exit is coming up."

John sat on a bench inside the train station and sipped coffee from a deli container. The station was larger than he'd imagined. A dozen tracks, several places to eat and shop, a large news-stand and bookstore. People came and went, mostly in one big hurry. Commuters with important things on their minds. He sat, sipped, and watched.

Across the terminal, he could see the reader board. Trains were scheduled for just about everywhere. He still had seven hundred dollars in his pocket and could afford a ticket to any destination he wanted, except for the fact that he had no idea where he wanted to go.

A uniformed police officer walked through the terminal. The man was a veteran of the job, an older man who probably should have retired, but for reasons of his own didn't. John watched him stroll through the terminal, stop to answer a few questions, directions probably, then continue on until he reached the exit door to the street.

John looked at the reader board again. Trains were going to Dallas, Houston, Fort Worth and Austin. Others were traveling as far west as Denver or east to Atlanta. A northbound train was headed for Kansas City.

Which Kansas City, John wondered. Missouri or Kansas? You would think people would want to know that before buying a ticket.

He took another sip of coffee, stood up and walked to the exit. Outside, he stood in front of the terminal to smoke a cigarette. The air was hot and heavy with car fumes. He'd barely lit the cigarette and taken a puff before he started to sweat.

Across the street from the terminal stood a movie theater that resembled an old Western saloon, complete with overhanging facade and wood balcony. The roof was dated 1885. Diagonally across the street from the theater, an old church rose up three stories high and dominated the skyline. It was Spanish in design and probably predated the Alamo.

A few people went into and out of the old church.

John watched them come and go. Fascinated by the look and design of the church, he stared at the intricate details carved into the stonework.

It reminded him of something.

The building had stood for two hundred years. A stucco gate surrounded it and the landscape, protecting it from invaders. Its pink roof stood out from the otherwise dull color. Tall palm trees swayed gently from warm ocean breezes. He could almost smell the salt from the nearby bay. Atop the roof stood a tall, gold-colored crucifix. Bright sunlight reflected off the crucifix, blinding you if you looked directly at it.

A bell from inside the building started to ring.

John tossed the spent cigarette to the sidewalk, stepped on it, then crossed the street at the light and stood before the church. There was something about the old structure that called to him. Maybe he was religious? Maybe he just liked old buildings?

He walked up the steps to the massive wooden doors and pulled one open.

"Nice to see you tonight, John," the man said. He was dressed all in black and had kind eyes and a warm smile. "Will you be staying for Mass?"

John could hear the man's voice in his head, although he couldn't see his face. The voice was soft, almost soothing to listen to as he invited you to come inside and join him for Mass.

John entered the church and closed the door. The interior was so quiet; it was as if a veil of silence had been dropped. He walked past the holy water font to the center aisle and all the way to the first pew in front of the altar and took a seat.

An old woman dressed in black sat across from him on the other side of the altar. She held rosary beads and prayed with her head bowed. Several rows behind her, a young woman with two small children sat in silence. To John, she appeared to be wishing for something, maybe for a husband to help raise her kids.

It struck him, wasn't a prayer nothing more than a wish?

Some candles at the altar were lit. A glass collection box was mounted on each guardrail for donations. John went to the altar, lit a candle and stuffed a twenty-dollar bill into a collection box. He couldn't explain why, but the simple act of donating the money had a calming effect on him. It was as if he was visiting an old, familiar friend who was always glad to see him, even though the two acts weren't connected in any way.

John returned to the pew and looked at the large crucifix on the altar.

"Every night you come into the church and put what little money you have into the collection box," the priest said. "For years I have

never asked why, John. Maybe you would like to tell me?"

"It makes me feel good," John said. "Inside."

"That is a very good reason," the priest said. "Maybe the best reason of all."

John turned away from the crucifix and looked at the stained-glass windows. Sunlight shining on the glass brightly illuminated the colors of each window, and one was more beautiful than the next. Yet, for all their beauty, the windows were depressing to look at. They told the story of the Stations of the Cross. Each window depicted a different scene of the crucifixion of Jesus Christ and the hell he was put through before ultimately being hung on a wooden cross.

John faced front again. Odd, how the windows bothered him. Odd, how he felt compelled to sit in a church when he wasn't sure if he was a religious man or not, if he even believed or not.

"Then leave me alone," John said.

"I'm afraid I can't do that, John," the funny little man said. "You're a hero."

Hero. What did he mean by that?

Actually, what did *who* mean by that?

John suddenly felt very uncomfortable inside the church. He stood up and walked to the exit, pushed open the heavy door and walked out into bright sunlight that momentarily blinded him. He sat on the steps to wait for his eyes to adjust to the brighter light and lit a cigarette.

Across the street, four men in dark suits huddled in front of the entrance to the train station. One man raised his left wrist to his mouth and appeared to be speaking into his watch. The other three men seemed to be scanning the streets as if searching for something, or someone, or maybe both.

A fifth man came out of the train station and stood next to the man talking into his wrist. The fifth man was large and imposing, and like the other three men, he seemed to be searching the streets.

John puffed on the cigarette and studied the fifth man's face. It was hard angles with a strong jaw and wide forehead. He reminded John of the drill instructor in the movie *Full Metal Jacket,* maybe a bit younger.

There was something else. The fifth man reminded John of somebody he knew. Maybe their paths had crossed at some point in the past? Or maybe he was just thinking of that movie?

Then a sixth man exited the train station and stood next to the fifth man. John immediately recognized the sixth man as the FBI agent who spoke on the phone in front of his motel room.

At that moment, John realized what they were looking for. They were looking for him.

Cone said to his agents, "You men join the others. Make sure every ticket seller is interviewed."

Cone's four FBI agents entered the terminal.

Freeman said, "It's possible we beat them here. She's driving an old car and we broke every speed limit by twenty miles an hour."

"He could have changed his mind," Cone said. "He could be at the bus station or even have gotten off somewhere en route."

Freeman sighed as he lit a cigarette. "John, John, John, where the fuck are you?"

One of Cone's men poked his head through the terminal door. "Sir, we got something."

John watched as they raced inside the terminal. He lit another cigarette off the butt of the spent one and felt no desire to move. He knew he was the target of their search, but having no idea why they were looking for him diminished the sense of urgency to run and hide.

More than anything else, he was curious as to what they would do next.

He puffed on the cigarette and waited.

A basement room inside the terminal building served as a small holding jail for the metro police. Freeman and Cone met the uniformed police officer in the cramped room. His name was Carter and he was a twenty-eight-year veteran of the job. He held the rank of lieutenant, but enjoyed street work too much to sit behind a desk.

Cone started the conversation. "My man said that you spotted a man fitting the description of the fugitive we're tracking."

"About six four, broad shoulders, dressed in black, short dark hair," Carter said.

Cone and Freeman exchanged a glance.

"He was sitting on a bench with a cup of coffee," Carter continued. "Looked like anybody else waiting for a train, maybe a bit more disconnected."

"Did you see where he went?" Freeman said.

Carter shook his head. "I went outside for about ten minutes," he said. "When I came back in, he was gone. I assumed he caught a train."

"He didn't," Freeman said. He looked at Cone. "Have your men do a car-by-car search of every train in the station. He could have bought a ticket for cash, and the clerk doesn't remember."

"What did this guy do?" Carter said.

"Nothing," Freeman said. "It's what he might do."

Freeman and Cone returned to the terminal, where Cone gave instructions to his men to search every train in the station.

"I need a smoke," Freeman said.

On the street, Freeman removed his cigarettes from a jacket pocket and lit one. Standing next to him, Cone said, "Maybe he changed his mind about taking the train."

"You still don't get it," Freeman said. "John doesn't have a mind to change."

"That may be, but he still had the wherewithal to make it this far," Cone said. "So some cylinders are firing."

"I didn't say he couldn't think," Freeman said. "And buried deep are his instincts."

"Then what are you saying?"

Freeman took a puff on his cigarette and let his eyes scan the street until they settled on the church across from the terminal. He looked directly at John Tibbets and they made eye contact. John didn't show recognition, but neither did he look away.

"Hey, Cone, are you a good runner?" Freeman said.

"Three miles every morning," Cone said. "Why?"

"Because he's sitting on those church steps watching us," Freeman said. "Waiting for us to do something."

Cone turned to look at John. At that moment, John stood up, turned and opened the church door.

"Go," Freeman said. "I'll take the back through the alleyway."

Freeman and Cone ran across the wide street, dodging traffic, to the church. Cone ran up the church steps while Freeman darted through the alley.

As soon as he set foot inside the church, Cone experienced several seconds of darkness as his eyes adjusted to the dim lighting. Once he could see again, he slowly walked down the center aisle to the altar. An old woman sat praying. Cone tapped her on the shoulder, showed her his ID and asked her to leave.

As he waited for the old woman to stand and make her way out of the church, he slowly scanned the interior. The stained-glass windows were intact. On the right side of the church, three confessional booths hugged the wall. Cone pulled his weapon, a Glock .40 pistol, and approached the booths.

Each booth had two sliding doors. Cone chose the center booth first, slid open the left and then the right door, then moved onto the remaining two booths without results. He looked forward at the altar, then past it to the left where a door was located.

Cone walked to the altar, stepped up to the marble floor and walked to the door. His footsteps echoed loudly. The door had a window at eye level. He peered through the glass into the dark room on the other side. Slowly, Glock at the ready, Cone opened the door and stepped inside.

There was a light switch on the wall. Cone flicked it on. Raised a Catholic, he knew this was the room where the priest changed into his vestments prior to saying Mass. A door on the opposite wall of the room probably connected to a rectory office. Cone tried the door. It was locked from the inside.

John waited for the FBI agent to enter the vestment changing room before he wiggled out from under the first row of pews. It was a tight fit and it took him nearly thirty seconds to free himself.

Before he stood up, John peered over the edge of the first pew and looked at the open door of the vestment room. The FBI agent was still inside. John ducked down and waited.

Cone reasoned that Tibbets must have found another way out of the church . . . or that he was still inside, hiding somewhere Cone had missed.

Cone walked to the open door of the vestment room, stepped out with his Glock in his right hand and came face to face with Tibbets.

There was split-second eye contact, a moment of complete silence.

Then Tibbets moved. Cone was well versed in hand-to-hand combat, having taken most courses offered by the FBI and the military. That said, he quickly discovered firsthand what Freeman had meant by his Rambo reference.

Tibbets snatched Cone by his gun hand at the wrist, bent and twisted downward. Cone's Glock fell into Tibbets' right hand. At that moment, Cone knew he was no match for John Tibbets.

They looked at each other.

Cone moved forward, hands up to protect his face and ready to slash at Tibbets.

Tibbets took one step backward, dropped the Glock and slashed through Cone's defense with a cupped right hand that struck Cone in the soft flesh of his throat. It took a second for the blow to kick in. Then Cone hit the door behind him and slumped to his knees as his throat swelled and closed up.

Cone knew then that Tibbets could take his life as easily as breathe.

He didn't. He lowered his hands to his sides and spoke softly. "Why are you after me?" Tibbets said.

Cone tried to speak, but all he could produce were some low rumblings from deep inside his throat.

"Hold still," Tibbets said, and was about to do something when the church doors burst open.

Cone and Tibbets turned to look at Freeman as he filled the door frame. "John," Freeman yelled.

Tibbets dashed past Cone into the vestments room as Freeman ran down the center aisle to the altar. Freeman reached Cone, and the FBI agent motioned for him to follow Tibbets.

Weapon drawn, Freeman raced into the vestments room only to find the connecting door kicked in. "John, it's Ben. Ben Freeman," he yelled as he approached the door. "Don't shoot me, John. I just want to talk."

Freeman went through the door ready to fire his weapon, but in the time it took him to say those fourteen words, Tibbets went out a window in the connecting hallway and was gone.

Freeman holstered his weapon and returned to Cone.

Freeman wasn't sure what John had done to Cone, but he was sure that without adequate oxygen the FBI agent could die. He lifted him and helped him walk to the first pew, where Cone flopped like a sack of potatoes.

"Can you talk?" Freeman said.

Cone wheezed and tried to suck air into his lungs.

"What did he do? Show me," Freeman said.

Cone cupped his right hand and stabbed at the air. Freeman was familiar with the move, having seen Tibbets use it in the past.

"Okay, okay," he said, and checked Cone's throat. Gently reaching for the sides of Cone's neck, Freeman massaged the soft tissue. After a few seconds, Cone's traumatized throat muscles started to relax. He pitched forward against the front of the pew and gasped like a man on his deathbed. "Easy, easy," Freeman said and held onto Cone.

Cone continued to suck in great amounts of air until his breathing slowly returned to normal. He looked at Freeman and snapped his fingers. "That's how quick he could have killed me if he wanted to," Cone rasped.

"I've been on the other end of it a few times myself," Freeman admitted.

"He asked me why we were after him," Cone said.

"What did you tell him?"

"Besides gasp, wheeze and a quick Hail Mary?" Cone said. "Nothing."

"Right," Freeman said. "Can you walk?"

"Let me get my gun."

Six

John ran down the alley to the street, turned to his right and slowed to a quick walk. Within a few steps, he blended in with heavy pedestrian traffic. At the corner, he glanced at the terminal building across the street. None of the other FBI agents were visible. He made a sharp left and walked to the end of the block, crossed the street and continued walking at a normal pace.

On the next block, he came to a park, turned and entered it. He walked for several minutes, then selected a deserted bench in the shade of some trees and sat. He lit a cigarette and tried to get clear in his mind what had just happened.

The FBI, for reasons he was unclear about, were after him. That much he was sure of, if nothing else. They'd broken into his motel room and followed him to El Paso, so a chance encounter at the church was out of the question.

It was the other guy, the big one who called him by name and identified himself as Ben Freeman. He'd expected John to, what . . . stop, turn around and shake his hand? It appeared to John that Freeman had expected him to do just that.

Ben Freeman.

Was he FBI like the others?

He wasn't at the motel, or if he was, he didn't show himself. Judging by the way Freeman ran across the street and then into the church, he didn't strike John as the sort to wait in the van for something to happen.

When he was sitting on the church steps and they made eye contact, John saw recognition in Freeman's eyes. That would explain his request to stop and talk, even telling John his name. It didn't explain the FBI manhunt across two states or shed any light on what they wanted with him, but it did tell John he was at least known to Freeman.

But it didn't tell him what Freeman wanted.

Except for John, of course, but again . . . why?

What had he done?

To whom?

And if he did do something to warrant interest from the FBI, why did he do it?

A police siren sounded in the distance. John resisted the urge to run and stayed put on the bench. As far as he knew, local law enforcement wasn't after him. The police officer in the train terminal didn't so much as glance at him, but that was before they chased him into the church. By now the FBI and the locals would have chatted.

The siren grew louder.

John kept his seat on the bench.

A man came running into the park. He looked left and right as if trying to decide where to run, then took off to his left. He raced past John without looking at him and ran down a path.

A few seconds later, two uniformed police officers ran into the park. They spotted John and ran to the bench. "Did you see a . . . ," one officer said.

Before the officer finished his question, John pointed to the path to his left.

"Thanks," the officer said, and he and his partner took off down the path.

The siren reached its pinnacle, then suddenly cut off. A moment later, four more uniformed police officers entered the park. One officer held a German shepherd on a leash. They ran toward John, and John pointed to the path.

They took off running.

John stood up. The park was suddenly getting very crowded and he decided it was the kind of company he should avoid for the time being.

He exited the park, turned left and walked along the street. Several blocks past the park, the neighborhood took a sharp decline in appearance. Seedy shops replaced the boutiques that had lined the streets near the train station. He passed several liquor stores and diners, then paused in front of an aging hotel.

The ten-story, hundred-year-old structure seemed oddly familiar. To his limited knowledge, he'd never set foot in El Paso before today, so the hotel must resemble another hotel from his past.

What past?

The one with palm trees and churches, or the one where FBI agents chased him through the streets?

Which one?

He didn't know.

Regardless, it wasn't safe to stay on the streets.

Freeman and Cone regrouped at a coffee shop across the street from the train station terminal. Neither man was hungry, but Cone ordered tea with lemon and honey for his throat. Freeman drank black coffee.

"Now you've had a taste of John Tibbets," Freeman said. "And that was just the tip of the iceberg, believe me."

"I believe you," Cone said. "My question is, what do we do now?"

"Send your men home," Freeman said. "We won't need them after today. I'll have my office send me a crew once we figure out where we're going."

"You don't think the locals can help us catch him before he

leaves El Paso?" Cone said.

Freeman shook his head. "Locals want facts before they agree to get involved," he said. "I can't give them that. Besides, I wouldn't know how to explain the trail of dead cops John would leave in his wake."

Cone took a sip of tea. He felt his throat respond to the hot, lemon-and-honey-flavored liquid, and his voice returned to normal. "It seems to me we could use my men to get a manhunt under way, as long as they're here."

Freeman took a sip of coffee. "Wouldn't do a bit of good," he said. "John has gone under by now."

"You're sure?"

"He's scared."

Cone took another sip from his cup. "He didn't look too scared to me."

"According to Monroe, John's mind is a blank slate with snippets of his past popping up at random," Freeman said. "Monroe can't predict what those snippets will be, but he suspects they will be recent memory to oldest. So he's out there without any idea of who he is or how he got here, with a mind full of bits and pieces of information that don't make sense to him. He's been chased through two states by people he doesn't know for reasons he doesn't understand, so right about now I'd have to think John is pretty scared. Maybe not of us, but of himself. And a man of John's ability is most dangerous when something frightens him."

Cone sipped his tea as he mulled that over. "You said he's gone under. You mean into hiding?"

"John's training and ability will kick in, even if he doesn't understand or know why," Freeman said. "He'll do what he knows how to do. He'll change his appearance, move at night, stay away from people and crowded places. He has some cash in his pocket, but getting more won't be a problem for him. He can stay out as long as he wants, provided he doesn't implode."

"Implode?" Cone said.

"Monroe feels that if too much information floods John's mind too quickly, it could have a reverse effect," Freeman said. "Instead of restoring his memory, his mind could protect itself from overload by shutting down."

"This Monroe sounds like an interesting guy," Cone said.

Freeman grinned. "You don't know the half of it."

"Based on what you just told me, our next move is what?"

"If Monroe is right, John's mind will take him to his most recent memory," Freeman said. "San Diego, the mission district."

"San Diego is four states from here," Cone said. "That's quite a distance for a man in his mental condition."

"Anybody else, I'd agree," Freeman said. "Not John."

"So that's where we're headed?"

Freeman nodded as he sipped coffee. "We need to get there before John, set up surveillance and bring him in."

"Question," Cone said. "What happens if he regains his memory intact?"

Freeman tossed some bills on the table. "We won't talk about that disaster just yet," he said.

The room was typical flophouse. Bed, chair, dresser with cigarette burns, television, a phone for incoming calls only, bathroom. Well worn and faded, the dark rug had darker stains. John paid in cash for two nights in advance.

He wasn't hungry, but he did pick up two containers of coffee from the deli across the street. He sat on the bed with his back against the headboard, lit a cigarette and sipped coffee from a container.

Ben Freeman, who was he? What did he want with John? The FBI, what did they want with him? That church, why was he drawn to it?

Questions without answers.

John felt the pistols press against his back. He removed them and set them on the bed. Twin Ruger .22 pistols with silencers. Why did he have them? Was he a criminal? That would explain the FBI. Maybe he'd robbed a bank, kidnapped someone or committed some other federal offense?

John removed the cash from his pocket. He counted a little more than six hundred dollars in a mixture of old and new bills. Hardly enough to warrant an FBI chase across two states.

Maybe he killed someone?

He checked the pistols. They had been recently fired. He removed the magazines. Each had a capacity of twenty rounds, but only held ten.

Had he shot someone?

Who?

And where?

For what reason?

He lit a fresh cigarette off the butt of the spent one. His head was spinning and he had to shut it down. Stop and regroup. Take it one step at a time. Step one was to find out exactly who John Tibbets was.

Find out who he was, and the rest should fall into place.

It should be so easy.

He smoked the cigarette down to the filter, squashed it out in the cheap ashtray on the nightstand, rested his head against the pillow and closed his eyes.

She was everything a woman should be, but so rarely is. Beautiful, kind and smart. At least, that's how she appeared to him. He could see her face and almost hear her voice, but just as she spoke, it all went fuzzy and he lost it.

She laughed at something he said, and her voice sounded like church bells ringing.

He looked up and there really were church bells ringing. Evening Mass was about to begin. She said good night and walked to her car that was parked at the edge of the mission.

The mission.

He watched her walk to the car, enter and drive away. He turned and looked at the gathering crowd outside the mission church.

The mission church.

He walked to the crowd and fell into line.

As a group, they entered the church.

John's eyes snapped open. At first, he didn't know where he was. Then slowly the room came into focus and he remembered that he was in a hotel in El Paso, Texas. He lit a cigarette and smoked while looking at the ceiling.

The dream, what little there was of it, slowly filtered into his conscious memory. The church bells ringing, the woman at the curb. The mission. He could see palm trees around it, their tops gently swaying from a soft ocean breeze.

He watched her walk to her car, a convertible with the top down.

A convertible with . . . California license plates.

He could almost see her face. Even blurred, he knew she was beautiful.

Who was she? What was his connection to her?

John took a final puff on the cigarette, stubbed it out in the ashtray and stood up. He needed a shower, not just to cleanse his skin, but also to clear his head. He entered the small bathroom, stripped off his clothing and turned on the shower to its hottest setting.

As the heat from the needle spray penetrated his skin, he felt the stiffness in his neck and the soreness in his muscles start to fade. If nothing else, he would be able to walk around without listening to his own bones creak like a rusty old door hinge.

After twenty minutes under the shower, he turned the water off and toweled himself dry. He stood in front of the mirror and inspected his face. It occurred to him that he didn't know how old he was, what day or month he was born, but judging from the deep circles under his eyes and the deeply etched lines in his skin, he figured his age at around fifty.

The speckling of gray in his short hair didn't mean much. Some men went gray by age thirty, so that wasn't a good barometer. He opened his mouth to inspect his teeth. His gum line showed some recession, especially around the upper front teeth, an indication his guess of around fifty was correct.

He stepped out of the bathroom and stood before the dresser mirror. The hair on his chest, as on his head, was speckled with gray. That didn't concern him. What did concern him were the deep-rooted scars on his chest and abdomen.

The scar on his chest just above the right pectoral muscle was star-shaped and deep. He touched it with a finger. It was from a gunshot wound. He twisted and inspected the scar on his abdomen. It was nearly identical to the one on his chest.

The scar on his chest appeared older, thickened by time. The abdominal scar seemed fresh, maybe a year at most.

John reached for his cigarettes, lit one and sat on the bed. He'd been shot twice that he knew of or at least reasoned out, but by whom and for what?

What had he done to warrant two bullets?

And why?

He didn't know much, but he knew the answers weren't in El Paso, Texas. His dream, coupled with what little memory he had, pointed him in the direction of California. The palm trees told him southern California. The church and mission narrowed it down to San Diego.

Six hundred dollars to his name. That was more than enough

for a train or bus ticket, but he knew instinctively public transportation was too dangerous. Flying was out of the question.

He would have to find another way.

Exhaustion suddenly washed over him, both mental and physical. He put the cigarette out, turned back the covers and slipped into bed. Within seconds, he fell fast asleep.

Thankfully, his mind stayed blank and he didn't dream.

SEVEN

They took off from the private runway at the El Paso airport that was reserved for traveling dignitaries and such. The jet seated twelve and was far more luxurious than what Cone was used to at the Bureau. Besides Cone and Freeman, just a pilot and copilot were onboard. Unlike commercial jets, the seats faced each other and were capable of swiveling one hundred and eighty degrees to accommodate face-to-face conversations.

Freeman and Cone occupied the first two seats and turned them so they could speak directly to each other without getting stiff necks.

"When we land, we'll be picked up by one of my people and driven to the mission where John has lived for the past year," Freeman said. "We'll meet with mission director Julie Warner, one of ours, and plan a strategy."

"How sure are you Tibbets will go to San Diego?" Cone said.

"I spoke to Monroe before I left my hotel room this morning," Freeman said. "His diagnosis is that John should be remembering snippets of events in his life from latest to earliest right about now. That takes him to San Diego. Hopefully, we won't have to wait too long for him to show up."

"He can't fly and if he's as smart as you say, he won't ride the bus or train," Cone said. "What are his options: hitch a ride, steal a car, walk?"

"With John, his options are what he says they are," Freeman

said, and stood up. "The same for his limitations. Want a Coke?"

John came through his hotel room door with three large paper bags. After he locked the door, he set them on the bed.

One bag had a label from a local drugstore chain. The bag contained an electric razor for cutting hair, soap, deodorant, toothbrush and paste, eyedrops and dark sunglasses.

The second bag contained a three-pack of underwear, a six-pack of white athletic socks and a three-pack of white tank-top style T-shirts.

The final bag came from the Salvation Army store on the next block. Two dark-colored shirts, two pairs of pants, black walking shoes and a small leather suitcase that was large enough to hold everything, plus the two pistols if need be.

John went to the bathroom, stood before the mirror with the electric razor and trimmed his hair down to a buzz cut. That short, he noticed more gray in his hair than when it was longer.

He gathered the cut hair from the sink and flushed it down the toilet. Next, he took a long hot shower and used the soap to wash his hair to remove any loose strands. After toweling dry, he dressed in new underwear, shirt, pants, socks and walking shoes.

He checked his appearance in the dresser mirror. He looked exactly as he felt, down and out with little prospects. Before leaving the room, he packed his new belongings into the small suitcase, old clothing into a paper bag.

Although the sun was setting, he didn't remove the sunglasses as he walked to the end of the block and tossed the paper bag with his old clothes into a Dumpster outside a store.

He walked several blocks and paused to look into the window of a pawnshop. He went in and exited with a used watch that the clerk assured him kept perfect time, and a Leatherman Tool that he slipped into a pocket rather than carry on his belt.

At a newsstand, he picked up the evening paper and took it with him into a small pub-style restaurant that specialized in— what else—roast beef.

One hour later, John left the restaurant and walked dark streets until he came upon what he was searching for, an outdoor parking lot. A two-foot-high silver guardrail surrounded the square block parking lot, except for the entrance and exit where a guardhouse sat with a motorized gate on each side of it.

The lot was three-quarters full. The attendant on duty appeared to be sleeping in his chair. John walked to the end of the block where it was darkest and stepped over the rail into the shadows of the large building across the street. He bent down and crawled to the first car in front of him. Using the Leatherman, he removed the rear license plate and stuck it into his suitcase, then did the same for the front plate.

Then he crawled to the guardrail, stepped over it and walked down to the next block. After a few more blocks, he noticed a change in the neighborhood. High-rise apartment buildings and upscale condos replaced the seedy hotels and flop houses. Bars and pubs lined the streets. Country-and-western music flowed from every pub and bar.

John watched four men, boys actually, exit a late-model BMW in front of an upscale club. They wore country-and-western garb, and one of them handed the keys to a valet parker on the sidewalk.

John watched as the valet parker drove the BMW around the corner to an open lot. After parking the BMW, the valet parker unlocked a small guardhouse on the lot and hung the BMW keys on a rack. Then he locked the guardhouse and walked back to the club.

While the valet parker waited for the next car, John walked around the block and entered the parking lot. He wasn't interested in the flashy BMW. In a back row, he spotted a green Ford Taurus, several years old.

He ducked behind a van and waited for the valet parker to arrive with the next car. The man parked it behind the BMW and opened the guardhouse to hang the newest set of car keys on a vacant peg on the rack.

Once the valet parker left the lot, John walked to the guardhouse and used the knife blade of the Leatherman Tool to slip open the cheap lock on the door. He stepped in, scanned the peg board and removed three sets of keys for Ford vehicles. He closed the door and located the three Fords. Two were pickup trucks. The third was the Taurus.

With the Leatherman Tool, he removed the license plates of the Taurus and replaced them with the stolen set. Before the valet parker returned, John was behind the wheel of the Taurus and half a mile away.

At the first gas station he came to, John pulled in to fill up the gas tank. He took the old license plates, bent them in half and buried them at the bottom of a trash can. When he paid for the gas, he purchased a road atlas, two containers of coffee and two packs of cigarettes.

Before driving away from the gas station, John scanned the atlas. I-10 West was just down the road. He estimated a four-hundred-and-fifty-mile drive before switching to 60 West. After that came I-40 West, then US 93 North. All told, about seven hundred and thirty miles, a trip he could make in thirteen hours, depending upon stops for gas, food and maybe a quick nap.

He would be gone five hours before the owner of the Taurus knew his car was stolen, six before the police circulated the plate number and out of state before anybody started looking.

Freeman and Cone were met at the airport by two of Freeman's men in a dark Ford sedan. They drove directly to the mission where Julie Warner, the mission director and a member of Farris' department, met them in her office.

Julie served coffee and sat behind her desk. "It's late," she said. "I was asleep."

"Couldn't be helped," Freeman said. "I explained all that."

Julie took a sip from her cup, then picked up a pack of cigarettes from her desk and lit one with a match. "Yes, you did," she said and blew smoke. "And I'm still trying to understand how he managed to take down the entire extraction squad right under their noses and make a clean getaway."

"Don't go bitchy on me, Julie," Freeman said. "You remember last year, New York, what it took?"

Julie nodded and took a puff on the cigarette. "I do, but after all the work Monroe did with John, I thought he was one-hundred-percent controlled."

"I guess Monroe needed a bit more fine tuning," Freeman said.

"I guess," Julie snapped.

"What happened in New York?" Cone said. "I know about saving the police officer's life, but what happened after that?"

"We couldn't risk exposure," Freeman said. "We came to bring John home and he escaped. Took out two teams of my best men, and he'd still be out there if it weren't for Julie's quick thinking."

Cone looked at Julie.

"He trusts me," Julie said with a touch of sarcasm.

"I know," Freeman said. "And I'm sorry."

Cone looked at Freeman, then at Julie. "Sorry for what?"

Julie took another puff on the cigarette. When she exhaled smoke, it was almost a sigh.

"Sorry for what?" Cone said again.

Julie looked at Freeman. "He doesn't know," she said. "You didn't tell him."

"Tell me what?" Cone demanded.

"John is to be decommissioned," Julie said. "With extreme prejudice."

"You mean kill him," Cone said. "That's what you mean."

"The decision isn't mine," Freeman said.

"But you didn't argue the point," Cone said.

"There is no point to argue," Freeman said. "And if there were a point, I wouldn't win it."

"For the life of me, I don't understand you people," Cone said. "Tibbets is a . . ."

"A what?" Freeman said. "An American citizen? A patriot? Protected by the Constitution? Entitled to his rights? What? You tell me."

"I don't know what the hell he is," Cone said. "But you made him and now you want to destroy what you made because he . . ."

"Not want," Freeman said. "Need."

"Because he knows your secrets?"

Freeman exchanged glances with Julie. She shrugged. "The truth is, we don't know what John knows at this point," she said. "Monroe feels that as time passes, John could regain his entire memory. It isn't that he knows our secrets, it's what he might do with them."

"Payback," Cone said. "You're talking about revenge for being kept a homeless, mindless idiot."

"Not of our choice," Freeman said. "But, the damage John could do to the country would be irrevocable. He has to be stopped before that happens."

"Killed," Cone said. "Is what you mean."

"Get off your high horse, Special Agent Cone," Freeman said. "All kinds of things you wouldn't approve of are done to protect this country and its people."

"Are you going to give me the 'you need me on that wall'

speech, because if you are, I've already heard it," Cone said.

Freeman stared at Cone for several seconds before he cracked up laughing. The tension relieved, Julie said, "If you two are done comparing your testosterone levels, maybe you can tell me when we might expect John to show up."

"I have a dozen men standing by," Freeman said. "Six will assume staff roles from inside. The other six will set up perimeter surveillance around the mission. Cone and I will set up a command post inside the mission. We need you to clear out the mission population until this is over."

"Two hundred people?" Julie said. "Send them where?"

"Tell them there's a gas leak," Freeman said. "Call around to the other missions for help. Do whatever it takes, but vacate the place by tomorrow."

"You expect him that soon?" Julie said.

"Monroe said John will remember things from latest to earliest," Freeman said. "Going backwards, he'll remember this place first. How long that will take is a guess, but Monroe thinks it will be soon. A matter of days."

"John won't go easy," Julie said. "And even with scrambled eggs for brains, he'll be difficult to fool."

"I know," Freeman said. "So we have to make this look good. No surprises except for the one we spring on him. Otherwise, it will get messy."

Julie shrugged. "I'm more or less just a maid around here, anyway," she said.

Three hours to daybreak. Since pinching the Ford, John had driven nearly three hundred and fifty miles. As he ate his breakfast sandwich and washed it down with coffee, he looked at the restaurant in the rest stop. It was unusually busy for so late an hour. From the picnic table in the parking lot, he watched patrons come and go by the dozens.

A family traveling late exited a white van and made their way into the restaurant. A young couple on a motorcycle pulled in. Another family, another young couple, a tour bus, another motorcycle.

Eighty travelers came off the bus. John scrutinized each one and picked out a man of about fifty. The man was tall with graying hair. He wore a sports coat over a casual shirt, slacks and loafers.

John took a final bite of his sandwich, washed it down with coffee, then lit a cigarette. He bided his time and finished the cigarette before standing up and reentering the restaurant.

The line to the counter was long and controlled by winding velvet ropes on stanchions. The man from the bus with gray hair was nearing the front of the line. He chatted with the man behind him until it was his turn to order.

John stayed behind the line as the man placed his order, then reached into the inside jacket pocket for his wallet to pay the bill.

John walked around the line to the soft-drinks station. He picked up a cup, filled it with ice from the dispenser and waited. When John spotted the man with gray hair approaching the soft-drinks station with both hands holding a tray, he filled his cup to the rim with water.

As the man with gray hair approached the soft-drinks station, John spun around and bumped into him, splashing the man's jacket with water.

"I'm sorry, I'm sorry," John stuttered. "I didn't see you."

"It's just water," the man said. "I'm fine."

"Your jacket," John said, and reached for some napkins. "It's wet."

"Only water," the man said.

John dabbed at the water on the man's jacket with the napkins, and as he did so discreetly removed the wallet from the inside pocket with his left hand, covering it with the napkins.

"That's fine," the man said. "It will dry. No stains."

"I apologize for my clumsiness," John said.

"Sure thing," the man said. "No worries."

John turned and exited the restaurant. He walked quickly to the picnic table, where he removed the driver's license and cash. He tossed the napkins into a nearby trash bin. On the way to the Ford, John deposited the wallet by the closed door of the tour bus.

In the Ford, John counted the cash and added it to his own. The extra three hundred brought his total back up to seven hundred and twenty dollars. From the glove box, he removed a pen and the car's title and registration. On the back of the registration, John transferred the title to the name on the license. Joseph William Specter.

"Thanks, Joe," John said and started the Ford. "For having gray hair. I owe you a big one."

"How is he doing?" Freeman said to Julie.

They were in the dining hall of the mission. Nearly every table was occupied. At the serving line, Charles supervised breakfast.

"Charles has never been a problem," Julie said.

"Breakfast any good?" Freeman said.

"I eat here," Julie said.

Freeman grabbed a tray, as did Julie. They walked through the serving line, then found an unoccupied table by the window. Freeman selected scrambled eggs, bacon and potatoes. Julie opted for pancakes. Both took orange juice and coffee.

"Where is Agent Cone?" Julie said.

"At the command center we set up in the vacant office next to yours," Freeman said. "How are you doing with the evacuation?"

"Three missions have agreed to take the entire load, but for no more than a week," Julie said. "After that, they'll either send them back or look to relocate them somewhere else."

"My guess is John will show within forty-eight hours," Freeman said.

"If Monroe is correct," Julie said.

"His program, he ought to know," Freeman said.

"If he's wrong?"

Freeman ate some of his eggs and washed them down with coffee.

"That bad?" Julie said of Freeman's silence.

"In all likelihood, worse," Freeman said.

Away from the glitz and glamour of the Vegas strip, the residential section of town was much like any other residential area across America. Working-class homes, mowed lawns, patio furniture and barbecue grills.

John drove the Ford along side streets to a wide boulevard filled with shops, car washes and used-car dealerships. He selected a dealership at random, turned onto the lot and parked.

He barely had time to exit the Ford and light a cigarette before a salesman emerged from an office and approached him.

"Morning, friend," the salesman said. "Buying or selling?"

"Selling."

The salesman, about John's age, wore a white shirt with a blue tie and fiddled with the knot while looking at the Ford. "What did you in?" he said.

"In?" John said.

"Blackjack, dice, slots, what's the poison that brought you to my lot?"

"Does it matter?"

"No, I guess not," the salesman said. "I've seen them all. Pop the hood and start the engine, I want to have a look."

John got behind the wheel, started the engine and flipped the hood-release lever. The salesman stood over the engine and said, "Give her some gas."

John pressed the gas pedal, and the salesman waved for him to stop. John turned the ignition off and stepped out. "Mileage?" the salesman said.

"A bit over sixty," John said.

"Engine sounds good, nice and steady," the salesman said. "You have the title and registration?"

"In the glove box."

The salesman circled the Ford, inspecting it as he walked. "No visible rust or dents. You kept her in good condition."

"Runs like a top," John said. "I hate to part with it, but . . ."

"Right," the salesman said as he pulled a small blue book from his back pocket and flipped through the pages. "Let's see now," he said. "The car is worth forty-five hundred as is. I'll give you twenty-nine."

"It's worth forty-five, but you'll give me twenty-nine," John said.

"Best offer in town," the salesman said. "You want to get home or not?"

"Cash?"

"On the barrel."

John nodded as he tossed the cigarette and stepped on it.

"Grab your papers," the salesman said. "It's cooler in the office."

John walked ten city blocks before stopping at a diner for lunch. He read a copy of the Vegas newspaper while he ate and avoided eye contact with everyone in the diner. He left the standard twenty-percent tip for the waitress. Big tippers in small diners tend to be remembered by those on the receiving end of the tip.

After lunch, John walked another mile along the wide street

until he arrived at a horseshoe-shaped motel that advertised cable, adult channels for an extra fee, vibrating beds and a swimming pool. He checked in, renting a room for one night.

Her face was cast in shadow as she stepped naked from the bathroom into the hotel bedroom. He pretended to be asleep because he wasn't sure if she wanted him to look at her.

She made her intentions clear when she slipped into bed next to him and kissed him on the back of the neck. Her skin was still warm from the shower, and her wet hair smelled of perfumed shampoo.

She sat on top of him, moaned softly and threw her head back. Her hair away from her eyes, he could see her face clearly.

She was . . .

John gasped as he opened his eyes. He sat up, reached for his cigarettes by the phone and lit one with a match, then turned on the lamp.

The woman in his dream at the church was the same woman from his dream in the hotel room. They were intimate, or at least they were in the dream. Maybe it was just wishful thinking on his part.

He tried to see her face in his mind, but the vision of it was hazy, much like the dream. But you don't dream of the same woman twice in different circumstances without it meaning something.

But what?

John stood up, went to the large window, and opened the drapes. Outside was dark. Night had fallen. The air was cool. He looked at his pawnshop watch. It was just after eleven P.M.

John stood with hundreds of other tourists outside the Bellagio Hotel and watched the famous water dance of lights in the fountains. Controlled by a computer, the fountains rose up in timed sequence, changing colors to the delight of the onlookers.

John turned away and walked along the main drag of the strip, Las Vegas Boulevard South. The crowds were thick, traffic clogged the street, the lights turned night into day.

At the entrance of the glitzy Golden Nugget, John spotted the man in charge of valet parking and approached him. The man wore a jacket with a bow tie and stood behind a highly polished podium.

John said, "I need a ride to San Diego."

The man gave John a quick once-over. "Don't we all," he said. "But as luck would have it, I have a young couple at the bar looking for gas money to Los Angeles. Want me to get them?"

"Yeah."

The man entered the hotel, and John smoked a cigarette while he waited. After five minutes, the man returned with a couple in their mid-twenties.

"Young broke couple, this is a man needing a ride," the man said as an introduction. "Take it to the street."

John and the couple walked to the sidewalk.

"I'm Tom and this is my wife Holly," the young man said.

"I'm John," John said, and shook Tom's hand. "He said you need gas money to Los Angeles."

"Like the man said, we're broke," Tom said.

"I need to go to San Diego," John said. "Can we work something out?"

"How much?" Holly said.

"What do you figure, two full tanks of gas to Los Angeles?" John said.

"At least, maybe three," Tom said.

"Four to San Diego," Holly said. "Then it's another hundred and twenty miles north to LA. Call it an even five."

"That's about two hundred and fifty dollars," John said.

"Sounds right," Tom said.

"I'll give you a thousand to take me to San Diego," John said.

Tom and Holly exchanged looks. "Mister, you can fly there for half that."

"I'm afraid of flying," John said. "And I dislike buses. We have a deal?"

"Pay up front?" Holly said.

"Yes, and I'll do some of the driving."

"Let's get started," Tom said.

"I've never been good at playing the waiting game," Cone confessed.

"Nobody is," Freeman said.

They were in the makeshift command center inside the mission offices. Freeman's men had installed surveillance cameras with night vision around the perimeter of the mission grounds, roughly an area of four acres. The night-vision feature wasn't needed, not really. Normally, floodlights were left on overnight to illuminate the grounds as a security measure. John knew that, and if he arrived to find the mission totally dark, he would be very suspicious.

"Except for John," Freeman said.

"Except for John what?" Cone said.

"Good at waiting," Freeman said.

"How so?"

"Well," Freeman said as he glanced at a monitor on the desk in front of him. "The Congo, back in the late unrest of nineteen ninety-seven. At the time, the country was named Zaire, which means the river that swallows all rivers." Freeman paused to light a cigarette. "Anyway, we had intelligence reports that Kabila had plans to overthrow Mobutu, and he did just that. First thing he did was change the name back to the Congo.

Soon after that, we received word his former allies were going to overthrow Kabila and take control of the country. We had the opportunity to take out a high-ranking general whose elimination might have averted a great deal of bloodshed. Word was he was traveling by convoy across the jungle to the capital. We had a perfect position to take him out from his open jeep. Fifteen hundred yards, a shot John and very few others could make."

Freeman paused to sip coffee and take a puff on his cigarette.

"What happened?" Cone said.

"He must have gotten word somehow, because his convoy never showed," Freeman said. "We dug in and waited eighteen hours before canceling the operation. And John, once he took position, he never moved. Eighteen hours at the ready, didn't so much as blink, even when the bugs were so big they could take a burger-size bite out of your ass. Can you do that, eighteen hours without so much as taking a piss? I can't. And five million people have died because a general decided to take a different route."

"So you're saying he can wait us out if he wants to?" Cone said.

"For as long as he wants to," Freeman said. "So we better make this shot count, because if we fuck up and he goes under, it will be one hell of a long time before he surfaces again."

"You're assuming he'll act as if he is still the same man," Cone said. "What if his mind is shot, his memory only bits and pieces?"

"A bit and a piece of John is better than the both of us combined," Freeman said. "Remember that when the time comes to take action."

EIGHT

Tom drove the first hundred miles before relinquishing the wheel to John. Holly did her best to stay awake and keep them company, but fell fast asleep in the backseat. John didn't bother with setting cruise control and kept a steady speed of sixty miles an hour. Nearly an hour of silence passed before Tom said, "You don't talk much, huh."

John glanced at Tom. "No, I guess not."

"Can I ask if you have any cigarettes?"

John reached into his shirt pocket for his pack and gave it to Tom. "Light me one, too," John said as an afterthought.

Tom used the dashboard lighter to light two cigarettes, then he passed one to John. "I suppose I should be thankful you're not asking me a bunch of questions," Tom said. "I've already heard it all from Holly, not that she isn't right, but how many times can I admit I was wrong?"

John blew smoke as he glanced at Tom. "You were up and thought you could ride it out to the finish," he said. "Until your luck turned and the house finished you."

"Guess it's nothing new, huh," Tom said.

"Kid, everything about Vegas is designed to separate you from your money," John said. "And to make you feel good about losing it by giving you free drinks, water displays and glitzy lights, but in the end the house never loses."

Tom took a puff on his cigarette and glanced at John. "How about you?"

"Me?" John said.

"Did you win or lose?"

"Neither. I'm passing through and my car broke down. I have a meeting I can't miss. I needed a ride."

"Must be important," Tom commented.

John glanced at Tom.

"Right," Tom said. "None of my business. Want me to drive?"

"I'm good for the rest of the way," John said.

"Are you sure?"

"I'm sure."

Tom stubbed his cigarette out in the dashboard ashtray. "Guess I'll join Holly," he said and closed his eyes.

Freeman opened his eyes when his watch alarm sounded at six-thirty in the morning. His back ached and his neck was stiff from a very uncomfortable night spent on a cot in the office.

He stood up, went to the desk, sat in the chair and reached for his cigarettes. As he smoked, he scanned the monitors. He called one of his men on his cell phone; the agent told him the night had passed quietly without incident.

Freeman left the office and walked across the courtyard to the dining hall for coffee. Two of his men had pots of coffee on the burner. They were preparing breakfast on the flat surface griller when Freeman walked in.

"Choose your poison, skip," the man behind the griller said.

"Doesn't matter." Freeman filled two mugs with black coffee. "Be back in a while," he said and left the dining hall.

Cone was still asleep when Freeman entered the office and closed the door just a bit too loud. The noise stirred Cone and he opened his eyes.

"I brought you some coffee," Freeman said, and held a mug out to Cone.

Cone sat up and took the mug. "Thanks." He took a sip and

looked at Freeman. "These cots are not made for sleeping. Anything from last night?"

"No, but I wasn't expecting anything that early," Freeman said. He sat in the chair behind the desk and lit a cigarette. "This afternoon, this evening, early morning for sure."

"What if your Monroe is wrong?" Cone said. "What if Tibbets is clear across the country by now?"

"I've thought of that," Freeman said. "But I've got to go on the premise Monroe is correct in what he tells me. John will come here first because he will remember here first. Want to get some breakfast?"

Cone sipped from his mug. "Yeah."

"Who is paying for this?" Holly said.

They were in a large, well-lit diner just a few miles west of downtown San Diego. John and Tom ordered extra-large portions of several breakfast items on the menu. John looked at Holly and smiled. "I am," he said. "So don't eat like a bird."

Holly smiled and ordered nearly as much as John and Tom did.

"Mister, we can't thank you enough for helping us," Tom said.

"Other way around," John said. "Just do me a favor and stay out of Vegas."

"We learned our lesson," Tom said.

"We?" Holly snapped.

"Me, I did," Tom said, looking at Holly. "I learned my lesson."

"How long have you two been married?" John said.

"Seven months," Holly said.

"You have a long way to go," John said. "If you have to pay off gambling debts along the way, you'll never get there."

"At least we'll make the rent this month thanks to you,"

Holly said. "Are you sure we can't drop you someplace closer to your meeting?"

John shook his head. "I like to walk off breakfast," he said.

John had no idea how he knew where he was going, but as he walked through the residential neighborhood, he knew instinctively it was the right direction. Not that anything looked familiar, because it didn't. If he had to describe his sense of direction, he would call it traveling by radar. It's just that it felt right.

As he walked, cool ocean breezes swayed the tops of tall . . . palm trees. Palm trees that looked all too familiar in their shape and sway.

He suddenly became aware of the great many pink rooftops on the seemingly endless rows of Spanish-style homes.

It occurred to him that he was walking his dream.

He lit a cigarette. *Let's see where this dream takes me to,* he thought as he blew smoke.

"Ben, you're being ridiculous," Julie said by phone. She was in her home office, at her desk.

"Take it up with Farris," Freeman said. "His orders."

"Based on what?"

"Monroe's evaluation of the situation."

"Come on, Ben, what the fuck does that mean," Julie snapped.

"How the fuck do I know?" Freeman snapped back. "I just follow orders. Call him yourself if you want an explanation."

"I'll do just that," Julie said, and hung up the phone.

The mission sat in the basin of a slight hill. San Francisco is usually associated with steep rolling hills, but San Diego itself is deep canyons, often separating entire neighborhoods.

John sat on a bench in a small park that overlooked the mission. In itself, the mission appeared peaceful enough, with nothing out of the ordinary taking place. Yet something nagged at him, told him to hang back and wait a while.

He smoked a cigarette and tried to identify exactly what was bothering him, but nothing jumped out at him. The mission, the church and surrounding grounds appeared much as they had in his fractured, truncated dream.

He stood up from the bench and exited the park. He walked several blocks to a small business section of the neighborhood, where he located a small sporting-goods store and purchased a pair of ten-by-fifty-power binoculars.

He returned to the bench, stood on it and used the binoculars to take a closer look at the mission and grounds. Everything appeared normal, except that he wasn't sure what normal was since his only memory of the place came from a dream.

He lowered the binoculars and sat on the bench. He lit a cigarette and stared into the park. The grass was green; the breeze was slight and smelled of salt sea air. A hundred yards away, a crowd of children played on swings and a jungle gym.

John closed his eyes and visualized the dream.

He opened his eyes and looked at the kids playing.

That's what was missing, what was nagging at him. He stood on the bench again and carefully scanned the mission and grounds with the binoculars. In his dream, the grounds and church were populated with crowds of homeless men and women living at the mission, milling about, talking and killing time between meals.

There wasn't one person anywhere on the mission grounds. Not at the church, the dining hall, the sleeping quarters. Breakfast would have just ended. A hundred or more mission regulars should be milling about, smoking, talking, fighting, something.

John moved the binoculars to the steps of the office where

she should be standing, watching the beginning of another day at the mission in her care.

She?

She, who?

John lowered the binoculars and closed his eyes. He could see her face and hear her voice. The plaque on her desk read . . .

Julie Warner—Mission Director.

John opened his eyes, stepped down from the bench, tossed the binoculars into his small suitcase and slowly walked out of the park.

"James, I disagree with your decision to keep me away from the mission," Julie said. "I am, after all, responsible for bringing him in last time. If it weren't for me, he'd still be running loose."

She could hear Farris sigh on the phone.

"You disagree?" Julie said.

"No," Farris said. "It's just . . ."

"Just what?" Julie demanded.

"Monroe feels . . ."

"Oh, fuck Monroe," Julie said. "It's his stupid experiment that got us . . ."

"Would you shut up and listen," Farris said, cutting her off. "I mean it, Julie. Don't fuck with me on this."

Julie buttoned it. She knew that with a whisk of his pen, she could be reading newspapers for terrorist code words in Lebanon, or worse.

"You were intimate with Tibbets and . . ."

"That was in the line of duty, James," Julie cut in. "It isn't fair to . . ."

"And Monroe feels that if Tibbets were to see you under these circumstances, it might trigger a violent reaction," Farris said. "He's very unstable and we can't risk him having a major blowup because somewhere locked away in his memory he believes you two were lovers and you betrayed him. It's Monroe's diagnosis and I agree with it. So stay put for a few days, eat junk food, work on your tan and catch up on the soaps."

"Soaps? What the fuck are you talking about?"

"Am I clear?" Farris said.

"Yes, goddammit, you're clear."

"Good. I'll have Ben call you with updates."

"Yes, sir," Julie said in her best good-little-soldier voice.

John wandered around downtown San Diego for about an hour and stumbled upon Balboa Park by accident. He entered through a wide gateway and paused for a moment as the size and scope of the park took him by surprise. The place was huge and beautiful to look at, with soft rolling hills, green grass and interesting people.

John walked the park with thousands of others. He looked at gardens, museum buildings, carousels, a miniature railroad and golf course. At an outdoor restaurant, he paused for an early lunch, then walked to the far end of the park where the San Diego Zoo more or less bordered it.

He took a seat on a bench, smoked a cigarette and watched the crowds of pedestrian traffic wander through the park. Many were headed into the zoo. Others seemed out to enjoy a beautiful day in the sun. No one seemed to notice him on the bench, or if they did, they paid him no mind.

The sun moved across the sky, lengthening the shadows cast by the many trees. John looked at his watch and was surprised to see the time was four in the afternoon. He'd been in San Diego eight hours and was no closer to learning the truth than before he left New Mexico.

One thing was clear, however. He wasn't going to figure it out on a park bench. John stood, walked toward the first park exit he came to and started looking for a place to stay. He didn't have to go far before he stumbled upon several cheap hotels in a seedy neighborhood in the downtown district.

Twenty-seven fifty bought him a room for the night on the tenth floor of a twelve-story hotel that sat between two fleabag mission churches. The room was as expected, but the double bed was comfortable and the television had limited cable access.

John stripped down to T-shirt and underwear, turned on the television and found an old Western on the classics channel. He fell asleep ten minutes later, just as drunk cowboys on horseback started shooting up the town.

Charles grilled chicken and burgers on the large barbecue grill in the backyard of the Spanish-style home. The grill, patio table and chairs sat on a brick patio just outside sliding double doors that led to the kitchen.

John and four other men from the mission were on the roof, replacing worn shingles. The house itself was just twenty years old, but shingles rarely made it that long, especially when baked by the harsh sun. To wait any longer meant risking serious damage to the roof and water leaks inside. Two more men from the mission worked below, cleaning up the torn shingles and feeding eighty-pound bundles to the men on the roof.

Charles called lunch, and John and the others came off the roof. Julie appeared in the double sliding doors and told them they could use the bathroom off the living room to wash up before eating.

They worked another four or five hours, then Charles drove them back to the mission in one of the mission-owned vans. John sat up front next to Charles because Charles had a terrible sense of direction, and John read hand-written directions given to him by Julie.

John opened his eyes.

Night had fallen. He changed into his clean shirt and pants after a hot shower. He wore the dark windbreaker to conceal the twin Ruger pistols in the small of his back, and left the hotel room.

He opted to walk. Cabs kept records, and he didn't know the bus routes well enough to avoid getting lost on some cross-town transfer. Besides, he needed the time to try to sort things out in his mind.

For instance, who the hell was Charles and what was his connection to Julie Warner? For that matter, who the hell was Julie Warner and what was her connection to him?

And the mission, why did he know it so well?

The questions kept coming, but the more questions he asked himself, the fewer answers seemed to materialize.

He walked for two hours, then quit asking himself answerless questions. He walked another half hour, concentrating on the directions he seemed to remember from his dream.

Then he stopped.

The street in front of him was the street in his dream. He turned and walked until he reached a large cul-de-sac of homes set back off the dark road. The homes were stretched out, some as far as a hundred yards or more apart.

In all, John counted seven homes. Julie Warner's was the one in the middle. He walked along the narrow sidewalk of the cul-de-sac, avoiding the dim lighting of well-placed streetlamps.

One home was well lit, the one farthest from Julie Warner's. John checked his watch. They must be watching late-night television. He walked closer to Julie's house. All the windows were dark. She must be in bed, sound asleep or watching Leno with the lights off. She didn't strike him as the Letterman type, but as he knew almost nothing about her, that wasn't a fair judgment.

He walked past Julie's front door, looked down the alleyway

that led to the backyard, turned and walked to the rear of the house. Even in the dark, he could see the lawn needed mowing. To his immediate left was the patio and just past that, the sliding double doors.

He stepped up onto the raised brick patio and approached the doors. He gently pulled on the handle. The doors, as he expected, were locked and the lock was a good one. Running the length of the doors on the floor inside, a telescoping steel bar snapped the doors closed so tightly, the only way in was to shatter the glass. It looked three quarters of an inch thick.

John walked around to the right side of the house's rear, where he knew the second bathroom was located. The window, a horizontal slider, was halfway up, more than enough room for him to squeeze through.

Sipping coffee at the desk in the mission office, Cone looked at the monitors and said, "So what's next, leave out a big hunk of cheese and see if it brings him in?"

At the other desk, Freeman looked at Cone. "Ever hear that patience is a virtue?"

"Ever hear that pride is a sin?" Cone said.

"Meaning?"

"Maybe the woman knows some things we don't," Cone said.

"Julie?"

"Yes, her," Cone said. "She's had him for years to study. Isn't it possible she knows his habits and personality a great deal better than you do?"

"Farris wants her off the . . ."

"Did he say you couldn't call her?"

Freeman knew Cone was right. Julie did know John better than John knew himself at this point. "No, he didn't say that,"

Freeman said and reached for the phone. "He didn't say that at all."

An extremely light sleeper, Julie answered the phone on the nightstand before it had the chance to ring twice.

"Yes," she said without a trace of sleep in her voice.

"Julie, it's Ben," Freeman said on the phone.

"You got him?" Julie said, looking at her alarm clock.

"No."

"Then what the fuck are you calling me for at one in the morning?"

"Talk."

Julie sat up, reached for her cigarettes next to the alarm clock and lit one. "You mean pick my brain?"

"Yeah."

"Well, that must have hurt to swallow a crow that big, huh."

"Keeping you out wasn't my idea," Freeman said. "Calling you unauthorized is."

"Give me an hour," Julie said. "I need a shower and some coffee."

"We can talk on the phone," Freeman said.

"No, we can't," Julie said and hung up. She swung her legs over the edge of the bed and grabbed her robe to cover her naked body. Then she went to the kitchen to brew a pot of coffee.

As he came out of the second bathroom, a light suddenly went on in the kitchen just down the hall. John paused to listen for a moment. It sounded like Julie was making a pot of coffee, an odd thing to do at this hour.

John turned and entered her dark bedroom, saw the chair opposite the bed and sat in it to wait. Five minutes later, Julie entered the bedroom and clicked on the wall switch. The recessed ceiling light came on.

Julie saw John in the chair and gasped. She hugged the robe and said, "John?"

John stood up. "Do you know me?"

"Yes, of course," Julie said, backing away. "What are you doing in my house?"

"How do you know me?"

"You live at the mission," Julie said. "I'm the director. Now tell me what you're doing here?"

"I can't seem to remember anything," John said.

"That's because you have amnesia, John."

"For how long?"

"What do you mean?"

"How long have I had amnesia?"

"Two, three years," Julie said. "Nobody is really sure."

"That doesn't explain it."

"Explain what, John?"

"I woke up in the New Mexico desert two days ago," John said. "That's all I remember, the last two days."

"I don't know anything about that, John. Like I just told you, you suffer from amnesia."

"Two, three years," John said. "What about since then?"

"I don't understand."

"You said I've been living at the mission for three years," John said. "Shouldn't I remember that? Shouldn't I remember what I was doing in New Mexico?"

"Not necessarily," Julie said. "We don't know how, but you suffered severe blunt force trauma to the head. Your memory comes and goes, and sometimes you suffer severe blackouts. I think that's what's happened now."

"Blunt force trauma?"

"Yes."

"To my head?"

"Yes. John, listen, I have a pot of coffee on. Let's go to the kitchen and talk. I'm not comfortable in here. Okay?"

John nodded and followed Julie to the kitchen. She poured mugs of coffee and they sat at the table. John pulled out his pack of cigarettes and looked at Julie. She nodded her approval. "One for me," she said.

John lit two and passed her one.

"I should call the mission doctor and have him meet us there," Julie said. "He'll want to examine you."

"Now?" John said.

Julie laughed. "You live there, John. Now is as good a time as any."

"He can help me? Remember, I mean."

"I'm afraid not, but he does know your history," Julie said. "And maybe that can help you piece together the past few days."

"I had a dream about the mission and you," John said. "That's how I knew where to go. I fixed your roof, didn't I?"

"Yes, several months ago," Julie said. "Since dreams are nothing more than a memory, that's your mind trying to recall actual events. Now, how about I go get out of this robe and into some clothes?"

John nodded.

Julie stood up. "I won't be a moment."

John picked up his mug. "Okay if I have some more?"

"Help yourself. There are some leftovers in the fridge, but I'm afraid I'm not much of a cook."

"That's okay. I'm not hungry."

Julie turned and entered her bedroom. "Everything will be fine, John," she said from inside. "Wait and see."

John stood up and carried his mug to the kitchen counter where the coffee pot rested on its burner. "I live there, right?"

From the bedroom, Julie said, "You stay there, John, because you have no place else to go at the moment."

97

John picked up the coffee pot and filled his mug. He took a sip and leaned against the counter. "Every night?"

"I can't say, John," Julie said. "Most days I leave by six, but I would guess that you sleep at the mission almost every night."

John took a sip from the mug, then stared down into it as he thought. "I have possessions there? I mean, things that I own?"

"You have a footlocker with some belongings in it," Julie said. "Clothes and personal items."

John took another sip. "What about friends? Other people at the mission. I must have some."

"Not many that I know of, John," Julie said. "You're pretty much of a lone wolf."

"Nobody?" John said.

"There is Charles," Julie said. "He's our cook. You might say that he is your friend. And me."

John sipped, then stared down into the mug again as he thought for a moment. "Charles is my friend?"

"And me," Julie said.

Slowly, John raised his eyes to look at the hallway that led to Julie's bedroom. "And you?"

"Yes," Julie said.

"Then why didn't you know I was gone?" John said. "A friend ought to know that."

He waited for a response, but his question was greeted with silence. "I said, why didn't you know I was gone? How come if you're my friend, you said you didn't know anything about me being missing?"

There was a soft noise from the bedroom. Footsteps on the rug. John looked at the wall in the hallway and slowly removed a Ruger pistol from the small of his back. A bullet was already chambered and he switched the safety to the off position. "Julie?" he said. "Did you hear me?"

Julie's shadow suddenly appeared on the hallway wall. It

wasn't elongated, which meant she was close. In her right hand, John could see the shadow of a pistol made longer by a silencer attached to the barrel.

"Julie?" John said.

"Be right there, John," Julie said.

She came out of the hallway quickly and took dead aim at where she thought John was, but wasn't. As she shifted the pistol from the kitchen table to the counter, John shot her once in the chest, knocking her against the wall. His silenced Ruger made little more than a cough. Against the white robe she still wore, a red stain appeared and spread quickly. Julie came off the wall, looked at the stain, looked at John and fired a shot. Next to John, the glass coffee pot exploded.

John fired twice more. Two more red stains appeared on Julie's bathrobe. She gasped as the pistol fell from her hand. John looked at her. "Why?"

She managed to move away from the wall and get to a chair. She looked at John. "For the credit," she said.

"I don't understand," John said.

She managed a tiny smile. "Gut shot is no way to go out."

"No, it isn't," John said softly. He looked at the expanding puddle of blood at Julie's feet.

The light went out in her eyes and she slumped to the table. John walked to her, lifted her head to look into her cold eyes, then gently lowered her head.

He picked up her pistol. It was a Glock nine-millimeter with a fifteen-round magazine. He stuck it down the front of his pants, then entered the bedroom. A dresser drawer was open. In it, John found two additional loaded magazines and three thousand dollars in small bills in a white envelope.

He pocketed the magazines and cash, then looked around the room. He went to the window and checked the blinds. They were venetian, with the slats made of thin metal. With the Leatherman, he cut the rope holding the slats and removed one.

He entered Julie's bathroom, took a face cloth and wiped his fingerprints from everything he'd touched in the house, then quietly left by the front door.

Forty-five minutes after Julie's stated one hour had passed, Freeman looked at his watch and said, "She's late. Almost an hour late."

"Call her," Cone suggested.

Freeman used the desk phone to dial Julie's number. He allowed it to ring six times until the answering machine picked up, then he hung up the phone.

"She's on her way?" Cone said. "Just late."

Freeman smoked two cigarettes and waited another fifteen minutes. Then he said, "No, she's not late. Let's go."

Freeman lifted Julie's head by the hair and looked into her lifeless eyes. "Jesus Christ," he said softly.

Looking at Julie, Cone said, "This tears it, Freeman. I'm calling this in and putting the Bureau on full alert to pick up Tibbets for murder and . . ."

"Shut up, Cone," Freeman said as he lowered Julie's head to the table. "Shut up and think."

"Think?" Cone said. "This woman is dead. Killed by your out-of-control man. How many more is he going to kill before he's stopped?"

Freeman pulled his smokes and lit one. "You want the total in body bags?"

"Is that supposed to be funny?" Cone said.

"No, it isn't," Freeman said. "Now if you will shut the fuck up for a second, I'm going to call Washington and advise them of the situation."

"Advise them of the . . . you're out of your fucking mind,"

Cone said. He reached into a suit pocket for his cell phone. "This ends now."

"Don't you make that call," Freeman said.

"We'll see who . . ."

"Don't make that call," Freeman said.

"Or what?" Cone said as he dialed a Washington DC area code.

Freeman walked to Cone, pulling his Glock pistol. Just as Cone hit the first digit for his office, Freeman stuck the pistol against Cone's temple and cocked the hammer.

"Or this," Freeman said.

Cone froze. "You're kidding."

"No, I'm not."

"You'll kill me for doing my job?" Cone said.

"I'll kill you for putting our country at risk, just like I'd kill anybody else who put our country at risk," Freeman said. "Now put the phone down or join her on the table."

Cone hit the end-call button and lowered the phone. "Now what?" he said.

Freeman lowered the Glock, decocking the hammer. "Now we go to Washington and choke some information out of Doctor Monroe."

Cone looked at Julie Warner's body. "Her?"

"She no longer has anything to worry about," Freeman said.

NINE

John took a left turn at the end of the cul-de-sac and walked about a half mile before he reached a small park. He entered, found a bench hidden in deep shadows, took a seat and lit a cigarette.

He should have been visibly shaken by the fact that he'd just shot and killed the woman of his dreams, Julie Warner, but he wasn't. In fact, he was strangely calm, cool and collected. After she was dead, he acted as if he knew exactly what to do next . . . almost as if he'd done it many times before.

Maybe he had.

The FBI was after him for a reason. Maybe that reason was on display back at Julie Warner's home in the form of Julie Warner's corpse.

That didn't explain why she tried to kill him, or what she meant by "For the credit."

The credit for what?

For killing him?

Or for bringing him in?

It struck John that Julie Warner could have been an agent for the FBI. If so, was she undercover as the director of a homeless mission? That made no sense. What purpose did it serve to assign an FBI agent to a mission for derelicts and drunks?

John lit another cigarette off the butt of the spent one. What sense did it make for him to be in the middle of it, whatever *it* was?

Unless . . . the mission wasn't a mission, but some kind of government facility.

For what? It always seemed to come down to those two words. For what?

John sucked in smoke and exhaled slowly, calming his mind, forcing himself to push through the haze and see things clearly. He remembered Julie Warner, but didn't know why. He went to her house to ask for her help and in return, she tried to kill him.

Maybe she just wanted to capture him.

She shot at him with intent to kill. The use of a silencer proved that. The only reason for a silencer was to kill without detection. The fact that she used one meant she wanted to take him without alerting her neighbors.

There was also the fact that silencers were illegal for all but those with the highest government clearance, which meant Julie Warner possessed one illegally or there was far more to her than her job title indicated.

She'd said, "For the credit," when he asked her why. Her dying words.

Why do people want credit, was the obvious question?

For the recognition.

Maybe Julie Warner was tired of the mission and wanted her employers to sit up and take notice by . . . what?

Shooting him?

No, by upstaging the men who'd chased him halfway across the country. That's how you get noticed by your superiors, you accomplish something they can't, especially if you're a woman.

In Julie's case, bring down John Tibbets.

But who the hell was John Tibbets?

She'd said he suffered from amnesia. She knew that, what else did she know? John tossed the cigarette and stood up. He'd left her house too soon. If she knew his name, knew he was a resident of the mission, knew about his amnesia, what else did she know?

Enough to want to kill him for the credit.

There had to be something in Julie's house, some documents or records of who she really was and possibly, what her connection was to him.

John left the park.

The cul-de-sac was lit up like a Christmas tree. Ambulances at three in the morning will do that to a neighborhood, especially when they are carrying out the dead body of a neighbor.

Every home was awake, the residents on their front lawns and steps. John stayed back a hundred yards in the shadows of some tall hedges and watched paramedics load a stretcher with Julie's body on it into an ambulance.

Four men in dark suits and sunglasses stood by Julie's front door. They had the look of the FBI or another government agency. Maybe the agency Julie was employed by that she so desperately needed to impress.

Loaded and ready to go, the ambulance drove around the turnabout to the road and past John. If the driver spotted him, he paid John no mind.

The four men stayed put in front of Julie's house. One of them spoke on a cell phone. The residents of the neighboring homes didn't approach the four men, but they didn't go inside, either. Curiosity was a more powerful driving force than common sense, at least when it involved a neighbor or a movie star.

The four men filed into Julie's house and closed the door. John waited and watched. After fifteen minutes, when there was nothing left worth watching, most of the residents of the cul-de-sac called it a night. John waited another fifteen minutes until lights inside the homes extinguished. Then he slowly walked toward Julie's home.

At the lip of Julie's driveway, he turned and walked toward the rear of the house. He stopped midway to peer into a window. The four men were sitting on the sofa, watching television, drinking coffee.

Searching the house was out of the question. The four men were going nowhere. They were waiting for him to return to the scene of the crime. John took another peek at the four men to memorize their faces, faces he'd never seen before, then turned around and left the driveway.

"You really would have shot me, wouldn't you?" Cone said.

"It comes with the job," Freeman said.

Cone looked out the window of Freeman's jet. They were at thirty thousand feet, racing toward Washington DC. "Seems a bit dramatic, don't you think?"

Freeman and Cone were seated opposite each other on the small, private jetliner. Freeman held a Coke and took a small sip. "I always thought I would make a good actor," he said.

Cone turned away from the window and looked at Freeman. Together they cracked up laughing.

A mile from Julie Warner's home, the neighborhood descended slightly from upper-middle class to lower. The homes were replaced with apartment buildings. Tree-lined streets became car-lined streets. John walked up to a ten-year-old Buick parked in the middle of the block. It was a massive car, probably terrible on gas, but a powerful beast and it suited John's purpose.

He removed the venetian blind slat and his Leatherman Tool from inside his jacket. Using the Leatherman's sharp knife, he cut an inch-long notch into the slat. Pressing the slat tight against the driver's-side window, he shoved it down between rubber and glass and moved it around until he felt the notch catch. Then he yanked the slat upward. The door unlocked.

He slid onto the seat, closed the door and used the pliers on the Leatherman Tool to snap off the ignition cap, exposing the starter button underneath. Reaching into the exposed ignition hole with the pliers, he pressed on the button and the engine started. He put the Buick into drive and drove away from the curb.

John made a quick stop at his hotel for his suitcase and cash, then got back on the road. He linked up with I-8 West toward Phoenix, a six-hour drive. With one pit stop for gas and breakfast, he could reach Phoenix by eleven in the morning.

There was nothing in Phoenix he was driving to. Nothing that drew him to the city in the way of a memory. He just needed to drive a wedge between himself and San Diego and find a place to rest, think and sort things out.

Maybe in a day or two, he might be able to piece together enough of the puzzle to figure out who he was and why they were after him. It had to be for something more than *for the credit.*

Cone looked around James Farris' office. On the way in, there were no markings to indicate they were entering a government building. The same was true of the office. James Farris smiled at Cone and said, "If you're looking for some kind of identification, I assure you that there is none. So, let's have breakfast."

Farris had sent out for breakfast or maybe had it catered, Cone wasn't sure. In any event, places were set at the large conference table centered in the room by two windows. Small burners placed underneath kept silver trays of food hot.

"Help yourself," Farris said.

Freeman removed the lids from the serving trays, filled a plate with eggs, bacon, potatoes and toast, and set it on the conference table. He looked at Cone. The FBI agent shrugged and grabbed a plate.

"We'll wait for Doctor Monroe so I don't have to repeat myself," Farris said. "And eat as much as you want or it will only go to waste. I dislike waste, especially when the taxpayer foots the bill."

John put the remains of his breakfast, two egg sandwiches with potato patties, into the paper bag it was served in and tossed the bag into the trash barrel beside the picnic table at the rest stop.

He removed his cigarettes from the pocket of his windbreaker and lit one with a match, then took a sip from his coffee container. Another three hours to Phoenix, maybe a bit more. After that, he had no idea what to do next. Find a room and hole up for a while, probably. Think, wait and sort things out seemed to be the safest and most logical move at this point.

He had nearly five thousand dollars in his pocket. How long would that last? How far would that take him? He needed . . .

A noise from the next picnic table distracted him. An old woman sitting alone talked to herself while she smoked and drank coffee. She was maybe seventy years old, dressed in rags, and had the glazed look in her eyes of a lifelong alcoholic.

Transfixed by the old woman, John felt something in his gut that he couldn't describe. Although he was certain he'd never laid eyes on her before, the old woman was strangely familiar to him. Not her physical presence, something else. Something he couldn't put a name to, yet he felt it like the sting from a slap in the face.

John stared at her as she held a two-way conversation with herself. Then she tossed her cigarette away and reached for her pack on the picnic table. She felt around inside the pack, then crushed it into a ball and tossed it to the ground. She looked at

John, saw the cigarette in his hand, stood up and walked to his table.

"Spare an extra one of those?" the old woman said.

John stared at her.

"Can you spare one of those?" the old woman said.

John looked across the table at her. She was filthy, with matted hair, yellow rotting teeth, and rags for clothes. Her eyes were red and swollen from a lifetime of cheap liquor and wine.

"Come on, John," she said. "Be a good guy. You're not a prick like those other bums around here."

He dug out his pack and slid it across the table to her. She grabbed it like a greedy child and tried her best to hide the fact that she'd removed three cigarettes from the pack when she only asked for one.

"Got a light?" she said, smiling, displaying her yellow, rotting teeth.

"Hey, mister," the old woman said. "What the fuck's wrong with you? Are you deaf, dumb or just plain stupid? I asked you a question."

John snapped from his reverie and looked at the old woman. "What?"

"I asked you for a smoke," the old woman said. "You got one or not?"

"Yeah, yes," John said and pulled his pack from a pocket. He held it out to the old woman. She removed a half dozen cigarettes before returning the pack, making no effort to hide the extra five.

"Thanks," she said, and turned away.

"Wait a second, please," John said.

The old woman spun around and glared at him. "Ain't none of your fucking business," she snapped.

"What?" John said.

"Whatever the fuck you're gonna ask."

"You remind me of someone," John said. "All I want to know is your name."

"Margaret fucking Thatcher," the old woman said. "What's it to you?"

"It's . . . like I said, you remind me of someone," John said. "Have we met before?"

"When was the last time you had a really good blowjob?" the old woman cackled.

"I . . . I don't know," John said, somewhat shocked at the old woman's crudeness.

"Then we never met," the old woman said, laughing as she walked away.

Monroe nibbled on some toast as he read a thick file of notes. "I can't tell you when John will remember events from his life, or what he'll recall," he said. "I can tell you that my treatment is wearing off a little bit more each day."

"Treatment?" Cone said.

"For lack of a better word," Monroe said. "It's an entire series of treatments, actually. Some hypnotic, some mind-altering, some drug programs mixed in . . ."

"Doctor, please," Farris said.

"Right," Monroe said.

"So what you're saying, if I understand you correctly, is that you have no idea what's going to happen next?" Cone said. "Or when."

"I didn't say that," Monroe said.

"Then what the fuck are you saying?" Freeman said, his patience wearing thin.

Farris glanced at Freeman. "Ben, come on."

"It's okay," Monroe said. "I understand his frustration with all this."

109

"Frustration?" Freeman said. "I've lost count of the bodies, Monroe. I'd say frustration doesn't quite cut it for me anymore."

Monroe chewed a piece of toast and washed it down with a sip of coffee. "What I can tell you is that John is slowly regaining his memory," he said. "Much of it will be in bits and pieces. Little snippets of his life in jagged memories that won't make much sense to him. The longer he stays out, the quicker this will happen. Then something will pull the trigger, and the floodgates will open. The little snippets will align themselves into what we can safely call long-term memory."

"Trigger?" Freeman said.

"A name, a place, maybe something in the news will strike a chord," Monroe said. "Possibly even a smell or something he eats. It's difficult to say, even with real amnesia patients, what will return the memory."

"A trigger," Freeman said, and shook his head.

John watched her smoke, the old woman. Once she returned to her picnic table, all rationality seemed to leave her. A washed-out, glazed look came over her eyes as she started talking to herself again. She pointed her right finger in the air and made stabbing motions, and John realized that she wasn't talking to herself at all. She was deeply engaged in a two-way conversation with a figment of her imagination, somebody who wasn't real except inside her mind.

"Margaret fucking Thatcher," she said to him. "What's it to you?"

Nothing. Not a thing. Except the longer John stared at her, the more familiar the old woman seemed to him.

"Why don't you come down to the bridge and share a bottle with me, John," the old woman said.

"I wouldn't be good company tonight, Maggie," John said.

"In that case, let me have a few more butts," Maggie said.
Maggie.
That was her name.

"What happens if John finds a trigger, as you called it?" Farris said.

"It could be an isolated memory," Monroe said. "Or it could open a floodgate. Either way, his memories will be earliest to latest. That much I can say for certain."

"Glad you're certain about something," Freeman said. "Because I'm certain about something, too. John is like Jaws out of water. Get too close and he'll bite your fucking head off."

Her name was Maggie. Not the old woman talking to herself at the picnic table. The old woman John saw in his mind.

The question was, who was Maggie?

"Nice day today, John," Maggie said. "What say we gets us a bottle and head over to the park?"

"I promised Julie I would fix her roof," John said. "Me and some others."

"Her roof?" Maggie said. "What the fuck for? It never rains here. That's why all the goddamn palm trees, they never need rain. These assholes paint their lawns green."

"I promised," John said.

"Suit yourself," Maggie said. "I'll see you later, maybe for dinner."

"Sure thing," John said.

A horn tooted. John turned around and saw Charles behind the wheel of the mission van. "Gotta go," he told Maggie.

Julie, Charles and Maggie were all at the San Diego Mission with him, of that John was now certain.

But when?

He lit another cigarette and tried to work out the problem, but the more he tried to put pieces of the puzzle together, the less they seemed to fit.

Julie.

Charles.

And now Maggie.

What did it all mean?

Monroe had a bad habit of underestimating Ben Freeman's intelligence. Freeman could be crude sometimes, and most times downright arrogant, which sometimes led Monroe to believe the man was a boorish oaf.

However, Freeman was no oaf and sometimes his arrogance was warranted. He would not have risen through the agency ranks to become second in command at so young an age if his intelligence and ability weren't above the ordinary. He had better get used to being barked at by Freeman, Monroe surmised, because Farris wouldn't be around much longer and it was obvious how the torch would be passed.

"It seems to me," Freeman said, "that John's progression will take him on a course back to the mission in the Bowery section of Manhattan."

"Yes, that would be how I see it as well," Monroe said.

"What we can't . . . what *you* can't predict is how long that progression will take?" Freeman said.

"Not with pinpoint accuracy, but I can tell you that in another few days John Tibbets will regain enough of his memory to act upon it," Monroe said.

"What does that mean?" Farris said. "Act upon it?"

"Unless I misunderstand the doctor," Freeman said, "I think he means John will try to put the pieces of his life back together in a sequence that makes sense to him. Isn't that right?"

"Yes," Monroe said.

"What are you driving at, Ben?" Farris said.

"We don't know where John is at the moment," Freeman said. "But if the doctor is correct, and I have no reason to believe that he isn't, John is headed for the Bowery Mission and we'll be right there to greet him."

Farris nodded. "When will you leave?"

"Right now," Freeman said. He looked at Cone. "Right?"

Cone, in this all the way now, nodded his head in agreement.

John drove the Buick into Phoenix and parked it in the first municipal parking lot he came across. It was a six-story building and even though spots were open on the third level, he drove to the sixth. As he came out of the turn from the fifth level to the sixth, he realized the sixth level was the roof and nearly empty of cars. He left the Buick standing alone against a wall in the sun.

Carrying his small suitcase, he walked along the streets of downtown Phoenix. Rush hour was in full force and the sidewalks were crowded with pedestrian traffic. What struck John about Phoenix as he made his way through the crowds was the sheer size and scope of the city. It was massive and not at all what he expected. As modern as any city in the country, it seemed to him out of place in the cowboy folklore of the West. Not that he expected outlaws and gunfights, but the city as it stood seemed as if it had been picked up on the East Coast or West Coast and dropped off here. Urban, with skyscrapers and modern buildings everywhere he looked.

Also, it was hot, with a dry, arid breeze that filled your lungs with warm air.

John turned a corner and found himself on Central Avenue, which he soon discovered was the dividing line for the city. As he continued walking, the skyscrapers were replaced with lofts, small buildings, prewar hotels and far less affluent pedestrians.

Some of the buildings were dilapidated from years of neglect and even fire. Just like with New York, that invisible dividing line distinguished wealthy from the less well-off.

He kept walking until a mile further down Central Avenue he came upon a six-story hotel that had seen far better days. He turned and looked across the street, and spotted a deli of Spanish origin. He turned back around and entered the hotel.

TEN

The pilot announced over the system that they would be landing at Kennedy Airport in fifteen minutes. Cone looked out his window at the sprawling expanse of New York City. At night, the city's lights told the story. The Brooklyn Bridge, the George Washington Bridge, the Empire State Building and Chrysler Building, they all stood like shining beacons of what man can do when he isn't busy trying to blow up his fellow man's accomplishments.

"I haven't flown into New York at night in a while," Cone said. "I forgot how it looks after dark."

Freeman grinned at Cone. "You mean how you can't see the filth from this high when it's all lit up like a Christmas tree?"

"That's not what I meant," Cone said.

"Wait until we land," Freeman said. "It will be."

John sprawled out on the lumpy hotel room bed and closed his eyes. Exhaustion washed over him and he was asleep within a few seconds.

It was a hot summer night and he couldn't sleep. He went for a walk and found himself under the long ramp to the Brooklyn Bridge. The street was wide, cobblestoned and dark. Many from the shelter slept in the street or on the sidewalk inside cardboard boxes, the tall kind used for refrigerators. Where they got them was a mystery to him, but he

115

didn't really care. He preferred the warm bed and hot food of the shelter.

Under the bridge overpass, he paused to smoke a cigarette. The air was hot and still, smelling of the sickly combination of garbage and salt off the ocean. He heard a noise and turned to locate the source. It came from about a block further down. He walked quietly toward it, thinking some of the men from the mission were at it again. Fighting over bottles of cheap wine or loose change that they begged for on lower Broadway.

As he neared the source of the noise, John stopped and hid in the shadows of an overpass pillar. This was different from the normal fights among the men living at the mission. A police cruiser with its lights flashing was parked in the middle of the street. Three men were beating a uniformed police officer senseless. The officer, a strapping man, put up a valiant fight, but only in the movies does one set of arms and legs win against three.

They were beating the officer to jelly. Still, it was no concern of his. He turned and was about to walk away when he heard the officer plead for his life. "Please," he begged. "I have a family. I have daughters at home."

For some reason, that struck a chord with him. He slowly emerged from the shadows to confront the three men. He recognized them from the mission, although they weren't regulars. One of them had the officer's gun and he aimed it at the officer's head. He was laughing, as were the other two.

They saw him then as he moved from shadow to the dim light of a streetlamp. The one holding the gun told him to mind his own business. When John moved, it was with the precision of a finely turned athlete. He put the three of them down, killed one, but not before the one with the gun got off a shot that put a hole in his side.

He used the radio in the cruiser to call for help. Two ambulances arrived, along with a dozen uniformed police officers and six detectives. While EMTs administered first aid to his bullet wound, a detec-

tive questioned him.

What were you doing there?

How did you defeat three armed men with a bullet in your side?

What is your name?

Where do you live?

Where did you learn to fight like that?

What is your name?

Where do you live?

"I don't know," he said over and over again.

You saved his life, the detective said.

His life.

Whose life?

What is your name?

John opened his eyes and for a moment, he didn't know where he was. He stared at the dark ceiling until slowly it came back to him. He reached over to turn on the bedside lamp, sat up and grabbed his cigarettes.

He picked up his cheap watch. It was just after two in the morning. He stood up to look out the window. The deli across the street was open twenty-four hours. His stomach rumbled.

Cone stood next to Freeman on the sidewalk outside the Bowery Church and Mission in lower Manhattan. "This is where he lived when you kept him under wraps?" Cone said.

"Not very glamorous, I admit," Freeman said. "But it was the perfect spot to keep John away from the public."

"Not see the forest for the trees," Cone remarked.

"So to speak."

Cone looked at the large, old church, the connected building used as a sleeping quarters and dining hall, the litter on the streets and the overall rundown appearance of the property, and he was not impressed. "Fallen on hard times?" he said.

"So to speak," Freeman said. "A lot of its expenses were picked up by us. We had three agents in residence, plus Julie Warner."

"Now it just has the homeless," Cone said.

"Not our problem anymore," Freeman said.

"But John is."

"Yeah." Freeman paused to light a cigarette, then pointed to the front steps of the church. "After he escaped from the hospital, we tracked him to the church. I had four men with me that night, all highly trained agents. He came out of the church right there," Freeman said, pointing to the church steps again. "He went through my men like a hot knife through butter. Any other man would have been trapped, but not John. Anyway, we pursued him through the Bowery and lost him under the bridge."

"And now we're set for a rematch," Cone said.

"It appears so," Freeman said.

"If he remembers," Cone said.

Freeman tossed his cigarette to the sidewalk and stepped on it. "He'll remember," he said, and turned away. "And even if he doesn't."

Surprisingly, the pastrami on whole wheat was excellent. So was the side order of thick fries with the skins left on, finished off with salt and vinegar. He polished off the late-night meal with a sixteen-ounce mug of coffee and a massive slice of creamy cherry cheesecake that wasn't dry and flaky, but so moist that liquid dripped off the fork.

The deli was divided into two sections. To the left of the entrance stood a wide counter filled with meats, breads and pastries. To the right of the entrance were a dozen tables overseen by a single waitress. Tonight, as every table was occupied, she had her hands full with hungry late-night drinkers.

"Refill?" the waitress asked John as she brought him his check.

"Touch it or I won't sleep," John said.

"It's three in the morning," she said, looking around. "Who sleeps."

John waited for her to add to his mug, then said, "Would you know where I can find a library?"

"A library," she said. "Let me think a second. We don't get many readers in here."

John sipped his coffee and waited. The waitress said, "Make a left out of here and go about a mile down Collins to Seventh Street. A block to your right is the library. It's not the main branch, but it's a big one."

"Thanks."

The check was for eleven dollars. John left the waitress a twenty and told her to keep the change.

Freeman and Cone sat in the backseats of a Lincoln Town Car as the driver, one of Freeman's men, drove the massive vehicle across the Verazzano Narrows Bridge onto Staten Island. Next to the driver sat another of Freeman's men. His name was Anthony. The driver was Parker. Neither man asked questions when Freeman told them to head to Staten Island. They just did as they were told. It was the only way to get ahead in the agency, keep your mouth shut and do as you're told. And never question authority, even when tempted.

Freeman lit a cigarette and leaned forward to speak to Parker. "Put this address in the GPS," he said, and gave Parker the address.

Anthony was good, Freeman noted. When they touched down on the Staten Island side of the bridge, he glanced at the GPS in the dashboard, made an immediate left and didn't look at it again until they reached a quiet, tree-lined street ten miles away. "This is it," Anthony said and killed the engine across the street from a two-story, Tudor-style house.

"Take a good look, gentlemen," Freeman said. "This will be your new home for as long as it takes."

Anthony and Parker looked at the house. There wasn't a For Sale sign on the front lawn, but it was obvious by the lack of drapes in the windows and the overgrown lawn that the house hadn't been occupied for quite some time. "We set up surveillance here?" Parker said. "In this house?"

"You do," Freeman said.

"Who is our target?" Anthony said.

"Gary Nevin," Freeman said. "He lives in the house directly behind us."

"When do we start?" Parker asked.

"Tomorrow morning."

"Any cover?" Parker said.

"What would you like?" Freeman said.

"I'll tell you what I don't like," Parker said. "The last operation you had us as a gay couple living together. I don't like that, having to hold hands with this ape." Parker nodded toward Anthony.

"Fair enough," Freeman said. "That cover wouldn't work in this neighborhood anyway. Okay, let's go."

Anthony started the engine. Cone waited until they were halfway across the bridge before he said, "So who is Gary Nevin?"

Upon rising, John shaved carefully, showered and dressed in clean trousers and shirt. He packed the pistols in the suitcase and slid it under the bed, double-checking the door lock on the way out.

In the lobby, he paid for an extra night's stay. Famished, he crossed the street and ate a hearty breakfast in the deli before venturing on foot to the library.

The library, as described by the waitress, wasn't the main branch, wasn't new or even in good condition, but it was big. Massive, in fact. Red brick with gargoyles adorning the roof, the old building was more like a fortress than a home for books. As John entered the library, he realized why when he paused to read a small brass plaque that read *Donated from the National Guard to the City of Phoenix Library System.*

A woman on the first floor sent John to the second floor when he inquired about the use of a computer. A woman on the second floor took John to the computer room, where a dozen terminals were set up on two railroad tables.

"I'm afraid I don't know much about computers," John told her. "I need to look up some old newspaper stories. Maybe you could show me how?"

It turned out to be not very difficult. Mostly type, click and click some more. The woman told John that thirty minutes was the limit for a terminal, but as today wasn't very busy, he could stay as long as needed.

At the librarian's suggestion, John tried the Nexis Lexis database system. Simply requesting a search of newspaper articles concerning a New York City police officer saved by a homeless man in the Bowery brought up dozens of stories by every newspaper in the city. The *Times, Daily News, Post, Newsday* and the *Wall Street Journal* had covered the story for weeks.

John read account after account of how he came to the rescue of uniformed police officer Gary Nevin, who was savagely attacked by three homeless men under the Brooklyn Bridge. *The hero, John Tibbets, also a homeless man, is an amnesia victim and refused the hero treatment offered by the mayor. Shortly after Tibbets was admitted to New York Hospital, he disappeared.* The stories, along with John, faded away after that.

He Googled Gary Nevin and read follow-up stories on the man. After Nevin's release from the hospital, he'd transferred from the Police Department to the Fire Department, much to the relief of his wife Susan and their daughters. There was some mention of Nevin's uncle, a career detective named Howard Taft. There were photographs of the uncle and Tibbets taken at the hospital. Young and old together. Taft and Tibbets. Neither smiled for the camera.

John sat back in his chair for a moment. Disappeared. Then reappeared in the desert of New Mexico with the FBI on his tail. None of it, not one word of it, made sense to him.

But he'd bet Gary Nevin knew what the hell went on. John clicked search and then print when he found a decent photograph of Officer Nevin alongside a photograph of himself. Nevin was a bloody pulp, but so damn happy to be alive he smiled through the pain as he shook John's hand.

John folded printouts of the news stories and photographs and tucked them into his back pocket. He thanked the librarians for their help on the way out.

In his hotel room, John read the printed news stories several times searching for some clue, some hidden meaning that might ring a bell in his head and provide some answers to his many questions. More questions arose than answers provided. Why was he living at the shelter in the Bowery? How did he lose his memory? What was he before he suffered blunt force trauma? Why was he able to take on three armed men in such handy fashion? How did he wind up in New Mexico? Why was he living in the San Diego Mission? What was Julie Warner's role in all this and why did she feel it necessary to kill him? Why was the FBI after him now?

Questions.

No answers.

He had to go to New York and find Gary Nevin. He didn't know why, but he knew Nevin was a key factor in unlocking the secrets sheltered away inside his mind.

John sprawled out on the bed, lit a cigarette and stared at the ceiling.

There was one nagging question left to be asked.

Did he really want to know?

He was safe for the moment, had some cash in his pocket and could lose himself somewhere deep in the West. Grow a beard, change his name, find some work and eke out an existence until he was forgotten, then come out of hiding and start life anew. He wasn't old, although time wasn't on his side, but there was enough left in the calendar to find a good woman, settle down, grow old together.

Did he really want to know?

He puffed on the cigarette and blew a smoke ring. The tiny ring widened as it rose toward the ceiling, spread and vanished into nothing.

Did he really want to know?

The answer was yes.

ELEVEN

Across the divide on Collins Avenue, John walked along Seventh Street and found a trendy men's clothing store where he purchased two medium-priced suits, four white shirts, two ties and two pairs of shoes. One block down, he picked up a decent suitcase—with a handle and wheels—to store it all in.

In his hotel room, John showered and changed into one of the suits, a lightweight gray wool. He selected a white shirt, dark tie and black loafers. Then he packed his remaining belongings into the new suitcase and sat on the bed to count his money. Thirty-nine hundred in mostly small bills remained, but that was more than enough to take him to New York.

In front of the hotel, John flagged a passing cab and asked the driver to take him to the Amtrak station.

"John's instinct for survival coupled with twenty-five years of training will take him to New York," Freeman said. "Even without his marbles, he's better equipped to stay alive than any man I have working for me now."

Cone took a sip of his drink, scotch and water over ice. The ice, mostly water now, weakened the drink to the point that the scotch had lost most of its flavor. "If he's that good, why not try to bring him back? Better to have him fighting for us than against us."

"He does fight for us when we need him," Freeman said.

"I don't mean as some kind of mindless zombie," Cone said.

"And besides, look how good it's worked out for you this way."

Freeman sipped his drink, bourbon neat, and thought for a moment. "If it were only that easy," he said.

Cone looked at Freeman. "What are you holding back?" he said. "What aren't you telling me?"

Freeman looked out the window. They were in the revolving bar on the fifteenth floor of the Marriott Hotel in Times Square. The bar turned slowly, giving the impression it wasn't moving until you glanced out the window and noticed that the giant neon billboard was replaced by the time and temperature clock of the Times reader board.

"You put a gun to my head," Cone said. "I think that earns me your trust or at the very least, the truth."

Freeman sipped his drink and set it on the table. "John wasn't just picked for Monroe's program because he went sour. Hell, half the men in the field do the same thing, just not as well as John did. What set John apart from the others, me included, is his ability." Freeman paused to take another sip of his drink. "And not just his physical ability, which is off the scale, but his mental capacity."

"Are you talking about his IQ?" Cone said.

"No, although it's been recorded at one-fifty-nine," Freeman said. "I'm talking about his mental toughness. What Monroe put him through would have broken a normal man in a few weeks. John didn't turn for a year or more."

"Turn?"

"Brainwashing to the layman," Freeman said. "His ability to resist under the harshest, toughest conditions. What they did to John McCain would seem like dealing with ants at a picnic in comparison."

"You mean memory eradication," Cone said. "That's what we talked about."

"What we talked about is the salvation of our country," Freeman said. "Look, you do a fantastic job at the Bureau, but it isn't enough. Maybe for now, you can hold things at bay, maybe even gain a little ground, but in fifteen years when the rest of the developing world catches up to us, what then?"

"You're talking about terrorism," Cone said.

"I'm talking about infiltration," Freeman said. "Don't think for one minute our enemies aren't working on Americanizing an entire generation of good little America haters as we speak. Young boys and girls who will grow into men and women with one specific goal in mind. Become citizens and blend into the system. Work for the government, big business, even run for political office on a local scale. Ever see an apple rot? It rots from the inside out. The skin still looks red and shiny while the inside turns to pulpy mush."

"Do unto others, only do it first," Cone remarked.

"And why not?" Freeman said. "We should sit around while some foreign-born scumbag gets elected to the Senate and feeds his motherland our military secrets and infrastructure weaknesses and flaws in our defense systems? No thanks, Mister FBI."

"I didn't say I wasn't with you," Cone said. "I'm just having a hard time digesting what you're saying."

"None of this is new," Freeman said. "Remember *The Manchurian Candidate*? Soldiers come home from Korea brainwashed by the Chinese. A code word is spoken over the phone; they try to kill the President."

"That was a movie," Cone said.

"And this isn't."

Cone paused to sip his drink and gather his thoughts. "John Tibbets is the key, isn't he?"

"And the lock and the barn door," Freeman said. "If Monroe can not just break a man like John, but totally erase his living memories, think what he can do with the average Joe walking the streets. Steal his identity and give him a totally new one. Implant a suggestion to take action five years down the road when the clerk in a Tehran office is now a high-ranking official. A normal day at work until he picks up an assault rifle and takes out his superiors, but not before transmitting their secrets to us, of course."

Cone stared at Freeman for several seconds. "And this is possible? I mean today?"

"John was programmed to commit assassination at one A.M.," Freeman said. "A post suggestion kicked in at two to erase the memory of it. That is why John has no memory of waking up in the desert. It was erased."

"Yet he ran," Cone said.

"I didn't say Monroe perfected his program," Freeman said. "He feels that's still a good year to eighteen months away. However, by the time the rest of the world catches up to us, you and I will be on Social Security and they will be on the bottom of a tall ladder looking up."

"That's why the urgency to catch him before his memory returns," Cone said. "He's useless to you if he knows who he is, isn't he?"

"No," Freeman said. "If John regains his memory intact, what he is, is a danger to us. All of us."

He opened his eyes, and the detective was with him inside the mission church. What did he want? Why didn't he just leave him alone? That's all he really wanted, to be left alone.

"I can't do that, John," he said. "You're a hero. The city wants to show its gratitude for saving the life of a police officer."

He went to leave and the detective placed a hand on his shoulder. His instincts kicked in and took control. With a snap of his wrist, he disabled the detective, then took off running and exited the church.

On the church steps, a uniformed police officer and Charles waited for him. He took the officer down and was about to run off when Ben Freeman arrived in a sedan.

"There," Freeman yelled. "Get him."

What the hell was Freeman doing there?

John opened his eyes to the sound of a recorded voice announcing stops along the Amtrak route. The train was entering the terminal at Oklahoma City, Oklahoma. There was a long way to go. Two more full days, in fact.

The train stopped. Doors opened, passengers rushed to get off as if the doors would snap closed any second and trap them onboard. A conductor came through and announced there would be a one-hour layover.

With his luggage locked securely in his stateroom, John went up to the street for some fresh air and a cigarette. The heat of downtown hit him in the face like a blast from a furnace. The street noise—a combination of cars, buses, trucks and construction—was deafening. Pedestrians, as they did in all major cities, moved along at a nerve-racking pace, seemingly unaware of the noise, heat and traffic.

There was nothing of note to see. John returned to the station, boarded the train, stopped by the dining car for some coffee and entered his stateroom. At the small desk, he opened an envelope, removed the news articles about Gary Nevin, and read them one more time. He looked at the photographs of Nevin and his uncle, a police captain named Howard Taft.

Taft was the man from his dream, the man in the church with him. *"You're a hero,"* he'd said. *"The city wants to show its gratitude,"* he'd said.

John set the articles on the desk. "Gratitude?"

"That's him," Freeman said from the backseat of the sedan. "Gary Nevin."

Cone, seated next to Freeman, looked out the window at the hook and ladder company where Gary Nevin and some of his fellow firemen stood outside the open bay doors. "He used to be a cop?" Cone said. "What happened?"

"After John saved his life, he transferred over at the request of his wife and kids," Freeman said. "His uncle was a captain with the PD and led me to John about a year or so ago."

"Was a captain?" Cone said.

"I shot him," Freeman said.

"Dead?"

"Retired to some complex in South Carolina."

"Any chance he'll go there first?"

"Monroe won't give odds, but I have a team watching Taft's house," Freeman said. "If John doesn't show here within a week, we'll head on down."

"You should give frequent-flier miles," Cone said.

"Yeah," Freeman said, and lit a cigarette.

A siren suddenly went off, accompanied by flashing red lights. Nevin and the others raced inside for their gear. "Looks like they're getting a call," Cone remarked.

"Let's go," Freeman told his driver.

"Where?" the driver said.

"Nevin's house on Staten Island."

Wearing just underwear, John sat on the floor between the bed and bathroom in his stateroom and starting doing sit-ups. When he reached the count of fifty, his stomach began to ache. At seventy-five, a deep burn set in, but he didn't stop. He locked his feet under the bed and when he passed the one hundred mark, the muscles in his stomach cramped and he had to slow the pace. Somewhere between one hundred thirty-five and one-fifty, nausea set in, and when he reached one hundred and sixty, he stopped.

He sat up with his back against the bed and waited for the nausea to pass and his breathing to return to normal. Once recovered, John assumed the push-up position. After twenty-five repetitions, his chest and shoulders started to burn. When he passed the fifty-repetition mark, the muscles in his arms began to quiver from the exertion. Around seventy-five repetitions, he started to gasp for air, and the burn in his triceps cut clear to the bone. At eighty-five, each push-up felt as if an elephant was sitting on his back. The last five repetitions to the one hundred mark came slowly until, at one hundred, John collapsed in a heap and sucked in so much air, he again felt dizzy.

After ten minutes, he recovered enough to stand and enter the shower stall in the tiny bathroom where the hot needle spray returned feeling to his muscles.

"John Tibbets would rather die than quit," Freeman said as he peered through the closed drapes of the house across the street from the Nevins' home. He turned around and looked at Anthony and Parker. "Remember that."

After renting a locker in Penn Station to check his bags, John emerged from underground and stood on West Thirty-fourth Street in Manhattan. The city was a whirling mass of confusion, with cars, trucks, buses, cabs, bicycles and thousands of pedestrians all vying for their tiny spot on the great island. To a casual observer, New York City appeared as a giant playground for adults. To John, it was just another piece of bread in a trail of breadcrumbs.

He drank it all in for a moment, then looked about to get his bearings. It was a strange feeling, knowing where everything in a city was without any memory of having been there. It was a feeling he was getting used to experiencing, but strange nonetheless.

He headed east on Thirty-fourth. Sweat poured down his face before he reached the end of the block. He loosened his tie, removed the suit jacket, and slung it over his right shoulder. As he passed a storefront, he caught a glimpse of his reflection in the window. Not exactly Frank Sinatra material, but he was reminded of an old album cover from the sixties where Sinatra had his suit jacket slung over his shoulder the same way.

At Fifth Avenue, John turned left and walked uptown to Fortieth Street, then stood at the base of the steps of the main branch of the public library. The building was enormous, looking more like a Cold War–era bomb shelter than a place of learning. To the left and right of the giant archway doors, carved statues of male lions sat ever on guard.

He climbed the steps along with dozens of others, passed under the arches, and entered the world famous lobby. Tourists were everywhere, some part of a guided tour, others wandering on their own.

John found and read a building directory rather than ask a librarian for help. Even innocent questions are remembered if the right people ask them, and he didn't want to chance being remembered.

Inside an immense reading room, he found the phone directories for each of the five boroughs that composed the City of New York. He carried the five massive books to a table and started with Brooklyn. Although Nevin wasn't exactly a common name, there were plenty to go around in the Borough of Kings. None, however, with the first name of Gary, or with a wife named Susan. The results were the same for the Bronx and Queens. He saved Manhattan for last, figuring the chances that Nevin lived on Trump's island on a firefighter's pay were slim to none. He opened the Staten Island book. Half the size of the one for the other boroughs, a third the size of the Manhattan book, Staten Island proved to be the residence of the Nevin family.

John wrote the address and phone number of Gary and Susan Nevin on a piece of copy paper, then went to the research room on another floor to locate subway maps. On the same paper, he listed the subway route to the Nevins' Staten Island home.

"What do you have to eat in this place?" Freeman said.

"We picked up a week's groceries," Parker said. "In the kitchen."

Freeman, still at the window, turned around to look at Parker and Anthony. "Well?"

Parker and Anthony exchanged looks, then got the hint. Together, they walked toward the kitchen.

Cone joined Freeman at the window and peered through a slat in the blinds at the Nevin home across the street. "We're staying the night?" Cone said.

"Looks like," Freeman said. "My guess is, John will show within the next thirty-six hours."

"Then I'm going to take a nap," Cone said.

"Should I wake you for some food?"

"Can those guys cook?"

"We'll find out."

"I guess so," Cone said.

Alone at the window, Freeman peered through the blinds at the Nevin home. Absolutely nothing was going on. That's what scared him the most.

John walked a few blocks to a coffee shop, where he sat at the counter and ordered lunch. While he waited for his meal, he went to the pay phone located between the men's and women's bathrooms and dialed the number for collect calls.

"Operator," John said when a female voice asked him how

she could be of assistance. "I'd like to make a collect call to Gary or Susan Nevin at the following number. My name is Howard Taft."

TWELVE

Susan Nevin was about to prepare an after-school snack for her daughters when the phone on the kitchen wall rang. When Gary was still on the police force, she dreaded a ringing phone whenever he was working. Every call could be the one telling her she was a widow, that her husband died in the line of duty and she should be proud of his dedication and service to their city. They bought an answering machine and she screened every incoming call. For ten years, the call never came . . . until it did.

Gary had been beaten by three homeless men in the Bowery. Gary's uncle Howard told her; he made the call himself, rather than pawn it off on some PR officer at One Police Plaza. On routine patrol, Gary stopped to help an unconscious man in the street, only the man wasn't unconscious and Gary had walked into a trap. Only the brave actions of another homeless man who came to Gary's rescue saved her husband's life. His name was John Tibbets and he suffered from amnesia. Because he was wounded by a gunshot while saving Gary, the city tried to make Tibbets a hero against his will. He disappeared after Howard got shot and nearly killed by unknown assailants and hadn't been heard from since.

Gary being a firefighter was marginally better than being a cop. Not that the life of a firefighter was a safe profession by any means, but Gary only worked two twenty-four-hour shifts per week, which gave him five days out of every seven to spend at home with the girls, and her.

In any case, the last voice Susan expected to hear when she answered the phone belonged to John Tibbets. At first, she was confused. The operator asked if she would accept charges for a collect call from Howard Taft. Unless something terrible had happened, why would Gary's uncle be calling collect?

Susan accepted the charges, and she was shocked when a voice said, "This isn't Howard Taft calling. It's John Tibbets, do you remember me?"

For a moment, Susan thought she would faint. There was a second or two of light-headedness as the memory of Gary's near death in the hospital flashed through her mind. She recovered enough to say, "Yes, I remember you." To her own ear, her voice sounded weak.

John picked up on the stress in Susan's voice. He said, "I didn't mean to frighten you, I'm sorry. If this wasn't important to me, I wouldn't be calling."

"We thought you were . . . dead," Susan said.

"I'm not."

"You disappeared a year ago," Susan said. "After Howard was shot."

"I don't know anything about that," John said. "In fact, I don't know too much about anything at all."

"The amnesia, yes," Susan said.

"Is he alive, Captain Taft?"

"Yes, and he's retired now."

Susan could hear John pause. A moment later, she heard him exhale, probably cigarette smoke.

"Why are you calling?" she said.

"I need to talk to your husband."

"John, I will always be grateful to you for saving Gary, but we don't need any more trouble in our lives," Susan said. "We have two daughters that need their father. I'm sorry if that sounds selfish, but . . ."

"It doesn't," John said. "But it doesn't change the fact that I need to speak to your husband. I wouldn't ask if it weren't important."

Susan sighed. She knew this wouldn't go anywhere good. However, if it weren't for John Tibbets she'd be collecting a widow's pension and scraping by to raise two daughters on her own. "Just talk?" she said.

"Yes. Just talk."

"He's at work, at the fire station."

"I'll call him myself. Give me the number."

Susan gave John the number, then added, "You're in some kind of trouble, aren't you?"

"Yes."

"Don't bring it here," Susan said. "For the love of God, don't bring it here."

"I'll do my best."

"We should have surveillance cameras and wiretaps for this job," Parker said from the window.

"We don't," Freeman said. He was on the sofa, eating a burger.

"But we should," Parker said.

"A lot we should that we don't," Freeman said. "Wiretaps means judges and judges mean explanations." He bit into his burger and washed it down with a sip of coffee from a mug. "Surveillance cameras won't see anything you won't, and besides, they make you lazy. You come to rely on them and lose your eye for the street. Once that happens, you're finished."

Seated in a chair opposite Freeman, Anthony said, "Anything happening out there? I hear a noise."

"School bus pulling up," Parker said. "A couple of girls getting off. The mother's at the door. How exciting is that?"

Cone, also on the sofa eating a burger, looked at Freeman. "How much longer are we going to wait?"

"Another day, then we'll head down to South Carolina," Freeman said. "But I don't think it will take a day."

"Only thing missing is a plate of cookies," Parker said. "They're in the house, the door is closed. Now what?"

Freeman bit into his burger and wiped his chin with a napkin. "Don't be in such a hurry to meet John Tibbets," he said.

"Yeah, why is that?" Parker said.

"Most don't live past hello," Freeman said.

Parker and Anthony stared at him.

Grateful for the brief lull in the action, Gary Nevin went for a nap on his bunk in the second-floor bedroom of the fire station. One of the busiest firehouses in all of Brooklyn kept him up sometimes all twenty-four hours of each twenty-four-hour shift. Today was exceptional in that calls were infrequent. Only two so far, twelve hours into the shift. Not one to argue with silence, Gary settled into his bunk for some much-needed sleep. In the first month after being nearly beaten to death and almost shot with his own gun, sleep was in short supply. Dreams, nightmares actually, had haunted him constantly. Slowly, with time, the nightmares had become less and less frequent until now they rarely happened at all.

He'd barely closed his eyes when Lieutenant Knoop shook him awake. "Hey, Sleeping Beauty, you have a phone call."

Gary was instantly awake, a habit born of a thousand middle-of-the-night calls. "Who is it, Lou?" he said.

"Man says he's your uncle from South Carolina."

"Howard?"

"Yeah."

"I'll take it here," Gary said. He rose and walked to the wall phone by the door and picked up. "Uncle Howard, is something . . ."

"This isn't your uncle," John said before Gary could finish his sentence. "It's John Tibbets. Do you remember me?"

A cold shiver ran down Gary's spine. Immediately, he was transported back to that night a year ago when he lay helpless and bleeding in the street just seconds away from certain death. He'd pleaded for his life, begging the man who held his own pistol to his head. Telling the man he had a family that needed him, little girls at home.

The man didn't care. He'd laughed at Gary, along with his two friends. Just before the man pulled the trigger, John Tibbets arrived on the scene.

"Mr. Nevin, are you there?" John said.

Gary snapped out of his memories. "Yeah, yes, I'm here," he said. "I'm just shocked to hear your voice, is all."

"I don't have much time," John said. "I need to see you right away."

"I don't understand," Gary said. "Where have you . . ."

"Not on the phone," John said. "In person."

"Where are you?"

"Manhattan. Listen, can you get away?"

"I'm on duty another twelve hours," Gary said. "Why don't you come by the station? We can talk here."

"People are after me," John said. "And by now, you're being watched."

"Watched?" Gary said. "What for? By who?"

"The people after me know that I'm going to retrace my steps," John said. "Don't ask me who they are or what they want. I don't know at this point."

"The people who shot my uncle?"

"That would be my guess, although I don't know why," John said. "Or what they want from me."

"Is that why you've been away all this time?"

"I have no idea," John said. "All I know is I need your help."

"How?"

"Any way you can," John said. "Start with what you know about me, but not on the phone. In person."

"Where?"

"Listen, I have an idea," John said.

"It's getting dark," Cone said. "How long do you want to sit here?"

They were in Freeman's sedan, parked across the street from the fire station in Brooklyn where Gary Nevin was assigned. For the past several hours, they'd watched the EMT ambulance being washed, oxygen tanks checked, hoses rolled, rain gear hung and other such off-call chores being performed.

"Give it a while more," Freeman said. "Then I'll call for a replacement crew."

"I suppose you have one handy?" Cone said, learning how Freeman operated.

"Not yet," Freeman said. "I have some men coming into Kennedy on a private flight. Should land within the hour. They'll call me as soon as they're on the ground. I'll have them meet us here. We'll take a break after that."

"Exactly how large is your organization?" Cone said.

"I can't answer that," Freeman said.

"Can't or won't?"

"What's the difference?"

"Trust."

Cone's remark drew a laugh from Freeman and he was about to reply with a snappy comeback when all hell broke loose at the fire station. Red lights flashed, sirens screamed, men dashed about, engines started, bay doors opened.

Behind the wheel of the sedan, Freeman started the engine.

"We're going to follow them?" Cone said.

"Where they go, Nevin goes," Freeman said. "And so do we."

It was Gary's turn to ride shotgun in the cab of the ambulance. Two of his fellow firefighters rode up front and the few minutes' travel time gave him the opportunity for the privacy he needed.

He pulled his cell phone and dialed the number for the disposable cell phone that John had given him when he called back the second time. John answered before the phone rang twice.

"Gary?" John said.

"I'm on a call to a warehouse fire on Tremont a few blocks from the station," Gary said. "Where are you?"

"I took the subway to Brooklyn," John said. "I'm two blocks from your station in a coffee shop. I'll walk over. Shouldn't be hard to find."

"I might be busy," Gary said. "I don't know if anyone is injured yet."

"Gary, be careful," John said. "We're probably being watched."

"Right," Gary said and hung up.

"What a fucking mess," Freeman said.

The warehouse held a large chemical factory that produced paint and assorted chemicals for thinning and removing it. The building stood two stories high and occupied most of the block. Due to the explosive nature of the fire, companies from several locations were called in and fire trucks blocked off the street as dozens of firefighters fought to keep the blaze under control.

Freeman parked the sedan around the corner, and he and Cone walked over to the scene. Uniformed police officers had cordoned off the street to keep pedestrians at bay.

"If those fumes get any worse, they'll have to evacuate the

area for ten blocks," Cone said.

Freeman wasn't interested in the fire or the fumes. His attention was on Gary Nevin, who was busy giving first aid to warehouse personnel and fellow firefighters at his ambulance.

"The man is good at his job," Freeman remarked.

Cone looked at Nevin, who was busy giving oxygen to several workers from the warehouse. "Ever want to do this job?" he said.

"Fireman?" Freeman said. "Never. You?"

"Thought about it a long time ago," Cone said. "Before my waist went from a thirty-two to a thirty-eight."

"You and me both," Freeman said as he scanned the crowd around him. Although night was quickly descending, the blaze illuminated the area well enough to see the eye color of those closest to him. "The man in the dark suit to our left thirty feet down, and the hippie-looking guy to our right wearing the *Honk if you love Jesus* shirt, see them?"

"What about them?" Cone said.

"Arson detectives," Freeman said. "They hang around a fire like this one and watch the crowd. They know that an arsonist who gets his nut off watching his handiwork will hang around. They spot a guy who looks like he's about to pop; he goes on their suspect A list."

"But that's not what you're looking for," Cone said. "In it?"

"No."

"You're hoping to spot someone breaking away from the crowd and approaching Nevin," Cone said. "That someone being Tibbets."

"Yes."

"Not three days ago, we left Tibbets two thousand miles from here," Cone said. "Alone, with little resources and no memory. Do you really think he's just suddenly going to pop up at a fire in Brooklyn?"

Freeman kept scanning the crowd, watching faces. He turned to look at Nevin, who was helping a man that appeared to need oxygen. The man's suit jacket was covering his head and Nevin held a plastic mask connected to a small tank as he helped the man into the ambulance. Once the man was inside, Nevin jumped in with him and closed the door.

Flames blowing out windows caught Freeman's attention and he looked away from the ambulance to watch firefighters scramble for safety as hot bits of glass flew in every direction.

John yanked the plastic mask from his face. "I'm okay," he said.

"Jesus Christ, you scared me half to death when I saw you running across the street like that," Gary said.

"I had to get your attention," John said.

Gary smiled. "You succeeded."

"I have very little time," John said. "What can you tell me about me?"

"I wish I could tell you what you want to know," Gary said. "But all I know is from our brief conversations at the hospital last year. You're homeless, you have amnesia and you saved my life. Plus, what I read in the papers and saw on the news, which you probably did the same. That's all I know."

"The mission?" John said.

"In the Bowery."

"I've seen it in my sleep," John said. "And you. That's how I knew who you are. I dreamed about saving your life."

"Listen, John, the man you need to talk to is my uncle," Gary said. "If anyone knows more about you, it's him."

"The police captain?"

"Yes, my uncle Howard. Captain Taft," Gary said. "Do you remember him?"

"Only from a dream," John said. "Where is he?"

"Retired, living in South Carolina with my aunt."

"Can you give me the address?"

"I'll write it down," Gary said, reaching for a notepad on the bench. He paused to look at John. "I have a few hundred bucks in my wallet."

"I'm good," John said. "Just the address—and, listen, I was never here."

"Sure."

"No, I mean it," John said. "These men aren't playing games. They're as serious as a heart attack."

By the time Freeman turned his attention back to Nevin's ambulance, four or five minutes had elapsed. The doors were still shut. Freeman's interest was piqued. "Cone, Nevin's ambulance doors are closed. He's got somebody in there with him."

"I caught the tail end of that," Cone said. "He was giving oxygen to somebody from the fire."

"Did you happen to notice the somebody is wearing a suit?" Freeman said. "Had the jacket pulled over his head."

Cone shifted his eyes to the ambulance doors. "They don't normally close the doors, do they?"

"No."

Freeman and Cone stared at the ambulance. The doors suddenly opened and John stepped out. He stood on the street for a moment. Then he turned and ran directly into the chaos.

"That's him," Freeman shouted. "That's John."

John darted past firefighters, turned to his left and raced into the night. Freeman pushed his way through the crowd with Cone at his back. "He crossed the street," Freeman yelled over his shoulder.

Another explosion in the warehouse sent thousands of shards of glass flying into the street. The police started pushing the crowd to the sidewalk, trapping Freeman and Cone in a sea of people.

"Clear the area," a fire captain yelled to the police. "Get them the hell out of here."

Along with the crowd, Freeman and Cone backed up until they were at the end of the block. Once free of the police blockade, Freeman grabbed Cone by the arm. "Let's go," Freeman said.

"He's a mile away by now," Cone said.

"I know," Freeman said.

The subway was just a few blocks from the warehouse fire. John caught the Manhattan-bound train after just a few minutes' wait on the nearly deserted platform. The train was a local and made every stop along the way toward the city. The added time gave John time to think. He became so engrossed in his thoughts, he didn't realize the train was above ground until they were crossing the Manhattan Bridge. The lights of lower Manhattan caught his eye and he snapped out of his funk. He stood and waited beside the door as the train slowly descended into the Canal Street Station.

At Canal Street, John switched to the uptown local into Penn Station.

Parker and Anthony nervously watched Freeman look out the window. They knew something had gone down that wasn't good, but Freeman had yet to bring it up, so they thought it best to keep quiet and wait it out. So they sat on the sofa with their mouths shut and waited for Freeman to tell them something.

Cone came out of the kitchen with a mug of fresh coffee and took a seat on the chair opposite the sofa. Like Parker and Anthony, he waited for Freeman to decide what his next move would be.

Freeman glanced at his watch, but didn't turn away from the window. "It's just after midnight," he said. "The house is dark. We'll wait until morning."

"For what?" Cone said.

Freeman finally turned away from the window and looked at Cone. "The fireman, what else?" he said.

The next train to South Carolina didn't leave until seven in the morning. John sat on a terminal bench to think it through. His options were to wait, rent a car using the driver's license he still had in his possession, or try for a bus. His options were severely limited.

Deciding on the train, John went to the counter and purchased a ticket. With six hours to wait, he returned to the street.

THIRTEEN

Freeman came out of the kitchen with a mug of coffee and a lit cigarette. He took a seat in a chair next to Cone and looked at Parker and Anthony. "Do you have my cell phone number?" he said.

"Of course," Parker said. "Why?"

"Because if John shows up at the Bowery Mission, I expect you to call me immediately," Freeman said.

Parker and Anthony looked at each other. At least it got them out of this goddamn house.

The stroll down Broadway took just over an hour. As he reached the block where the mission was located, John noticed the immediate change in the neighborhood. From West Fourth Street south, wealth had moved in, refurbished warehouses and old red-brick buildings, opened trendy shops and restaurants and driven the winos, junkies and hookers to a new location on the lower west side by the river.

John passed a few open bars that had sidewalk tables, mostly occupied by young men and women who didn't care about time or commitment, or so it appeared to him.

Then, just like that, the neighborhood morphed. Gone were the trendy loft apartments, bars and glitzy lights. Seedy warehouse-type buildings and dark streets took up most of the walk to the Bowery. Garbage and old newspapers swirled across the sidewalks on an evening breeze that smelled of salt, vomit and stale urine and was strangely familiar to John.

A man dressed in layers of rags approached from the dark doorway of an old warehouse building. "Got a dollar?" the man said.

John paused, looked at the man and removed his cigarettes from a jacket pocket. As he lit a cigarette, the man licked his lips. "Spare one of those?"

"I thought you wanted a dollar," John said.

The man, not small by any means, was nonetheless dwarfed by John and he apparently thought better of showing anger. "I'm just trying to get by," he said.

John held out the pack of cigarettes, and the man slowly removed one. "Thanks. Got a light?" he said.

John handed the man his book of matches. As the man lit up, John said, "I won't give you a dollar, I'll give you ten."

"Ten?" the man said suspiciously. "What for?"

"The homeless mission a few blocks from here," John said. "I figure you for a regular customer."

"So. What about it?"

"So what can you tell me about the place?"

"What do you mean, tell?"

"I used to know the place, but I've been away," John said. "There used to be a church and a building where you could sleep."

"Still is," the man said. "But I wouldn't know about the church. I just eat and sleep there in winter."

"Who runs the place?" John said.

"Some city-appointed dickhead," the man said. "Used to be some woman, but she left a few weeks after I showed up from the Bronx. A pretty woman, always smiling. Janie or Julie was her name, something like that."

"And the church?" John said. "Do they keep it locked?"

"You're kidding," the man said. "Around here they'd steal

the blood of Christ if it wasn't locked up."

John removed a ten-dollar bill from his pocket and held it out to the man.

The man looked at the bill for a moment, then gingerly took it and stuffed it into a torn pocket. "You say you used to know the place?"

"A year back or so," John said.

The man squinted at John. "Let me have a look at you," he said. "In the light."

John moved a few feet to his left where the dim light from a streetlamp pooled down. The man came a bit closer to John and studied his face carefully. "Had some long hair and a beard on you, I might say you're the man who used to talk to the cook a year ago. He left with the woman."

"What was his name?"

"Charles. A black fellow. Always talking, but could make a mean meatloaf and chicken stew, so it was worth listening to his never-ending bullshit."

John nodded. He removed a twenty-dollar bill from his pocket, folded it in half and tucked it into the man's shirt pocket. "Thanks," John said.

The man pulled the bill from his pocket and looked at it. "I wasn't always like this," he said. "There was a time."

"Do you remember it?" John said.

"Sure."

"Then you got a leg up on me, my friend," John said.

From behind the wheel of a Ford sedan, Parker fumed and chain-smoked as he crossed the bridge and entered lower Manhattan. The entire trip, he didn't say two words until finally, as he dodged a refrigerator-sized pothole and then swerved to avoid a collision with a yellow cab, his anger got the better of him.

"Motherfucker, motherfucker," he shouted in a sudden burst of fury.

Anthony, much more levelheaded, turned to look at him. "Take it easy," Anthony said. "I'd like to get there in one piece."

That seemed to have the reverse effect on Parker, who went nearly red in the face from anger. "That Freeman, that motherfucker Freeman," Parker shouted, and banged a fist against the steering wheel.

"You want to crash and burn in this piece-of-shit car, that's your business," Anthony said. "But as long as I'm riding shotgun, you watch the road."

Parker tossed his spent cigarette out the window and grabbed another from his pack. As he pushed in the dashboard lighter, he said, "Don't you get it? Don't you see what Freeman is doing?"

"No, I don't get it and neither do you," Anthony said. "I just do as I'm told, same as you."

"He's planning something," Parker said. "Something he doesn't want us involved in. Something he doesn't want us to see."

"Like what?"

"Like I don't know," Parker said. "But what do you think the odds are Tibbets will show up at the Bowery Mission just waiting for us to nail him? A million to one, a billion? Be easier to win the lottery."

"Freeman is covering his bases," Anthony said.

"Covering his ass is more like it," Parker said. "He had him at the fire and blew it. Now he wants us out of the way. Why?" The lighter popped out and Parker touched the red-hot coil to the cigarette between his lips. "Huh, why?"

Again, Anthony turned his head to look at Parker. "Do you want to be a lower-case field agent all your life? I don't. I'd like to lead a team and maybe travel some. Secure a pension. That ain't gonna happen if you act like a fucking spoiled brat every time the boss gives you an order you don't like. So shut the fuck up and drive us to this fucking mission where we will sit on our fucking asses until Freeman says otherwise."

Parker blew smoke from his nose. "Doesn't mean I gotta like it," he said, knowing Anthony was correct. "No, not one bit."

John stood before the church that was part of the mission compound. Separated by a small courtyard, the church towered over the dining hall and office facility. The sleeping quarters, once a hotel that was donated by its owner, loomed as tall as the church.

As he stood on the sidewalk and smoked a cigarette, John couldn't remember staying at the mission, yet he knew every square inch of the place. It was a strange feeling to know something without knowing why or where that knowledge came from.

He knew the massive oak doors in front would be locked and impossible to break into, but he also knew the single rear door that led to the priest's vestment room was thin and easy pickings.

He walked down the narrow courtyard to the rear of the church. A lone floodlight illuminated the area. The large backyard gardens were in complete disarray with overgrown weeds, neglected flowerbeds and broken planters. The lawn, what there was of it, was brown and dry. He remembered when flowers bloomed and thick, green lawn covered every square inch of the backyard.

He removed the Leatherman Tool from his right pants pocket, extended the four-inch saw blade and went to work on the wood frame around the door lock. Within seconds, the neglected wood crumbled and he was able to push the door inward and enter the vestment room.

150

Once he closed the door, the only light in the room came from the red emergency-exit sign above the door. After a few seconds, John's eyes adjusted to the added darkness. He opened the connecting door and stepped into the church behind the wide, marble altar. Except for a veil of white linen, the altar was bare. "*. . . they'd steal the blood of Christ if it wasn't locked up,*" the wino had said.

John walked past the altar, stepped down to the floor and turned to the rack of candles to his left. There were thin sticks in a bucket of sand, and he pulled out a stick and lit the end with a match. He lit a dozen candles, then extinguished the stick by placing it back into the sand bucket.

Walking to the first pew, his footsteps echoed loudly on the hardwood floor. He took a seat and faced the altar. He didn't know if he was religious or if he even had a religion, but nonetheless he was comfortable inside the quiet confines of the old church. The smell of incense and the eerie silence was as familiar as the handshake from an old friend, if he had any old friends.

He looked at the statue of the Virgin Mary, the baby Jesus in his manger, the stained-glass windows depicting the Stations of the Cross, and he knew every inch of it, even with his eyes closed.

He must have spent a great deal of time in this church.

But why?

He stared at the barren altar. It was here that he'd confronted the police captain. He saw the man standing before him. He wasn't here to hurt, but to help. John saw himself disable Taft with a blow to his throat and then run from the church, leaving Taft helpless on the floor.

Why would he do that, huh? Why? Hurt a man who was there to help.

John suddenly felt warm and uncomfortable. The air inside

the church was stale and heavy with humidity. He stood up, ascended the altar steps and entered the vestment room, then went outside to the courtyard.

Feeling the relief of the cooler night air, John sat on the steps of the church to smoke a cigarette.

"Fucking shit hole of a neighborhood," Parker said as he drove west of the bridge to the Bowery Mission.

"It's the Bowery," Anthony said. "What did you expect, red carpets and rose petals in the streets?"

"I expect not to have to dodge winos and junkies," Parker said. "Hey, there it is."

"Pull over," Anthony said.

Parker steered to the curb in front of the church and killed the engine. He reached for his smokes and lit one off the dashboard lighter. As he puffed, he and Anthony were silent for a moment.

Closest to the church, Parker turned and peered at the dark silhouette of the old building. The church steps, some thirty feet away from the car, were shrouded in shadows and impossible to see, which made the tiny red ember glowing in the dark easier to spot.

At first, Parker thought his eyes were playing tricks on him. Then the dimming ember moved and grew brighter, and he realized someone was sitting on the church steps, smoking a cigarette.

"Hey, Anthony," Parker said.

"What?"

"Somebody is sitting on the church steps, smoking a butt."

Anthony looked past Parker and spotted the glowing ember. "I see it."

"You don't think?"

"What, that it's Tibbets?" Anthony said. "No, I don't. I think it's some wino drunk on the steps, is what I think."

"Let's check it out," Parker said.

"Let's just sit here and wait for Freeman to call," Anthony said.

"Stay if you want, but I'm going," Parker said. He opened his car door and stepped onto the sidewalk, removing a small Maglite from his pocket.

"Shit," Anthony said and opened his door. He walked around the car and stood beside Parker. "This is really fucking stupid."

"Come on," Parker said.

They walked toward the steps, with Parker's flashlight aimed at the shadowed figure still seated. From ten feet away, they stopped short. The man was sitting there as quiet as you please, enjoying his cigarette and the cool breeze off the water, acting as if he had not a care in the world. John Tibbets on the hook and he was theirs for the taking.

"I don't fucking believe it," Anthony said as his right hand removed the holstered Glock from his hip.

"Believe it," Parker said as he pulled his own weapon.

Together, they aimed their pistols directly at John Tibbets.

"Don't you fucking move," Anthony said. "Not a muscle."

Calm as can be, John said, "I'm not moving. I'm sitting here."

His voice was deep and unruffled, as if he were used to guns being pointed at his face. They moved to within five feet of him and he watched them with mild curiosity, the way a child would watch his father when Dad was doing something he didn't quite grasp.

"It's him," Parker said incredulously. "It's really fucking him."

"I see him," Anthony.

"Stand up and put your hands on your head with fingers laced," Parker said.

"Why?" John said, without moving other than to take a puff on his cigarette.

"What, why? Because we said so, asshole," Parker said. "Now stand the fuck up and put your . . ."

"I don't think so," John said calmly.

"He doesn't think so," Anthony said.

"I don't give a rat fuck what he thinks," Parker said.

"I'm not bothering you," John said. "I'm just minding my own business and you two come along. I don't know who you are or what you want, but I'd appreciate it if you went away and left me alone."

"Really?" Anthony said, somewhat amazed.

"Who we are, are the guys with the guns, and what we want is for you to stand up with your hands on your head," Parker said. "Now do it, and I mean now."

"You really want me to?" John said.

"No, I'm just talking to hear my own voice," Parker said. He waved his pistol in an up-and-down motion and said, "Now get up slow and put your hands on your head."

John tossed the cigarette away and slowly rose up from the steps. "If you say so," he said.

"I say so," Parker said. "Hands on your head, laced. No sudden moves."

John placed both hands on top of his head and looked at Parker. "Are you cops?" he said. "You look like cops."

"Shut up," Parker snapped.

"What did I do?" John said. "I have the right to know."

"I told you to shut up." Parker looked at Anthony. "Cuff him."

Anthony holstered his pistol and removed a pair of handcuffs from behind his back. He walked behind John and said, "This won't hurt. Right hand first."

John looked Parker in the eye. The eye, as was often misquoted, wasn't the window to the soul, but a porthole to the brain. He could see the man was itching to pull the trigger and do some damage. Probably had something to prove like all those idiots who play paintball on weekends. Unlike vegetable dye, a bullet traveling seventeen hundred feet per second doesn't come out in the wash. "I'll bet you own a Hummer," John said. "Am I right?"

"What?" Parker said at the precise moment Anthony reached for John's right hand to cuff it.

The instant there was skin-to-skin contact, John smashed Anthony in the face with the back of his head. The sound was not unlike a ripe melon being struck with a blunt object. The force of the blow shattered Anthony's nose. He staggered backward, blood streaming from his nostrils.

Parker hesitated, not believing what he was seeing. Then he recovered his composure and hastily fired his Glock, but John was no longer in the line of fire.

John spun to his right and threw his body to the sidewalk as Parker opened fire and shot Anthony in the chest three times. Still in shock from the head butt, Anthony staggered backward as red stains appeared in a tight circle on his white shirt.

Anthony looked at the blood gushing down his shirt, then at Parker. "You stupid fuck," he said, and pitched face first to the sidewalk.

"Anthony?" Parker said in disbelief.

John didn't wait for Parker to regroup a second time. With the heel of his right shoe, he smashed Parker in the left knee. As Parker screamed in pain, John's left foot kicked the Glock from Parker's hand.

John bounced to his feet and faced Parker. "I don't want to kill you," John said. "Don't force me to."

Hobbled by the broken knee, Parker could barely stand. He looked into John's eyes and remembered Freeman's words: *"Don't be in such a hurry to meet John Tibbets. Most don't live past hello."*

"I don't want to die," Parker said.

"Good, because I don't want to kill you," John said. "Show me your chin."

Parker tilted his head upward and John uncorked a right uppercut that sent Parker into the next time zone.

Freeman rang the front doorbell of the Nevin home at exactly seven in the morning, just hours after the warehouse fire. Susan Nevin answered the door dressed in a white robe over a nightgown.

"Yes?" Susan said.

"What time does Gary come home from work?" Freeman said.

John was so exhausted he fell asleep fully dressed on the bed in his sleeping car before the train left the station. Just before his eyes closed, he saw Parker's face and heard the man's voice. "I don't want to die," he'd said.

Neither did John, not without some answers first.

"Who are you people?" Gary said.

"I'll ask the questions, Gary," Freeman said. "And you answer them. That's how this works. It's pretty simple, actually."

Cone stood in the background and watched Gary Nevin. He was a strapping man up close, well suited to his role of firefighter. There was fear in his eyes, but Cone could see it wasn't fear for his own safety. He was afraid for his wife and daughters. That concern would be his weakness, and both Freeman and Cone knew it. Hell, Gary probably knew it, too. That's why he'd switched from police to fire.

"Now let's save some time here," Freeman said. He stood in front of the sofa where Gary sat next to his wife and two daughters. "I already know you met with John Tibbets last night.

I also know he'll be on his way to see your uncle, the police captain. What I don't know, but what I would like to know, is what you two talked about."

"We have rights," Gary said.

"You fucking idiot, what do you think I'm trying to protect," Freeman shouted.

"Please don't swear in front of my daughters," Gary said.

Freeman glanced at Cone and smiled. "Hear this?" Freeman said. "He's worried about bad language in front of his daughters."

"I'm worried about the safety of my family," Gary said.

Freeman looked back at him. "As you should be, Gary. See, I want answers and if I don't get them, some really bad shit is going to happen here."

Gary's two daughters started to cry and Susan hugged them tightly. "For starters, I'll kill your wife where she sits, and then you, and I'll leave the two girls alive so they can carry around, for the rest of their lives, the scars of watching their parents being murdered. For starters."

Susan gasped at Freeman's threat and held her daughters tighter.

"So why don't we make this easy?" Freeman said.

"What do you want to know?" Gary said.

"Anything you and John talked about," Freeman said.

"He wanted to know what I knew about him," Gary said.

"And you told him?"

"Nothing, because that's what I know about him. Nothing."

"You wouldn't be lying to me, would you, Gary?"

"I swear on my family that I don't know anything about him other than what you already know," Gary said. "That's why I sent him to see my uncle."

"Did he say how he came to find you?"

"Yes. He said he dreamed about me," Gary said.

Freeman nodded his head as if that made sense. "Hopefully we'll pick him up before he reaches your uncle," he said. "But just in case, do you have a place to move to for a few weeks?"

"My sister in New Jersey," Susan said immediately.

"In case of what?" Gary said.

"In case John decides to come back," Freeman said. "We'll be using your house as a place to trap him."

"Is that legal?" Susan said.

Freeman sighed. "Nothing about this is legal, Mrs. Nevin."

John slept so soundly he didn't feel the train leave Penn Station, and didn't wake up until a conductor announced there would be a one-hour layover in Washington, DC. He stood, stretched and went outside to clear his head and smoke a cigarette in the fresh air and sunshine.

"We're ready," Gary said.

Freeman glanced at the packed SUV. Susan occupied the front seat, the daughters in back. The cab was loaded with family-type stuff, clothing and whatnot. "Remember what I told you," Freeman said.

"Don't come back until you call," Gary said.

"This is for the safety of your entire family," Freeman said. "Just keep that in mind if you're tempted to ignore what I told you. Also, and more important, remember we'll be watching you. All of you."

"I love my family," Gary said. "Do you think I would put them at risk?"

Freeman looked into Gary's eyes. He saw what he needed to see. "You'll hear from me," he said.

Gary got behind the wheel of the SUV and drove away. Cone, standing nearby, walked over to Freeman. "Do you think he'll stay away?"

Freeman lit a cigarette. "We'll know soon enough."

"If he doesn't?"

"Then we'll know he can't be trusted."

"And?" Cone persisted.

Freeman blew smoke and walked away toward his sedan. He paused to look at Cone. "You coming?"

"Come in, John. Have a seat."

He took a chair opposite the large desk and waited. Behind the desk, through the window, the Washington Monument dominated the scenery.

"We have a problem, I'm afraid," said the man behind the desk. "A serious one in need of immediate attention."

"Isn't that why I'm here?" John said.

The other man sat back in his chair and looked at him for a moment. "I suppose it is true I've never called you home just to shoot the shit," he said.

"No, sir."

"Would you like some coffee while we discuss details?"

"Is that your way of telling me this could take a while?"

The man grinned and sent for coffee.

They sat at the conference table and discussed details of the operation. The President was up for reelection. Most of his crime bills and gun legislation were dismal failures. "Hell, name me one thing the son of a bitch has gotten done," the desk man said. He sipped coffee from his expensive cup. "No matter. If we want to stay in business, keep our funding, we have to play ball sometimes."

The next day John left for the Mexican border where he would do what the border patrol could not, execute as many drug lords and gang members smuggling drugs into the country as possible to quell the violence and win points with the voters for the President.

Before he left the office, they talked some more. Weapons and expenses, that sort of thing. In the background, through the window, stood the . . . ?

Cone was behind the wheel of the sedan when Freeman took the call from Parker. Freeman listened carefully, nodded a few times, then asked him if he was okay. Agitated, Freeman hung up, closed his eyes and sighed deeply.

"What?" Cone said.

Freeman shook his head as he lit a cigarette. "John returned to the Bowery Mission," he said.

Curiosity piqued, Cone turned his head to look at Freeman. "And?"

"He was sitting on the church steps when Parker and Anthony pulled up in the car," Freeman said. "They couldn't believe it, but there he was."

"And?" Cone said again.

Freeman blew smoke. "He killed Anthony, but allowed Parker to live." Freeman looked at Cone. "I wonder why that is."

Cone glanced at his watch. As if reading Cone's mind, Freeman said, "By now he's gone, out of the city."

"The uncle?" Cone said.

"The uncle," Freeman agreed. He sighed. "I wonder why he let him live?"

John looked at the tower that stood above all others in the distance, the Washington Monument. There was a strange familiarity about it, and not the kind felt from seeing photographs or even taking a tour.

This felt intimate, as if he had some firsthand knowledge of some Washington Beltway secret. He tossed the cigarette to the ground, stepped on it and returned to the train. As it rolled out of the station, John thought some more about the monument.

Somewhere inside his head, the answers were locked away.

Maybe Captain Howard Taft was the key to unlocking the mystery inside his head.

Maybe.

FOURTEEN

Sixty is the new forty. Isn't that what they say on TV when they try to sell you diet pills and tiny cans of food?

Just like Anna Nicole married for love and used-car salesmen don't lie about the quality of their product.

Retired police captain Howard Taft set fire to a cigar and inspected his shiny green John Deere riding mower. That more than anything else summed up his retirement, mowing the lawn and letting a gas-powered machine do all the work.

He puffed smoke and looked around at the old men in their Bermuda shorts, black socks and golf shoes as they waited to tee off. Silly-looking creatures playing a ridiculous game in the hot sun so they could fib to their wives about what a great round they shot today and maybe convince them that today was the day to finally break out that prescription for Viagra.

Was seventy the new fifty? Because if it was, he didn't remember possessing such knobby-looking knees or blue spider veins on his legs when he hit the half-century mark a decade ago.

He looked at his brand-new house, a three-story, eleven-room, palatial tribute to modern architecture that turned his stomach to see. Not that it was ugly, it wasn't. It was like today's popular music. It lacked the feeling and soul of yesteryear.

Yesteryear.

The fact that such a word was part of his vocabulary made him feel older than his sixty years. As if he had a zoot suit hid-

162

den in his closet and couldn't wait to sneak the word Daddy-O into the conversation.

He checked the gas in the John Deere. It was close to full, as he knew it would be, but the urge to check was just too great. Too many years of being a cop, of checking things you already knew to be true just for the sake of checking.

He mounted the mower and pushed the automatic electric start button. The engine fired to life. The grass didn't need mowing, not really, but the homeowners association frowned upon lawns that didn't match the beauty of the nearby greens, for his house sat on the ninth hole of a golf course on beautiful Hilton Head Island off the coast of South Carolina.

They paid him a visit, three silly men representing the association. They told him his lawn was a half-inch too long and gave the course a shabby appearance that was unsatisfactory to association members.

"My house isn't a green," he told them.

They said it was in the bylaws.

"If someone is playing through my yard, they shouldn't be allowed to swing a club," he told them.

They said it was in the bylaws.

"Fuck the bylaws," he said.

Bad language in public was against the bylaws, they said.

He mowed the lawn.

At Christmas, he dug out the boxes of decorations Joan had collected through thirty-seven years of marriage and they came around again.

A public display of Christmas decorations was against the bylaws, they told him. Certain people might find them offensive, they said.

"Tell them not to look at it," he told them.

They couldn't do that, they said, tell people what they could or couldn't look at.

"But you can tell me not to decorate my own damn house," he said.

It was in the bylaws, they said.

"I don't give a flying fuck what's in the bylaws," he told them.

They said bad language wasn't permitted in public places and a member of the association disciplinary committee would be around to speak with him. A week later, Mr. Peepers knocked on his door to inform him the association committee had made the decision to levy a fine against him if he failed to comply with all association bylaws.

Taft blew his top and told Mr. Peepers he could shove the bylaws up his bony ass.

Another week passed and the committee, all seven of them, showed up at his door to inform him that he and Joan weren't welcome residents of their beautiful paradise. They suggested that maybe the Tafts would be happier living in a neighborhood more suited to their lifestyle.

"What lifestyle would that be?" Taft inquired. "The dead?"

Before things got out of hand, Joan intervened. She told the committee that after a lifetime of being a police officer, her husband was having a difficult time adjusting to retirement. He would mellow out and fit in if they would give him the chance.

For the moment, the committee was appeased and left them alone.

Spring arrived, not that you could tell the difference between winter and spring that far south, and Joan planted roses under the windows to give the place some color. The committee wasted no time in telling Joan roses weren't on the list of flowers allowed in the bylaws.

Joan, a woman who angered slowly, but like a watched pot eventually reached the boiling point, told them to stick their bylaws where the sun doesn't shine. The committee chairperson, a woman, told Joan that she and her husband weren't welcome in their community and that's when Taft stepped in and asked them to leave his property, never to return.

The committee said they would force them to sell and Taft all but threw them out.

He and Joan sat down and talked, maybe for the first time since he'd been shot, just over a year ago. Maybe it was a mistake to move here, Joan said. Maybe they should sell the place and return to Brooklyn, she said.

They decided to contact a Realtor, put the place on the market and retire where people still had a pulse.

In the meantime, the lawn needed mowing.

As he rode around on the John Deere, he thought about the problem. It wasn't the house, which was really quite lovely. It wasn't the association committee, not really. They were silly little people and didn't count for much in the scheme of things. It wasn't money, as his pension and investments gave them a six-figure income for life.

The crux—the root of his problem, if he were to be honest—was boredom. After a lifetime of work, of carrying a badge and prowling the city, investigating and arresting the bad guys, he had not one interesting thing to do, go to or see.

That, more than anything else, was what men over sixty died from . . . boredom. The feeling of not being useful anymore. Of wearing black socks with Bermuda shorts in public and not caring. Actually having favorite television shows and caring what news commentators said, yet not voting because it was too much trouble to get out of bed and drive to a polling place. Of getting a retirement hobby. To Taft, a retirement hobby was nothing more than marking time until you died.

Not making love to your wife for the simple reason that it was just too damn much work, and having her agree.

These are some of my favorite things, Taft hummed to himself as he rode in circles around the lawn.

Change.

That's what life was all about, really. Cradle to the grave, it was all about change. From infant to teen to man, and finally to old man. Each phase was nothing more than change.

What it boiled down to was the simple fact that he needed something to change in his life, and fast.

That, or die of boredom waiting for the next visit from Mr. Peepers.

They flew on the private jet to Hardeeville, where a sedan was gassed up and ready to go. Freeman drove, Cone rode shotgun, and they rolled into Hilton Head Island around noon. Freeman wasn't impressed. Unless you lived for golf and the beach, there was pretty much nothing else to do except hit balls, roast in the sun or play shuffleboard. His office had made a reservation at a local hotel on the island, and he didn't have his hopes up for that, either.

"How do you figure a man spends thirty-plus years a New York City cop, living on a golf course?" Freeman said.

"I doubt it's for the golf," Cone said. "It's probably a makeup to the wife."

"An apology for thirty years of missing birthdays and anniversaries?" Freeman said, and thought about that for a moment. "That's probably why I never married."

"Guilt?"

"More like hassle."

"There's two-seventy-eight," Cone said.

Freeman veered to his right and took the on-ramp for Interstate 278 South/East. Cone switched on the dashboard-mounted GPS unit and keyed in Taft's address. "We beat him here?" Cone said.

"Unless the train grew wings, no doubt."

They reached a bridge that connected the mainland to the

island. "How do you want to handle surveillance?" Cone said.

"Us for the moment," Freeman said. "If he took the train, as I believe he did, we're at least one full day ahead of him."

They crossed the bridge. Freeman glanced at his watch. It was just past noon. "What say we find a spot for something to eat?" he said.

The lawn was mowed exactly as the committee specified. Even Mr. Peepers would be hard pressed to find fault with it. Taft put the mower in the garage and sat at the patio table to admire his handiwork. Joan came out with two tall glasses of lemonade and sat with him.

Taft took a sip and reached for the cigar and book of matches in his shirt pocket. As he bit off the tip, he said, "I was just thinking what a great job I did on the lawn."

Joan looked at the freshly cut grass.

"And then I asked myself why I care," Taft said.

Joan watched him blow a smoke ring in the air. "Oh, Howard, I do owe you such an apology," she said.

"For what?"

Joan waved her hand in the air. "This," she said. "You weren't ready for this and I insisted. I should have known you weren't the type to be satisfied with a life of leisure, not after more than thirty years of police work."

"It's not so bad," Taft said.

"Yes, it is," Joan said and started to laugh.

What else could he do except laugh along with her? He loved her too much to do anything else.

Freeman ate a bite of his very tender, bloody steak and looked at the ocean below the extended deck of the restaurant. Cone had chosen a chicken dish with a green salad. That was the difference between the two of them, Freeman reasoned. He was a

167

bloody-steak man, while Cone chose the safety and boredom of chicken with salad.

The tide was out and the stench of the ocean reached their table. Not so bad it made him lose his appetite, but enough to make him hurry through the meal. "We'll head over to the course he lives on and check things out," Freeman said.

Cone took a sip of his soft drink, Dr Pepper on ice. Freeman did a quick memory search and decided he'd never sampled one. In fact, he never knew anyone who actually had. "Is that any good?" Freeman asked.

"What, my soda?" Cone said. "It's something I grew up with. I'm just used to it." He sipped some more and put the glass down. "You said we'd head over to where Taft lives."

"Soon as I finish this last bite," Freeman said.

"I haven't done much stakeout work the past few years, but two men in dark suits don't exactly fit in with the local ambience," Cone said.

"Exactly why I had my luggage transferred from the plane to the trunk of our car," Freeman said. "Like the card says, never leave home without them."

"And me?" Cone said.

"There's some stores over there," Freeman pointed out. "I think you'll look good in golf pants."

"Maybe if I had something useful to do," Taft said. "We could actually enjoy living here."

Joan laughed again. Her voice was like church bells ringing to Taft. She saw the look wash over his face. "Oh, no," she said.

"Why not?"

"It's the middle of the day."

"So?"

Joan sat back in her chair. That was exactly right, so? She stood up, turned and started walking toward the open sliding doors. She paused to look back. "You coming?"

Taft jumped to his feet. "Damned right," he said.

"Leave the cigar," she said.

Freeman and Cone strolled down Main Street of the quaint little town and appeared to fit in with everyone else. Gone were the dark suits, replaced with khaki slacks and white polo shirts. They wore loafers on their feet. To conceal their Glock .40 pistols inside the waistbands of their khakis, they wore the polo shirts tucked outside their belts.

"It strikes me that, besides the fact that we look like a pair of idiots in these clothes, it might be somewhat difficult to conduct surveillance of Taft's home," Cone said. "It is after all on the ninth hole, with no parking except for in his driveway and no cover whatsoever."

"True," Freeman said, lighting a cigarette.

"Which part?"

"That we look like a pair of idiots."

"Let me take a stab at this," Cone said. "We know the only way onto this dopey island is across that bridge. Your men will stake out incoming traffic for Tibbets on foot because it's highly unlikely he'll be renting a car."

"Unlikely, but not impossible," Freeman said. "But on the chance that he does, I'll have men on each side of the bridge looking for vehicles and walkers both."

"Okay, but that still leaves the house," Cone said.

"I know how the FBI likes to do it," Freeman said. "Obtain a warrant and a house with a visual on the suspect, and monitor until something breaks. Well, we don't have that luxury on this one."

"Meaning?"

Freeman took a puff on his cigarette and blew smoke through his nose. "Forget the FBI playbook for once. This is too important to play by them. Besides, they don't really want to know about it."

"We wait for Tibbets from inside the Taft home," Cone said.

"B-I-N-G-O," Freeman said, allowing himself a tiny grin.

"So we just throw the law and constitutional rights out the window?" Cone said.

"You haven't figured out by now that sometimes the only way to protect rights is to violate them?" Freeman said.

"It takes some getting used to," Cone admitted.

"Don't take too long making the adjustment," Freeman said. He paused to glance at his watch. "We have time to check into our hotel, then meet my men."

It was amazing how a fifteen-minute romp with his wife could send Taft reeling for thirty minutes of snooze time, but it never failed. Joan often joked that she didn't perform her wifely duties up to par if he didn't go comatose.

When he finally came to, Joan was toweling herself dry after a quick shower and made the suggestion they go into town for dinner. Revitalized, Taft thought it a wonderful idea, mostly because he awoke with a fierce appetite and not so much that town was anything special in the way of cuisine.

Wearing his snazzy, lightweight sports jacket over a short-sleeve shirt, tan pants and comfortable walking shoes, Taft backed the car out of the garage while Joan did whatever women did to get their faces ready for public display.

The hotel was on the mainland side of the island, with a bird's-eye view of the bridge from a sixth-floor window. The hotel itself was new, but constructed to showcase old Southern charm and hospitality. In that regard, Freeman thought it failed miserably, appearing cheeky and gauche. For one thing, decorating something to appear old didn't make it old, and for another, charm was something acquired over a long period of time. Not in the three years the hotel had existed.

Still, the place wasn't bad and would do nicely as a headquarters for the duration of their stay.

Freeman came away from the window and looked at the six-man team Farris had dispatched him. They were young, but gaining experience quickly, according to Farris. They would obey orders without question, act and respond without hesitation and would one day soon head up their own teams.

For now, Freeman needed them as his eyes and ears. They sat in chairs and on the bed, his surrogate children, waiting for his instructions. He held up the eleven-by-fourteen photograph of John Tibbets and passed it around.

"This photo is about five years old, but John hasn't changed a bit since it was taken," Freeman said. "The thing is, if you aren't tuned into certain traits John possesses, he'll blow right by you. For instance, he's an expert at disguise. Beards, hair, he can do it all. What he can't change or disguise is his height, which is six foot four, and his barn-door shoulders. Given that the average Joe of this gated community is eighty, wears his Bermuda shorts up to his neck and plays golf in black socks, Tibbets will stick out like a sore thumb if he goes hiking across that bridge. My guess is he will try to cross the bridge in disguise, possibly in a stolen or rented car."

The last man passed the photograph back to Freeman He set it on the desk beside the bed and looked at the six men. "Questions?"

"Sir, could he possibly come over by boat?" one of the six asked.

"What's your name?" Freeman said.

"Price, sir. Mark Price."

"Well, Price, he could," Freeman said. "Except a boat is a high risk for exposure and Tibbets knows that. Wherever there

171

are boats, there are generally a lot of people around, and his game is stealth."

"Sir, will we have three-man teams on both sides of the bridge?" another asked.

"Your name?" Freeman said.

"Locke, sir. Walter Locke."

"Two-man teams stationed on both sides of the bridge will commence right after this meeting," Freeman said. "Use of cell phones only, no radios for someone to spot. Casual clothing, sunglasses until dark, concealed weapons. If Tibbets is spotted, alert me by phone and then tail him to his destination. Agent Cone and I will be at an undisclosed location, and agents Price and Locke will accompany us. Any other questions?"

The six agents remained silent. "Good," Freeman said. "Get changed, gentlemen, work starts right now."

Old habits die a slow and painful death, exemplified by Taft's choice of retirement vehicle, a seven-year-old Ford Crown Victoria made for the deputy chief of the New York State Police that Taft purchased for slightly more than a song. A massive beast produced to police specifications such as three hundred horsepower, engine idle meter, heavy-duty frame and suspension, all-speed traction control, engine block heater, ballistic door panels that could stop a bullet and, of course, cruise control. All Taft had to do was give the Vic a paint job to remove the state logo and bring it home.

Joan chose a more sensible vehicle in the Mercury sedan that Taft found difficult to squeeze in and out of, so tonight they rode in the Vic to the restaurant in town. *Over the bridge and into town to grandmother's house we go,* Taft thought as they crossed the bridge to the mainland.

"Maybe we can take a walk around downtown after dinner?" Joan said as he slid into a space in the restaurant parking lot.

"Why not," Taft replied.

The restaurant Joan chose en route, an Italian place, sat across the street from the hotel with the fake Southern charm. There was a lobby bar in the hotel that they'd tried a few times and wasn't to their liking, but the Italian restaurant was. The owner, a sixty-two-year-old Italian from the Bronx, knew his way around the kitchen, served generous portions and balked at the idea of butter with bread, serving garlic-laced olive oil instead.

They exited the car, and it was a funny thing: Joan took his hand. A twenty-foot walk and she felt compelled to take his hand as if they were newlyweds. A year ago, she'd only link up to him if they happened to be caught in a windstorm, but since the shooting, she held onto him as if he were buried treasure. He supposed that if he had died that night, it would be tougher for those left behind to carry on. He knew that from having to tell many a victim's wife their loved one was gone. For the victim, the suffering was over. For those left to mourn, the suffering had just begun.

The restaurant was crowded, but a few tables remained. He and Joan were seated at the window with a view of the bridge and bay. "What shall we window-shop for?" Taft said as he dipped warm, crusty bread into a bowl of olive oil.

"I said take a walk through town," Joan said. "I didn't say anything about window-shopping."

"Explain to me the difference," Taft said.

The call came a little while later as they strolled hand in hand down Main Street to look at the latest in fashionable bedspreads that Joan had her eye on. At first, Taft forgot that he'd tucked his cell phone into the left-hand pocket of his sports coat. Then, when it rang, he debated if he should answer or not.

Finally, he removed the phone from the pocket and said, "Hello?"

FIFTEEN

Just after dark, Freeman drove along the road that circumvented the golf course and arrived at the Taft home without being seen by a single person. It occurred to Freeman that John Tibbets would note the same thing. "You see what I see?" Freeman said to Price and Locke, knowing that Cone had made the same observation as him.

"What's that, sir?" Price said.

"Think," Freeman said. "Look around and think."

Price and Locke looked out the back windows of the sedan. "There's nothing to see, sir," Price said.

"Ben," Freeman said.

"Ben," Price echoed.

"How about you, Locke?" Freeman said.

"Mark is correct, Ben," Locke said. "There is nothing to see and nobody here to see it."

"And?"

"And . . . Tibbets might realize the same thing, sir . . . Ben."

Freeman glanced at Cone, who was grinning into his hand. "Very good, Locke," Freeman said. He drove past the Taft home, found a shadowed spot to park, and killed the lights and engine. After a quick glance at the house, Freeman said, "Nobody's home."

Price and Locke looked at the Taft place. It was a modern, two-story house with a half acre of backyard lawn and half that out front. It was difficult to tell at night where the Taft property ended and the golf course began. Probably at the road.

"How do I know that from sitting here?" Freeman said.

Price and Locke concentrated on the house, searching for the same clues Freeman had picked up on. After a minute, Price said, "The outside floodlight is on, which is something most people leave on when they go out after dark."

"Good," Freeman said. "What else?"

"A light is on in the kitchen," Locke said.

"Also good," Freeman said. "A light is on in the kitchen, but there is no movement, nobody at the oven cooking, sitting at the table, nothing. So why is that light left on?"

Price and Locke looked at the illuminated kitchen window and thought for a moment, but they had nothing.

"Agent Cone?" Freeman said.

"The garage connects directly to the house via the kitchen," Cone said. "They come home from dinner or wherever, park the car in the garage and enter through a connecting door into the light."

Price and Locke realized the scenario was so simple they'd missed it because they were looking for the complicated. As if reading their minds, Freeman said, "Don't overlook the obvious when it slaps you in the face."

Price and Lock nodded their heads even though Freeman couldn't see them. He said, "Do you two think you can babysit the house while Agent Cone and I take a quick ride back to town?"

"Sure," Price said.

"From the inside, sir . . . Ben?" Locke said.

"That would be good," Freeman said.

"How do we get inside, Ben?" Price said.

"I'll take care of that," Freeman said. "What I want you to do is wait in the dark for Taft and his wife to return from dinner or wherever they went. Apprehend and sit on them, then call me on my cell if we haven't returned by then. Keep in mind Taft is a thirty-year cop with the NYPD. If he walks through that door and gets so much as a hint a hair is out of place, you lose your edge. Understand?"

"Yes," Price said.

"Understood," Locke said.

"I'm going to pick the kitchen-door lock and let you guys in," Freeman said. He opened his car door and paused to look at Price and Locke. "You coming?"

Freeman parked the sedan a hundred yards down the road on the soft shoulder. They had an excellent view of the Taft house. The road, on a slight incline, gave them the advantage of seeing a car's headlights at least thirty seconds before the car itself, more than enough reaction time.

Cone knew that what they were doing was entrapment by the Justice Department's standards, but he was enjoying operating outside the rules for once and he could see why Freeman had such disregard for them. The rules, such as they were, more often than not gave the bad guys an unfair advantage that lawyers could manipulate to their benefit. In Freeman's world, the rules were made up as they went along, with total disregard for individual rights. In Freeman's world, the bad guys weren't bank robbers, kidnappers or drug dealers. They were ruthless, faceless enemies, and in order to win, you needed to be equally ruthless. Rules neutered the war on terror, allowed child rapists to roam free and rape again, and had allowed the mob to operate with near impunity for a hundred years.

Freeman's was a different world.

Cone was starting to enjoy it.

"How much time do you want to give them after Taft and his wife return home?" Cone said.

Freeman, about to light a cigarette, paused to look at Cone.

"It's refreshing, isn't it?" he said.

"What?"

"Not having the FBI playbook dictate your every move." Freeman lit the cigarette, puffed and said, "To answer your question, until John shows."

"Those boys couldn't handle him," Cone said. "He'd kill them or they'd shoot themselves first and probably take out the Tafts in the process."

"That's why, after the Tafts are safely inside, you and I will take position opposite the house and take John down before he has the chance to enter," Freeman said.

"Ambush the ambusher," Cone said.

Freeman puffed on the cigarette and blew smoke. It rose to the roof of the sedan and vanished into nothing. "It would be nice to take him alive, but that may not be possible. Do you have a silencer for your Glock?"

"No."

"I have an extra," Freeman said.

Taft instantly recognized the voice when John Tibbets said, "Is this Howard Taft, the ex–police captain?"

Taft was so shocked at hearing the voice that he stopped short on the street and in doing so pulled Joan backwards. "What is it, the boys?" Joan said, referencing their sons.

"If this is Captain—" John said.

"It is," Taft said, cutting John off in mid-sentence. "I never thought I'd hear from you again."

"Howard, what is it?" Joan said, with growing concern in her voice.

"I wish I could say the same," John said.

"Still suffering from amnesia?" Taft said.

Hearing that, Joan knew who was on the other end of the phone. Her instincts, honed over thirty-plus years as a cop's

wife, kicked in and raised her concern level to near epic propor-
tions. "Howard, hang up," she said, knowing that he wouldn't,
couldn't.

"I'm suffering from a lot more than that," John said. "We
need to talk. In person, right away. I think the men who are
after me might come after you."

"I'm in South Carolina," Taft said.

"So am I," John said. "In fact, turn around."

Taft slowly lowered the phone and turned to look behind
him. There in the shadows of a pay phone outside a closed
women's clothing store stood John Tibbets. Joan turned and followed Taft's line of sight, and omitted a soft gasp.

"It's all right," Taft said to Joan. He returned the phone to
his ear.

"See me?" John said.

"Yes."

"There's a bar opposite the hotel on the corner," John said.
"It's dark. Find a table against the wall and wait for me."

John hung up, turned and vanished like a ghost in the night.
Joan said, "Howard?"

"I know," Taft said. "Come on."

"Where?"

"Have a drink."

"I'd rather not kill him," Cone said. "Given the choice."

"Given the choice, I'd rather not kill anybody," Freeman
said. "The thing with John is, he makes the choice for you."
Freeman turned to look at Cone. "Remember that when the
time comes."

"And you estimate that to be?"

Freeman glanced at his watch. "Even by local train, not much
longer."

"Provided he is on the way," Cone said. "He could have

178

changed his mind. He has resources. He could have decided it was safer to cross over into Canada and disappear."

"He wouldn't have gone to the trouble of contacting the nephew if that was on his mind," Freeman said.

"Maybe you frightened him off," Cone said.

"There's about as much chance of that as me being elected President," Freeman said. "No, he'll show. And soon."

Cone looked at the light in the Taft kitchen window, then glanced at his watch. "Let me have that extra silencer," he said.

Joan's hand trembled as she raised the glass of white wine to her lips. Taft watched her take a delicate sip, then lower the glass to the table, spilling some because her hand shook so much.

"Try to relax," Taft said. "We're just having a drink in a public place."

"Relax?" Joan said. "Excuse me, Howard, but you nearly died just one year ago because of this man, so don't tell me to relax."

"I didn't . . . there he is."

Joan turned her head and looked at John Tibbets as he strolled through the door of the bar from the street. She had seen his picture in the newspapers and once or twice on the cable news shows, but in person she wouldn't have recognized him. For one thing, he was a much larger man than she anticipated. Six three or four, his shoulders stretched his suit jacket to the limits of the fabric. For another thing, he was handsome and to Joan that didn't compute when you know a man to be capable of murder. She supposed she'd seen one too many episodes of *Law and Order,* where the killer is always a squat troll of a man. As he came closer, even in the dim lighting, Joan could see the intelligence in his dark, brooding eyes.

Dark, brooding eyes? She'd have to quit reading those romance/ mystery novels. Then he was at their table, towering over them.

"John, have a seat," Taft said. "This is my wife, Joan."

John lowered himself into a chair and extended his right hand to Joan. A bit surprised at his action, Joan took his hand in hers. It all but disappeared inside his massive palm. "If I've upset you, I'm sorry," John said. His shake was gentle despite the size of his hand.

Their hands came apart and Joan picked up her glass to take another small sip of wine before speaking. "My husband nearly died last year because of you, Mr. Tibbets," she said. "I'm not looking for a repeat performance."

"That wasn't his fault," Taft said. "I was a cop doing my job, and that's all it was."

"It's okay," John said. "She has every right to be angry. In fact, after I'm done telling you what I'm about to say, she'll probably be even more angry."

Taft glanced at Joan, then looked at John. "Want a drink before you get started?"

"I don't know," John said. "I can't remember if I have a favorite drink or when I last had one."

"I'll order you a Scotch and water," Taft said. "That's always a good place to start."

Cone looked at his watch. "It's after nine."

"Don't worry," Freeman said. "John is on his way, if he isn't here already."

"You know him that well?"

"Yeah."

"What aren't you telling me, Ben?" Cone said.

"You already figured it out," Freeman said.

"You and Tibbets were partners, weren't you?"

"For many years." Freeman turned to look at Cone. "Anything else?"

"No."

"And you're sure it was the same man as a year ago," Taft said. "The man who shot me and kidnapped you?"

"He has to be," John said. "Although I can't actually remember being with you that day, or any other day for that matter, it has to be him if what you tell me is true and he came after me at the Bowery Mission."

"I never actually saw him at the mission, but I'll never forget his face from that night on the street when he shot me," Taft said. "Not a big as you, but a large man with dark eyes and hair and a look to him that said he had no problem pulling the trigger."

Joan gasped softly at that, and Taft gave her hand a gentle pat.

"And you have no idea who Freeman is?" John said. "Even after a year?"

"The man doesn't exist and neither do you," Taft said. "But if he's chased you from New Mexico to Texas, I have no doubt he will eventually wind up here."

Joan spoke for the first time since John started his tale. "And you have no idea how you wound up in the desert in New Mexico?" she said.

John shook his head. "Just snippets of information, mostly in dreams. That's how I was able to track down your nephew and finally you."

"Mr. Tibbets, may I be honest with you?" Joan said.

"Please," John said.

"I will forever be grateful to you for saving my nephew's life, but I will also never forgive you for almost losing my husband's. That said, I wish you would just go away and never come back."

John and Taft looked at Joan. "I won't apologize for saying

that," she said.

"No apology is needed," John said. "I can't fault how you feel. What you said is true."

"And beside the point," Taft said. "Right?"

"Right," John said.

Joan turned to look at Taft. "Then what is the point?"

"John is here to warn us," Taft said. "That this Freeman will show up wanting to talk to us."

"I found you, and I have no marbles in my bag," John said. "He won't have any trouble locating you."

"But why?" Joan said. "What does he want with us?"

"Him," Taft said and nodded to John. "He wants him."

"Even if I hadn't come here," John said. "Freeman would still show up to find out if I had. His methods aren't . . . gentle."

Joan stared at John for many seconds. "He'd hurt us?"

"No," Taft said bluntly. "He'd kill us."

"Why?" Joan said. "We've done nothing to him. Why would he want to kill us, Howard? Why?"

"That answer," Taft said, and leaned over and gently tapped John's head. "Is locked away in here."

Joan stared at John. "I don't understand any of this."

"That makes all of us," John said.

Taft cracked a smile as he took a sip of his drink.

"I'm glad you find all this funny, Howard," Joan said.

"You're missing the point, my love," Taft said. "John isn't here simply to warn us this Freeman is on the way. He wants us to leave."

"Leave?" Joan said. "You mean our home? And go where?"

"Anywhere," John said. "The point is not to be there when Freeman shows up and to be someplace he can't find you."

The realization finally hit Joan in the face like a hard slap. "Oh, dear God, our sons. He would . . ."

"He would," Taft said. "Remember, this is a man who shot

me for no apparent reason simply to get to John."

Joan fought to regain composure. After all, she hadn't spent more than thirty years as a cop's wife without learning a thing or two about stress management. "What do you suggest we do, Mr. Tibbets?" she said.

"How far do you live from here?" John said.

"Fifteen minutes," Taft said. "Just over the bridge."

"And your sons?"

"Our youngest is in college in North Carolina," Taft said. "The oldest is an engineer with a chemical company in Georgia. Our daughter is traveling Europe for a month or more, part of a research group for her master's degree."

"I think your daughter's okay for now, but we'll need to get to your sons tonight," John said. "But, first, we'll need to go to your house so you can pack what you need."

"My car is right around the corner," Taft said. "Might as well go with us."

SIXTEEN

John waited in the lobby of the bar for Taft to retrieve his car. He had a clear line of sight to the bridge that connected the mainland to the island, and there were enough streetlamps along the way to illuminate the bridge clearly.

Something was wrong. He didn't know what, but something. Maybe he was just spooked at so many close calls, or maybe it was the eerie feeling of being watched or a combination of the two, but he felt it deep inside that something was wrong.

Taft arrived in his car, an old Crown Vic, and he was glad to see the massive sedan because that gave him ample room to hide on the floor of the backseat.

As Freeman planned, Taft's headlights shone over the slight incline at least fifteen seconds before his car did. "Time to punch in," Freeman said.

Taft's car, a massive Crown Victoria, slowed at his driveway, made a left turn into it, paused while the garage door opened by remote, then disappeared into the dark driveway. As the garage door closed, Cone said, "Two people. The passenger has to be his wife."

"Unless that's his mistress and he's bringing her home for a threesome," Freeman said as he opened his car door. He went around to the trunk, opened it and returned with two Kevlar vests. He sat and tossed one in Cone's lap. "Better suit up," he said. "I'd hate to have to fill out a report to the FBI."

Cone pulled the polo shirt over his head, then picked up the vest.

Taft waited until the garage door closed and locked before he opened his car door and got out. On her side, Joan exited and looked over the car roof at Taft.

"It will be all right," Taft reassured her.

Joan nodded, walked around the car to the connecting door and opened it. Taft looked into the Vic at John. "Would you like to come in while we pack a few things? Maybe have a drink or use the bathroom?"

"I'm good," John said. "I'll just stretch my legs and have a smoke."

"Okay, be back in a few," Taft said, and followed his wife inside the house. She must have gone directly up to the bedroom, because she didn't stop along the way to turn on lights, as was her usual habit.

So he followed her up and entered the bedroom, where she already had one suitcase on the bed. She looked at him as he came in, pausing as she opened the case. "Howard," she said softly.

"It will be fine," Taft said reassuringly. "Now hurry and gather what you'll need and I'll do the same."

Taft went to his closet and selected his largest suitcase, the one he'd used for the eight-day cruise they took on their thirty-fifth wedding anniversary. He set the case on the bed next to Joan's, then went to his dresser and slid open his top drawer for underwear. He heard Joan give a frightened gasp; he looked in the mirror and saw two men, one slightly taller than the other, aiming pistols at them. They were young and still had the soft neckline and skin of men under thirty, but Taft wasn't fooled by that. Their eyes were hard and cold, and the look in them said they had something to prove. He'd seen that look on many a man, and most of the time their story ended badly.

"Do not move," the shorter man said.

"On the bed, now," the taller man said, and motioned with his pistol.

Taft looked at them through the mirror. "Which is it, don't move or on the bed?"

"Did somebody say you could talk?" the shorter man said.

"This is my house," Howard said. "I'll speak if I want to."

"Howard, they have guns," Joan said. "Don't argue with them."

"Listen to your wife, Pop," the taller man said. "She's making sense. Now sit."

Taft glanced at Joan and nodded to her. She sat on the bed next to her suitcase. Taft walked to the bed, sat next to Joan, and patted her leg.

The shorter man looked at the suitcases on the bed. "Going somewhere?"

"Is that against the law, because if it is, I missed that one the past thirty years when I was a cop," Taft said.

The taller man walked to the bed, looked at Taft, then smacked him across the face with the barrel of his pistol. Taft fell backward to the bed as Joan screamed.

"You shut up," the shorter man said to Joan. "Or you'll get the same."

"Quit fucking around and make the call," the taller man said.

"Right," the shorter man said, lowered his pistol and dug out his cell phone. He was about to dial Freeman's cell number when there were two soft coughs behind him. He pitched forward to the rug.

It took a moment for the taller man to process what he'd just witnessed. Then he spun around just in time for John to fire two shots into his chest. As his pistol slipped from his hand, he looked at John. "You're Tibbets?" he said as blood ran from the holes.

John walked closer to him. "You're Freeman's man?"

"Fuck you," the taller man said and fell dead to the rug.

John looked at Joan. The woman was in shock on the bed. Next to her, Taft stirred and slowly came around. "Is he okay?" John said.

Joan stared at John.

"Is he okay?" John said, louder.

Taft sat up and rubbed his chin. "Joan, snap out of it."

Joan turned to look at Taft. Her entire body suddenly shook as she burst into tears. "Aftershock," Taft said to John.

"There's no time for this," John said. "If these two were in your house, Freeman isn't far away. Grab what you need and meet me downstairs."

Cone looked at his watch. Seated in the car as he was, the Kevlar vest limited his movements somewhat, and raising his wrist felt clumsy. "It's been fifteen minutes," he said to Freeman. "I thought you told them to call you when he came home."

"I did."

Cone looked at Freeman. "Maybe he got the upper hand on them?"

Freeman looked at the house. The bedroom lights were on. The Tafts went straight from the garage to the second-floor bedroom. So where were Price and Locke? "Let's go," he said.

From the dark living-room bay window, John spotted the sedan parked on the shoulder of the road a hundred yards to the right. The quarter moon shed just enough light to see the faint outline of the car, but not enough to make out any passenger. There was no doubt in his mind who that passenger was—but was Freeman alone, or were there reinforcements in the car with him?

"We're ready," Taft said from behind him.

John turned around. "Do you have a weapon in the house?"

Taft opened his jacket to expose the massive .357 Magnum revolver that had served him so well the last twenty years on the job.

John nodded. "Can you still drive like a cop?"

"I have a cop's car, don't I," Taft said.

"Get behind the wheel, start the engine, but don't open the garage door until I tell you to," John said. "Then drive out like it's a high-speed chase."

"You're not coming?"

"Pick me up at that phone booth where I called you from." John turned back to the bay window and saw the light from Freeman's car. It was on for just an instant, then shut off. "Go, there isn't much time."

Taft nodded and turned away.

John looked out the window. It took a few seconds, but then he saw them walking on the soft shoulder of the road toward the house. There were two of them. His eyes tracked their shadow-on-shadow movement, and he put them at a distance of two hundred and fifty feet away.

He waited and watched until they were turning down the walkway that led to the Taft home. Then he ran to the connecting garage door where Taft sat behind the wheel of his Crown Vic, his wife next to him.

John waited, then heard the sound of the front door slowly opening. He motioned to Taft, turned and went to the kitchen door, opened it and ran into the backyard.

Freeman and Cone were about to enter the house when the garage door opened and Taft's Crown Vic raced out, turned onto the road and sped off the way only a trained cop could handle such a massive beast.

Freeman and Cone did an about-face and raced to the sidewalk in time to see the red taillights of the Vic fade away into the distance. "We underestimated the old cop," Cone said.

From the corner of his right eye, Freeman saw movement on the road. He turned to look at a figure running toward his sedan. "No," Freeman said. "We underestimated John."

Cone looked at the dark figure closing in on the sedan. "Did you leave the keys?"

"No, but that doesn't matter," Freeman said. "John can start a car quicker than it takes to say it."

A moment later, the light inside the car came on, then went off. Seconds after that, the engine started and the car sped onto the road and vanished around a turn.

"He's good, isn't he," Cone said.

"You don't know the half of it," Freeman said.

"Should we check on your boys?" Cone said.

"Yeah."

They entered the house and found Price and Locke dead in the bedroom on the second floor. Price had been shot twice in the back, Locke twice in the chest. The entrance wounds were small, and Freeman didn't need a ballistics test to know they were made by John's .22 Rugers.

"These men never had a chance," Cone said.

"They were green," Freeman said. "That's why I assigned them the house."

"Tibbets must have been inside Taft's car," Cone said. "Do you think he made your men at the bridge?"

"He's running on instinct," Freeman said. "He smelled a trap without any evidence of one."

Freeman's cell phone rang. He answered the call, knowing in advance who would be on the other end. "Sir, this is . . . ," a young man's voice said.

"I know who this is," Freeman snapped. "What do you have to report?"

"We observed a Crown Victoria cross the bridge about twenty minutes ago. It just came flying back to the mainland with what looks like your car hot on its heels."

Freeman sighed. "I'm at the Taft residence. Retrieve my car and come get me."

"Retrieve it from where, sir?"

"From wherever the hell Tibbets dumps it."

Freeman hung up and grabbed his cigarettes from a pocket, lit one and sat on the bed. The bodies of Price and Locke were at his feet. He looked at Cone. "Call your office and request a file on Howard Taft and his family. I want to know who his relatives are and where they live."

Cone nodded and pulled his cell phone. Freeman stood up, went downstairs to the kitchen, and fished a can of Coke out of the fridge. He was delaying the inevitable. After lighting a fresh cigarette, he pulled out his phone and dialed the home number for Farris.

John spotted the Crown Vic parked alongside the pay phone and parked Freeman's sedan behind it. Although he'd removed the ignition system with the Leatherman Tool, he knew Freeman could start the car the same way he did. He exited, pulled the three-and-a-half-inch serrated knife blade from the Leatherman Tool and gave Freeman's sedan four flat tires.

He folded up the knife and entered the backseat of the Vic. "Go," he told Taft.

The callback from Cone's office came an hour later. He and Freeman were eating sandwiches made from cold cuts they'd found in the refrigerator. Lean cuts of pastrami with mustard on crusty rolls, kettle-cooked chips, washed down with icy cold bottles of Heineken, eaten with great appetite while two bodies grew colder one floor above them.

Cone had his phone, notebook and pen on the table anticipating the call and he answered it before the second ring. While he listened and made notes, Freeman fixed two more sandwiches, then took a call of his own. He hung up after a few minutes and waited for Cone, who spoke and made notes for several more minutes.

"They found my car parked next to a pay phone," Freeman said when Cone finally hung up. "Four flat tires. What do you got?"

Cone glanced at his notebook. "Howard Taft Junior is a chemical engineer in Virginia, just outside of Richmond," he said. "The younger son, Michael Taft, is a student in North Carolina living off campus. I have current addresses for both."

"He'll swing north to pick up his sons, then disappear somewhere and regroup," Freeman said. "He's an ex–police captain, so he's not without connections."

"You mean he's helping Tibbets?" Cone said.

"It's probably stuck in his craw all this time, an unsolved mystery," Freeman said. "Now he's got a second shot at solving the puzzle."

Cone mulled that over for a moment and hated to admit it, but he followed Freeman's train of thought. "It's an entire family you're talking about."

"They don't necessarily have to be killed," Freeman said. "They could cooperate and hand John over to us."

Cone nodded. "If we reach Howard Junior first, it's a good bargaining chip," he said.

"The jet is being refueled and should be ready to go within the hour," Freeman said.

"What about the two men upstairs?" Cone said.

"I called for a cleanup crew, and my men should be here in a few minutes to pick us up," Freeman said. "So we might as well eat these other sandwiches."

Cone picked up his second sandwich and took a bite. "Want another beer?" he said, sounding a great deal like Freeman.

SEVENTEEN

Thirty minutes after merging with I-95 North, Joan spoke her first words since leaving the house. She turned around in her seat and looked at John. "You murdered those two men," she said. "One in the back."

Taft glanced at his wife. She was on the edge. He'd seen it many times, even with experienced cops. A shooting occurs. Someone dies, but not you, even though it was close. Immediate relief is followed by aftershock at surviving such a narrow escape, then relief is followed by guilt for being lucky enough to have survived when someone else did not.

That guilt manifests in silent shock that can last for hours, days, weeks and even months. Some never recover. That Joan spoke so soon after the incident was a good sign. That she was hostile was an even better sign.

John said, "I'm sorry you had to see that, but my choice was limited as to what to do considering they were there to kidnap you or worse."

"So you killed them," Joan said.

"Joan, Mr. Tibbets did what he had to do in order to save our lives," Taft said. "You can't fault the man for that."

Joan turned back around and sat facing front. "I can fault him for bringing us this trouble. For putting our sons and us in danger. I can fault him for that, Howard."

"If there is someone to blame for that, it's me," Taft said. "I chose to involve myself in John's life after he saved Gary that night a year ago. More than three decades of cop training doesn't shut off that easily. If I'd stayed out of it, quit being Mr. Detective know it all, John and I would have parted company. No, Joan, if you're looking for someone to blame, it's your husband."

Taft's words seemed to have a sobering effect on Joan. She sat motionless for several minutes, giving him a chance to concentrate on his driving. "We'll need to stop for gas soon," he said. "We've another four hours driving in front of us."

"Do you have any maps in the car?" John said.

While Joan busied herself inside the rest-stop restaurant, John and Taft studied an atlas of Interstate 95 North on a picnic table in the well-lit parking lot. John smoked a cigarette. Taft lit up a cigar and hoped Joan wouldn't make him extinguish it when she returned with the food.

John traced a path with his finger north of the rest stop. "It's at least four hours from where we are now, eight to your oldest boy in Atlanta," he said. "By now Freeman has figured out where we are headed."

"What resources does he have?" Taft said, and blew a dark smoke ring.

"The FBI for one. I don't know about his area because I don't know what his area is as yet," John said.

"If he has the FBI running interference for him, you can bet it's federal," Taft said. "The question is how high up the ladder."

"Apparently, he kills at will without worrying about consequences," John said. "I'd say it's top rung."

"And you're mixed up in it."

"Apparently so, or he wouldn't still be after me."

Taft puffed clouds of cigar smoke as he mulled over something in his mind. "He shot me because he thinks I discovered something about you I shouldn't know."

"Or you had the resources as a police captain to eventually discover something," John added. "Either way, you had to be eliminated."

"I remember that night, we were under the bridge," Taft said. "I was taking you in to try to sort things out. He showed up, got out of his car and shot me in the chest without so much as a by your leave."

"I read about it in the library," John said. "I can't say as I remember it."

"I don't remember much after going down," Taft said. "I knew that I'd been shot and knew that it was bad. After a few seconds, I drifted in and out of consciousness until I woke up in the hospital after surgery. I do remember bits and pieces, though. Tiny snippets of information that've haunted me for a year."

"I know the feeling," John said.

Taft displayed a tiny smile. "I suppose you do."

"Maybe you still remember?"

"Like I said, snippets," Taft said. "I remember Freeman and the woman arguing about something."

"Julie Warner?"

Taft nodded. "I couldn't make out the words, but I think she was upset that he shot me. Then someone was screaming about the bad guy, but I don't know who. After that, the next time I open my eyes I'm wired to an EKG machine."

"The bad guy?"

"Yeah, the bad guy."

"Who was doing the screaming, can you remember?"

"It sounded like you, but I can't swear to it," Taft said. "I was in pretty rough shape at the time."

"We'll talk more about it later," John said. He tapped the

atlas with his finger. "I have an idea."

Michael Taft was finishing off a can of Red Bull as he studied for a midterm exam. Advanced Accounting, as boring a subject as ever invented, was still a necessity even in the modern world. He was torn between breaking for a pizza or a nap when his cell phone jangled on the dresser. He rose from the bed to answer the call.

"Michael," Taft said before his son had the chance to say hello.

"Dad, I was just . . ."

"Michael, there isn't time to chat," Taft said. "I need you to . . ."

"Is something wrong with Mom?"

"Michael, be quiet and listen to me," Taft said. "I need you to gather up as much clothing as you can in the next fifteen minutes, then drive your car to the first rest stop just over the border of South Carolina."

"Dad, what are . . ."

"Michael, there is no time for discussion," Taft said. "Our family is in danger. I need us all together. Now hurry."

"Danger? Dad, I don't . . ."

"I'll tell you about it in the car," Taft said. "Now hurry. Please."

"Okay, Dad," Michael said.

Howard Taft Junior, weeks short of his twenty-seventh birthday, had just come off a sixteen-hour day at the chemical plant, ordered a pizza and collapsed in front of the television to watch the Senators lose another one when his phone rang. Annoyed, assuming it was work calling about a new problem with a chemical mix, he allowed his answering machine to screen the call.

The phone rang six times before the machine picked up. He

sat through his recorded voice message before his father said, "Howie, are you there? It's me, Dad. Pick up the . . ."

Howard Junior picked up the wireless phone on the coffee table and pressed the talk button. "Dad, I'm here. I thought it was . . ."

"No time to chat, Howie," Taft said. "And no time to argue. Listen to me carefully now."

As Freeman's private jet descended toward the runway over Raleigh, Cone listened to Freeman's phone conversation with Farris and Monroe on speaker. The speakers, built into the overhead lights, had a slight feedback problem, causing a one-second delay in the conversation.

"For a guy with no marbles, he's been one step ahead of us all the way," Freeman said. "He's managed to find his way clear to the ex–police captain."

There was a pause before Monroe said, "I never said he couldn't think or reason, and removing a man's memory doesn't remove his instincts or his skills."

Freeman said, "Yeah, well, by now he's regaining more of his memory and that makes him even more dangerous. If he reaches the point of total recall, John will go under and he won't surface again until he's good and ready, if ever."

An echo sounded over the speaker, followed by Monroe's delayed response. "Not necessarily. I've been conducting some experiments on some other subjects. I've found there is a delay in recall when they reach the halfway point between memory and amnesia. Kind of a tug of war, so to speak, that results in a shutdown of function. Ben, are you there?"

"I'm here," Freeman said. "It's this damn delay. How long will this shutdown last?"

"Days, possibly," Monroe said. "I don't know, I'm still testing. But any delay buys us time."

Another second's pause, then Farris said, "Ben, it's critical to all involved that you find John before he causes any more damage. If by some chance he's picked up by some local PD and it becomes known he's the Homeless Hero from New York, well, I don't need to tell you how embarrassing that would be, and not just to us, but Congress and all the way to the top."

Freeman and Cone exchanged glances. Each knew the question had to be asked. "The police captain and his family?" Freeman said.

A pause, followed by, "Naturally we don't wish the innocent any harm. That said, bring them in for a consultation."

Freeman said, "The police captain, he's not stupid."

"Do what you can, Ben," Farris said after the delay.

"Ben," Monroe said over static. "Get to John as quickly as possible. If he shuts down, we may lose him forever."

"But you're not sure of anything at this point?" Freeman said.

A pause, then, "No. I can tell you he'll hit that midpoint, but after that, it's a crapshoot. He could be lost or he could be whole. I'll know more after I study my subjects."

There was another static-filled pause, then Farris said, "Ben, I do not want you to fuck this up. I do not want to see this on CNN. I do not want to read about this in the fucking papers. Are we clear?"

"Yes," Freeman said.

The speaker suddenly went dead and Freeman pushed the disconnect button overhead on the console. He looked at Cone. "No backing out now, Agent Cone," he said.

"I wasn't planning on it," Cone said. "I'm in it until the end."

"It will probably get even messier than it is now."

"I realize that, but there is no way I can back down now," Cone said.

Freeman smiled at Cone. "You want to see just how good he is, don't you?"

"The thought has crossed my mind," Cone admitted.

"That thought has crossed a lot of people's minds," Freeman said. "It's usually their last thought right before the lights go out."

The speaker crackled to life and the pilot said, "Guys, ten minutes to touchdown. Buckle up and all that good stuff."

Freeman and Cone drove from the private airfield near Raleigh to Michael Taft's off-campus apartment located a mile from the North Carolina State University campus where he was a junior.

The apartment complex was nothing special, a group of four-story buildings isolated by a wide boulevard from middle-class homes, shops and stores. The lock on Michael Taft's lobby door was broken; they walked right in and took the stairs to his third-floor apartment.

The hour was late, the hall was dark and quiet, and Freeman used a lock pick to breeze through the cheap lock. Cone went in first; Freeman followed and softly closed the door.

Michael Taft wasn't home. His small, one-bedroom apartment looked as if a professional burglar had tossed the place. Dresser drawers open, closet a mess, one piece of a three-piece luggage set missing.

"He's in the wind," Freeman said. "Off to meet his father."

"Probably the other son, too."

"No doubt."

"Half-eaten pizza on the bed, books on the floor; he was studying when the call came," Cone said.

"John will stash them somewhere safe, then go underground," Freeman said. "We may have to wait it out until John reaches that point Monroe talked about."

"How do you hide an entire family?" Cone said. "Even for a

veteran cop and an experienced field agent like Tibbets, that isn't easy. They need a place to hide, food, money, and all that leaves a long train behind you."

Freeman sat on the bed and lit a cigarette. He talked it through. "John convinces Taft and his wife their lives are in danger. When they return home, Price and Locke ice the cake. They hit the road and Taft calls his sons, and they arrange to meet up somewhere as a family." He paused, looked around for a moment, then looked at Cone. "Where?"

Cone glanced down at the textbooks and notepad on the bed beside Freeman. Michael Taft had left in a hurry, so big of a hurry that he left behind the note he'd scribbled on the top page of his notebook while talking to his father.

"There," Cone said, pointing to the notebook.

Freeman looked down at it. On the page was scrawled: *1st rest stop in S. Carolina, I-95 South.* "He's piggybacking the retreat."

"What?" Cone said, looking at Freeman.

"The rear advances toward the middle while the middle retreats toward the rear," Freeman said. "The point retreats to the middle where the rear and middle have regrouped, bringing you up to full strength. You now retreat or advance as a full squad."

"So instead of Taft driving four hours, he and his son each drive two and meet in the middle," Cone said.

"Exactly."

"So the first son drives where?"

Freeman and Cone studied a map of the East Coast from the front seat of Freeman's agency-provided sedan. Freeman traced Interstate 95 South with his finger. "Taft told his youngest boy to meet him at the first rest stop in South Carolina," he said. "The oldest son lives in Virginia and he meets Taft where?"

Cone studied the map. "Taft continues driving north while Junior drives south," he said. "They meet in the middle."

"Where's the middle?" Freeman said.

Cone traced a path south from Richmond and north from the border of South Carolina. "The rest stop on ninety-five near Rocky Mount."

Freeman studied the route. "Four-hour drive north, maybe three hours south." He paused to look at his watch. "We can fly in and still beat Taft by an hour. He won't go anywhere without his kid and that gives us an hour to play with."

Freeman started the engine and put the sedan in gear.

Cone looked at him. "Taft could be on his own by now," he said. "Tibbets could be in the wind and on his way to Mexico or Canada."

Freeman turned into the street, hung a U-turn and started back to the airfield. "No choice but to risk it at this point," he said. "And even if John did ditch Taft, my guess is Taft knows where he's headed. That means we'll know, too."

Cone nodded as Freeman turned left at the corner. As much as he hated to admit it, Freeman's world was addictive and he was becoming hooked. In the FBI, if you drew your weapon, ten forms had to be filled out afterward. In Freeman's world, it was expected for you to draw your weapon. And forms didn't exist.

John handled Taft's Crown Vic like an old pro, Taft observed from the front passenger seat. After picking up Michael, Taft conceded the wheel to John, and he drove the next one hundred miles with machine-like precision. His body never seemed to move as the speedometer needle held at a steady seventy miles per hour without the use of cruise control. He stayed in the center lane and never switched to the left or right, never passed and never slowed. No part of his body appeared to move except for the occasional flick of the wrist to accommodate twists in the lane. In his present mode, John could drive coast to coast on ten tanks of gas and eight hours' sleep without so much as a peep out of him. It was as if instinct born of a thousand hours of training took over and shut down his thinking process. It occurred to Taft that it probably had.

In the backseat, Joan and Michael slept with their heads resting against each other. When they picked up Michael at the rest stop, Joan, more clearheaded than hours earlier, hugged their boy while Taft explained the family was in danger from an old, active case he'd worked on in New York. Without diving too greatly into details, Taft told Michael that an underground organization had surfaced to hunt down John Tibbets and those close to him. Familiar with the Homeless Hero story from a year ago, thankfully, Michael did not ask too many questions.

After an hour in the car and given the late hour, Michael and Joan fell asleep. Taft resisted the urge to nap. He fought off fatigue by removing his shoes and clenching his toes, and by smoking a cigar, something Joan would never allow in the car had she been awake.

John just kept rolling on, though, and didn't say a word until they approached the next rest stop at Rocky Mount. As he took the entrance ramp to the rest stop, he veered off to the truck parking lot, killed the headlights and looked over at Taft. "Duck down until I find a parking spot," he said.

John cruised to the rear of the lot and parked behind a long row of eighteen-wheelers. When Taft sat up and looked out, the restaurant complex at the front of the rest stop was obstructed by a hundred or more trucks. "Hide in plain sight," Taft said.

"What does your boy look like?" John said.

"Like me, only thirty years younger," Taft said. "But I'm going with you."

"No," John said. "Don't underestimate Freeman or the FBI.

By now, they're on to us. Maybe even figured out where we'll be picking up your son. Keep your cell phone on and if I call, get the hell out of here. Drive south and figure out a safe place to go. I'll call back later, on your cell."

"I'll not leave my son," Taft said.

"If I make that call and you don't, you'll lose your entire family," John said as he exited the Vic. "And I can't save your boy if I have to save all of you."

Taft knew John was right, of course. You don't sacrifice all for the sake of the one, but in this case, the one was his firstborn son. Taft reached for his shoes and slid behind the wheel.

"Still have the Magnum?" John said through the window.

Taft raised his shirt to reveal the butt of the .357 revolver. "Might want to keep it next to you on the seat," John said. "For good luck."

The rest stop parking lot encompassed two acres divided into separate sections for cars and trucks. Although there were streetlamps, light was minimal as John made his way across the lot, zigzagging in between trucks and shadows until he arrived at the grassland area reserved for dog walking.

He paused in the shadows cast by a tall oak tree and allowed his eyes to adjust fully to night vision. He looked ahead at the lot reserved for cars. Despite the late hour, a third of the lot was occupied. Some kids tossed a Frisbee, other people walked their dogs, some ate outdoors on picnic tables on the grass. John walked to a nearby empty picnic table in the shadows and took a seat.

Resisting the urge to light a cigarette, he scanned the parking lot, his eyes moving from shadows to people, movement, faces, searching for something that stood out.

There was nothing.

At first.

Slowly, the overall picture came clear. In the dog-walking area, a man wearing a suit walked a large dog back and forth across the lawn. The man seemingly paid no attention to the dog, nor the dog to its owner. Instead, the man seemed more interested in watching the parking lot, and the dog appeared on alert instead of showing the usual sniff-and-pee behavior. Man and dog did not so much walk the dog-walking area as patrol it.

John turned his attention to the Frisbee players. At a glance, they appeared to be young men taking a break from the highway by indulging in a harmless game. Upon closer inspection, the group, although dressed in jeans, shorts and T-shirts, were not young men in their late teens and early twenties, but at least a decade older.

After a catch and toss, a Frisbee player knelt down to tie a shoelace beside a sedan. A man seated behind the wheel looked at the Frisbee player and they appeared to exchange a few words before the player stood up and made a catch.

A quick scan showed another eight men, each one sitting alone in his car, in the driver's seat, not eating or drinking or resting, but watching. A man in a Ford sedan raised his right wrist to his mouth, held it for a few seconds, then lowered it to the steering wheel.

John scanned the parking lot up to the restaurant complex. There in the window stood a man in a suit looking out. The man's right wrist was held to his mouth, and although John was too far away to see his lips move, he knew the man was speaking to somebody in the parking lot.

Another Frisbee player knelt to tie a shoelace. While doing so, he raised his right wrist to his lips and whispered into what appeared to be a watch.

More than a dozen men had created a tightrope around the parking lot. John looked at the long exit ramp that skirted a gas station. It was the only exit ramp back to the highway, even for the eighteen-wheelers that needed to circle around the lot on another ramp and merge with cars to gain highway access. Two sedans, each with two men occupying them, sat on either side of the first pump, ready to block egress in an instant.

With his head down, John turned to look at the dog walker behind him. The man, less than twenty feet away, wasn't the threat. The dog was. A Doberman of about eighty pounds, it was fast and vicious and could bring a man down in a heartbeat.

The light from a car door opening caught John's eye and he shifted his gaze toward it. A figure emerged from the car and for a fleeting second before the door closed and the light extinguished, his face was visible. There was no mistaking him for anybody other than Howard Taft Junior, Taft's oldest son.

Howard Junior stood beside his car, his eyes scanning the parking lot for signs of his family. That was an easy mistake recognized by even a mediocre professional. To Freeman's crew, it was blood in the water.

John quietly removed Michael Taft's cell phone from his pocket and made the call. Taft answered before the second ring. "It's a trap," John said. "Go, leave now."

"I'll not leave my son," Taft said.

"Then you'll lose everything," John said. "Back out the entrance ramp onto the highway. Don't turn your lights on until you've merged with traffic. Don't stop unless I call you. If I don't call you, don't stop."

"John, don't let anything happen to my boy," Taft said.

John hung up and tucked the phone away. Things were happening now, subtly, but in motion. The Frisbee players stopped tossing the disc around and gathered in a small group several car lengths from Taft Junior. Behind John, the dog walker came to a sudden stop. In the restaurant window, the man raised his wrist to his lips.

The tightrope grew tighter. The fishing net was ready, and he and Taft Junior were the targeted fish.

John closed his eyes and took shallow breaths. Slowly, an image took shape in his mind. He didn't know where it came from, a memory or some past training, but he suddenly knew exactly what to do and how to do it.

He opened his eyes and turned his head to look at the dog walker. Man and dog were deep in shadows, alone on the grassy area reserved for dogs. Intent on locating Taft Junior, the man was deeply focused on scanning the crowd in the parking lot.

John slowly removed one of the .22 pistols from the small of his back. Under the picnic table, he racked the slide and removed the safety, then checked the silencer. Quietly and with as little motion as possible so as not to catch the dog walker's eye, John stood up from the picnic table and started walking away. When he was out of the man's peripheral line of sight, John turned and backtracked along the grassy area.

Just as the man and dog caught sight of him, John shot the dog twice in the chest and the man directly through the heart. Man and dog fell dead to the grass in the dark shadows. John stepped around them and walked at a normal pace to the end of the dog-walking area, reached the parking lot and skirted around to the rear of the restaurant complex.

Several back doors were open. A kid was hauling green garbage bags to a Dumpster, listening to an iPod and in his own world. John whisked past the kid and entered a hallway. Heat from several kitchens hit him in the face. The noise of food being prepared and a dozen conversations going at once masked his footsteps. He walked down the hallway and paused at a set of double doors that had windows at eye level, tucking the .22 into his waistband and under his shirt.

The complex interior was composed of several fast-food chains and two sit-down restaurants. The place was only a third full, with a great many people at tables and in lines. John slowly opened the double doors and entered the complex.

Lines for the fast-food restaurants stretched for twenty feet. John eased through them and took a seat at a vacant table adjacent to the burger joint, facing the back of the man looking out the window.

John studied the man. Though he couldn't see his face, he was sure it was FBI Agent Cone. A quick scan of the interior revealed that at least four men at tables were either FBI agents or Freeman's men.

Cone suddenly raised his right wrist to his mouth. John couldn't see or hear what Cone was talking about, but he knew by the four agents' reactions that somebody outside had found the dog walker.

The four agents rushed out to join the manhunt John assumed was under way, leaving Cone alone in the complex. John stood up and walked over to Cone, who immediately became aware that someone was behind him. Before he could react, John pulled the pistol and shoved it into his back.

"I killed one man tonight, I don't want to make it two," John said.

To his credit, Cone remained calm and collected. "I'm FBI Agent Richard Cone," he said.

"I know who you are," John said. "I remember you from the motel in New Mexico and the church in Texas. The question is, who am I and what is so important about me it's worth a cross-country chase?"

"You're John Tibbets," Cone said.

"I gathered that already," John said. "That doesn't tell me who I am or what you want with me."

"I suppose not," Cone said. "Look, that gun is getting pretty uncomfortable. Why don't we go sit down and talk this through?"

"It will get a great deal more uncomfortable if I put a few

rounds in your liver," John said. "So let's quit playing games. Nobody is going to sit down and talk. What we are going to do is stroll on out of here, get in Howard Junior's car and drive away unobstructed."

"I'm afraid I can't allow that," Cone said.

"I see," John said. "Well, then, I suppose I should just give myself up."

"That would be wise," Cone said. "I'm sure you've seen the firepower out there."

"Let's talk about that," John said. "Are they your men or Freeman's?"

"Agents from the Virginia and DC offices."

"Freeman?"

"Just three," Cone said. "He and they are in cars parked beside the gas pumps."

"The question is, Agent Cone, will your men allow you to die or will they stand down to save your life?" John said. He reached around Cone's waist to remove his Glock and tucked it into his own belt. "And I think we both know the answer to that one."

"I can't control Freeman," Cone said.

"Then I'll die, but you'll die first," John said. "Call him on your little Dick Tracy radio and tell him that."

Howard Taft Junior grew more frantic by the moment as he stood beside his car and waited for his father. Without giving details, his father had stressed that this was a life-and-death situation, so as he waited it was only natural his imagination ran amok. On the drive south he had something to occupy his mind, but standing here was brutal. His entire family could be dead at this very moment while he watched kids toss a Frisbee around a parking lot.

Something caused the Frisbee game to break up. They walked across the lot to the grassy area, and that was fine with Howard

Junior. All that running around was a distraction. He took a few steps away from his car to search for his father, turned, and saw two men approaching him, one behind the other.

The man in front, dressed in a conservative gray suit, appeared about forty-five years old, fit and trim. The man behind him, about the same age and dressed more casually, dominated the scenery. At least six foot four inches tall, the second man possessed wide, barn-door shoulders and the body of a heavyweight boxer.

They stopped directly in front of him.

"I'm FBI Special Agent Richard Cone," Cone said to Howard Junior.

"Are you here because of my dad?" Howard Junior said.

"Yes," Cone said.

Howard Junior looked past Cone at John. "Who are you?"

"I wish I knew," John said. He pointed to Howard Junior's car. "Yours?"

"Yes."

"Keys in it?"

"Yes."

"Get in the backseat," John said.

"I don't understand what . . ."

"If you want to see your family alive, get in the backseat," John snapped.

Howard Junior opened the back door of his sedan and got in. John gave Cone a tiny shove. "Open the passenger door, get in and shove over behind the wheel."

"How far do you think you're going to get?" Cone said.

"If we get caught, you die," John said. "That's how far."

Eighteen

Behind the wheel of yet another company sedan, Freeman seethed with rage at having to allow John to slip through his fingers once again. He supposed, though, that John being who he was would have made good on his threat to kill Cone if they didn't comply.

Still, it burned his ass no end how John waltzed in and caught them all with their pants down around their ankles.

Despite his boiling anger, Freeman had to smile. Even with one marble in his bag, John Tibbets had proved once again just how great an agent he was and could be again if he could be salvaged somehow.

But how?

With each man John killed, he drove the nails deeper and deeper into his own coffin. If he wasn't taken down soon, Farris would almost certainly have him executed to avoid yet another government scandal. More importantly, John couldn't be trusted not to go completely off the deep end and engage in a countrywide killing spree.

Okay, the second scenario was remote, but they'd had the parking lot fishnetted and he still managed to kill an FBI agent—two, if you counted the dog—and waltz on out as if taking a stroll on the beach.

"Sir, what should we do now?" the agent seated next to Freeman said.

Freeman lit a cigarette and continued to gaze out the window.

"Sir?" the agent said when Freeman didn't respond.

Freeman turned his head to look at the man. He was about thirty, with soft eyes and a young face. "What's your name?"

"Maxwell, sir."

"Like the Silver Hammer?" Freeman said.

"I don't understand, sir," Maxwell said. "What hammer?"

Freeman realized just how young the next breed of agents really was. To Maxwell, Freeman was a dinosaur and Farris a fossil. They obeyed orders because that's what they were supposed to do in order to get ahead, but the generation gap was wider than ever.

"Ever shoot anybody?" Freeman said.

"No, sir," Maxwell said.

"Do you think you can?"

"It's what I was trained for, sir."

Freeman started the engine. "I guess we'll find out," he said.

"Where are we going, John?" Cone said.

"North on ninety-five," John said.

"Can you be more specific?"

"No."

"John, listen to me," Cone said. "You can't win this and even if you could, what would you win?"

From the backseat, Howard Junior said, "Where are my father and my family?"

"At the moment, I don't know," John said.

"That's no answer," Howard Junior said.

"It's the only one I've got right now," John said.

"Then what the fuck are we doing here?" Howard Junior shouted.

John turned his head to look back at Howard Junior. "Keep your cool, son. Don't lose it now or it's over."

"What is over?" Howard Junior said. "Who are you people?"

John looked at Cone. "Good question, Agent Cone. Care to answer it?"

"I can't answer it because I don't really know all that much," Cone said.

"Agent Cone, understand this," John said. "The only reason you're still alive is for the conversation."

Cone glanced sideways at John. "I'll tell you what I know on one condition."

"What's that?" John said.

"You surrender yourself to me," Cone said.

"Now why would I want to do that?" John said.

"I can protect you," Cone said. "The FBI can protect you."

"Protect me from what?" John said. "From Freeman?"

"If not the death penalty, at least life in solitary confinement."

"For what?" John said. "Defending myself? I woke up in a desert without knowing how I got there and have spent the last week running from you people. Can you explain any of that, Agent Cone?"

"Yes, I can."

"But?"

"You have to trust me."

"You mean give myself up?"

"Yes."

"So I should give myself up to you without knowing why," John said. "In my place, would you?"

Cone allowed himself another sideways glance at John. The .22 pistol was rock solid in his grasp, aimed directly at Cone's middle. His eyes returned to the dark road. "No, I wouldn't," Cone said.

"Then give me something, a reason to trust you," John said. "Then we'll talk about turning myself in."

"Fair enough," Cone said. "Where do I begin?"

"With what you know. Start with Freeman."

"Freeman is second in command of a highly classified government agency," Cone said. "So classified, I didn't know it existed until they brought me into the fold after the motel incident in New Mexico."

"What do they do?" John said.

"Military extraction, civilian interference, preemptive problem solving."

"What the hell does that mean?" Howard Junior said.

"Assassination," John said. He looked at Cone. "Is that what I am, an assassin?"

"Yes," Cone said. "Their very best, so I'm told, so I've seen."

"None of this makes a bit of sense," John said.

"You went rogue," Cone said. "They brought you in and salvaged you by . . . eradicating your memory."

"The amnesia?"

"Yes. A specialist by the name of Doctor Monroe treated you with a combination of drugs and techniques to block out your memory. They used a homeless shelter to keep tabs on you and keep you in the system."

"For what reason?"

"Reactivation."

"For what reason?"

"I can only speak of the one incident I'm aware of," Cone said. "A major player in the drug trade was bringing in shipments through a small airport in New Mexico. You were reactivated to take him and his partners out with extreme prejudice."

"You mean kill them?" Howard Junior said.

"That's what he means," John said.

"Speak fucking English, man," Howard Junior said.

"Did I succeed?" John said.

"Yes, but something went wrong," Cone said. "You were supposed to shut down right afterward, but instead you killed some FBI agents and took off on your own."

"I don't believe you," John said.

"It's true, John."

"I don't remember any of that."

"Why would you? You've been programmed to forget."

"What the hell does any of this have to do with me and my family?" Howard Junior said.

"Your father was a pretty good detective," Cone said. "When John saved the life of his nephew last year, he got involved, and was helping John when Freeman showed up and put an end to it."

"You mean this Freeman shot my father?" Howard Junior said.

"He couldn't risk the exposure of a national scandal," Cone said.

"So he shot my dad in cold blood?" Howard Junior said.

"And now he's after me again?" John said. "And Taft and his entire family this time."

"You have to understand something, John," Cone said. "I'm not the bad guy here and neither is Freeman. You are."

John kept the pistol aimed at Cone's stomach while he peered through the windshield.

"Is that true?" Howard Junior said. "Is he the bad guy in all this?"

"He doesn't have to be," Cone said. "He could give himself up right now and I'll take him and you directly to FBI headquarters in Washington."

"And my family?"

"We'll bring them in safe."

"Mr. Tibbets?" Howard Junior said.

John continued to stare out the windshield.

"Mr. Tibbets, is that true?" Howard Junior said. "Are you the bad guy in all this as he said?"

John slowly turned to look at Howard Junior. "No," he said. "I didn't shoot your father in cold blood and I'm not the one hunting your entire family right now." He waved the .22 pistol at Cone. "He is."

"That's not true, John," Cone said. "I'm not hunting anybody. I'm along for the ride and to see if I can help, and I can."

"By running down the entire Taft family," John said. "I don't believe you."

"I'm not sure I do either," Howard Junior said.

"Pull over onto the breakdown lane," John said.

"Why?" Cone said.

"I don't want to get your brains all over the kid's car," John said, and raised the .22 pistol to Cone's head.

"Jesus Christ, don't shoot him," Howard Junior cried.

"Shut up, kid," John said. To Cone, he said, "Now pull over or I pull the trigger."

"Pull over where?" Cone said.

"The shoulder," John said.

Cone slowed the car as he eased from the center lane to the breakdown lane and slowed to a stop. He put the car in park and then looked at John. "Now what?"

"Now, you get out," John said.

"Out?"

"Yeah, out," John said. He removed the magazine from Cone's Glock and gave him the empty weapon.

Cone stuck the Glock into its holster, opened the door and stood beside the car as John slid behind the wheel. "This is a big mistake," Cone said.

"I've made them before," John said and put the car in drive. "I think."

Cone jumped backward as John sped back onto the right

lane of the highway, merged with traffic and vanished into a sea of red taillights.

"Sir, how are we going to locate the suspect on the highway?" Maxwell said. "They have a big head start on us and we don't know if they've gotten off the highway or doubled back or what."

Cruising at eighty-five miles an hour in the left lane, Freeman suddenly darted across into the right lane and slowed to sixty-five. "Look for a clue as to what happened," Freeman said.

"Like what, sir?"

"Oh, I don't know," Freeman said and veered into the breakdown lane. "How about a stranded FBI agent?"

From the backseat of his car, Howard Junior said, "Now what?"

"Are you handy with tools?"

"I'm a freaking engineer, man."

"Good," John said. Less than five miles down the road from where they let Cone off, John veered into the breakdown lane once again and came to a stop behind a college kid fixing a flat on his beater.

John exited quickly and approached the college kid, who appeared to have no clue as to how to change a flat. Howard Junior came out and stood behind John. "Need a hand?" John said to the college kid.

"I think I have the wrong kind of jack," the college kid said. "This one doesn't seem to work."

"No problem," John said. "We'll try to fix it for you."

John knelt down beside the tire and gave it a quick once-over. "Maybe the tire can be saved, but you drove on the rim."

"What's that mean?" the college kid said.

"Rim's bent," John said. "You need a new one."

"So I'm stuck? Man, I gotta get to class in four hours. I've been studying all night at my mom's house to prepare for a . . ."

"Relax, kid," John said. "Take our car, drive to town and buy a new tire. We'll try to get the old one off for you by the time you get back."

The college kid looked at John. "Are you serious?"

"Yeah, we have nothing to do for a few hours," John said. "Bring us a couple of coffees on the way back."

The college kid looked at Howard Junior.

"Keys are in it," Howard Junior said.

"Thanks," the college kid said. "If I fail this test, I'm dead in the water."

"Then I would go get that tire," John said.

The college kid dashed to Howard Junior's car, got behind the wheel and drove off into the night.

"Now what?" Howard Junior said.

John pulled out the cell phone and dialed Taft's number. "We wait for your father to come pick us up. Get down behind the car."

"I'm Agent Maxwell, sir," Maxwell said to Cone, who was seated in the back of Freeman's sedan. "Like the silver hammer."

"What's this kid talking about?" Cone said.

"Never mind that now," Freeman said. "How big a head start do you think John has on us?"

"From where you picked me up," Cone said and looked at his watch. "At least ten miles by now."

"If he's even still on the highway," Freeman said.

Maxwell glanced out his window at the beater of a car with a flat tire. He couldn't see anybody changing the tire. They must have given up and walked to the next exit. "That sucks, getting a flat. You would think more people would have Triple A."

Ignoring Maxwell, Freeman said, "Cone, we've lost him. Without bringing in local law enforcement, we have zero chance of running him down. We can make Washington in a few hours.

I suggest we head back, regroup and work the problem. Your computer bank and ours is our best bet at finding John and maybe where the Taft family is headed."

"Agreed," Cone said.

Ten minutes after Freeman drove past John and Howard Junior, Taft showed up in the Crown Vic. "Whose car is this?" Taft said as John and Howard Junior got in.

"I'll explain on the way," John said.

"On the way to where?" Taft said.

"The one place in this entire country where Freeman would never look," John said.

"And where is that?" Taft said.

"New Mexico," John said.

NINETEEN

Less than one mile from where it all started, at least from John's memory, was the Desert Oasis Camp Ground. John remembered seeing the signs for it when he'd walked along the road to town from the motel.

Having had the good sense to remove his emergency funds from the strongbox in the bedroom closet, Taft had ten thousand dollars at his disposal. He figured living on the coast in a hurricane-watch zone, the money would come in handy for evacuation purposes. He'd never figured on using it to hide his entire family from the government, but the money could be replaced and they couldn't.

Taft rented a four-bedroom mobile home in the campground overlooking a small lake and river. He gave Joan nine thousand dollars, keeping one thousand for himself. Joan was not a happy woman, but her sons were alive and with her, and that was some compensation. Exhausted and bleary-eyed, Joan fell onto the bed in one of the bedrooms and was sound asleep before Taft left the room. He met with his two sons outside the trailer.

"After you drop John and me off at the . . ."

"You're not staying?" Michael snapped. "How the hell can you leave us now?"

"Michael, listen to me," Taft said. "This man is the key to something very important. Too important for me to walk away from, and there is a better chance they won't find you if I'm not with you."

"But you're retired," Michael said. "Besides, it will be dark soon."

"This isn't about retirement," Taft said. "It's about something bigger than ourselves, and I have to help him find out what that something is. Now drive us to town, and that's the end of it."

"Mom won't be happy when she finds out," Howard Junior said.

"No, she won't be, but she'll understand," Taft said. "She's a cop's wife, and that you never retire from."

"You're sure you want to stay here?" Howard Junior said, as he looked at the motel that to him was in the middle of nowhere.

"Yes," John said. He opened the rear door, got out of the car and looked back at Taft. "I'll wait for you over there."

Behind the wheel of the Crown Vic, Howard Junior looked at his father. "Why can't you just go to the police with this?" he said.

"I am the police," Taft said. "But, that aside, no police department would step on the toes of the FBI in an investigation. Now remember, don't drive the car unless you have to make a trip for food and don't use your cell phones under any circumstances. The only incoming calls you should answer are from me, and I'll text them. Did you bring your laptop?"

"No."

"Good. Those can be traced quite easily. Now for God's sake, take care of your mother. She tends to worry too much."

Taft and his two sons exited the Vic to hug each other. Then Howard Junior got behind the wheel, and Michael took the front passenger seat. As the Vic drove off into the night, Taft walked to John, who was smoking a cigarette in front of the motel sign.

"They're good boys," John said.

"That they are," Taft agreed.

"You'll have to wake the manager up," John said. "Pay cash for the room. If he asks if you're alone, tell him I'm your brother. He knows my face, so I won't go in with you, and he won't care enough to come out and look."

"What name shall I use to sign in?" Taft said.

"Freeman," John said. "Ben Freeman."

"You've been here before?" Taft whispered.

"Yes."

After checking into the motel and eating a quick takeout meal from the local diner a mile down the road, John suggested a walk to take the edge off so that they could sleep. The walk led them down the road and into the woodlands behind a small private airport where they now stood.

"When, John, when have you been here?" Taft said, his cop's sense on alert.

John stared at the hole in the chain-link fence. "I . . . don't know."

"But this place is familiar to you?" Taft said.

"Yes."

"What is familiar about it, John?"

John shrugged his shoulders as he stared at the hole in the fence. After nearly forty years of being a cop, after thousands of interviews with witnesses and suspects, Taft knew a few things about coaxing details from those who couldn't remember a thing.

"Is it the hole in the fence?" Taft said. "Have you seen it before?"

"No," John said. "Wait. Yes, but it wasn't there."

"The hole wasn't there?"

"No."

"Any idea how it got there?"

John stared at the hole. "I . . . I cut it. With bolt cutters. No, wire cutters I had in my pocket."

"And why did you do that, John?" Taft said.

John wiped his eyes with the fingers of his right hand. Even in the dark, Taft could see he was sweating heavily, although the desert night air was cool. "John, did you hear what I said?"

Either he didn't hear Taft or chose to ignore him, but John suddenly pushed through the hole in the fence to the other side.

"Where are you going?" Taft said as he followed John through the hole.

John walked a bit, then paused. "It was here."

"What was here?" Taft said, looking at John. A sheen of sweat made his face glow in the moonlight; his eyes were as focused as lasers. "Tell me."

John walked toward the airport hangar doors. He paused to look around again. "I shot them."

"Who did you shoot, John?" Taft said.

"I don't know," John said. "These men. More men followed through the fence. I shot them, too."

"Why, John, why did you shoot them?" Taft said. "You must have had a reason."

John felt a sudden, very sharp pain in his skull that started at the crown and seemed to seep downward directly into his brain. He gasped and laid a hand on Taft's shoulder to regain his balance.

"What is it?" Taft said.

"Headache."

"Maybe we should head back to the room?" Taft suggested. "Sleep is probably the best thing right now."

"No," John said as he sat on a chair outside the hangar doors. There was a second chair, and Taft sat on it. John pointed directly ahead. "They were there. I came out of the shadows and I shot them, all of them."

"How many men, John?"

"Four," John said. "No, six. Six men."

"Right here, you shot and killed six men?" Taft said.

"Yes."

"For what reason, John?"

John closed his eyes. He could almost see the event as it played out that night. Dressed all in black, he came out of the shadows with a pair of silenced Ruger .22 pistols, aimed and fired two shots into each man. The entire scene played out in a matter of seconds.

"John, did you hear me?" Taft said.

"Yes."

"Why did you kill them, John?" Taft said.

John rubbed his skull as if trying to massage the pain away. "It was . . . my mission."

"What mission, John?" Taft said. "What are you talking about, the FBI?"

"No," John said. The pain inside his head escalated to the point he thought he might have a stroke. Pressure bulged behind his eyes and he gently massaged them. "But they were here."

"The FBI?"

"They came through the fence after me."

"You mean pursued you?"

"No. Almost as if they were . . ."

"What, John?" Taft said when John paused to rub his temples. "Almost as if they were what?"

John lowered his hands and looked at Taft. "Almost as if they were supposed to be there."

"The FBI?"

"No."

"Then who?"

"I don't know."

"Okay, John, just relax," Taft said. "Maybe if we took things one step at a time it might help your memory."

John gently massaged his nose just below his eyes. "The pain is going away," he said. He pulled out his pack of cigarettes and lit one with a disposable lighter. Taft removed a long cigar from his shirt pocket and took the time to light it properly with a match. They smoked in silence for a few moments before John said, "My mission was to kill them all and that's just what I did."

"Who are them, John?" Taft said as he puffed on the cigar.

John thought for a second, trying to gain a clearer picture in his head of the men that he killed. "I don't know," he finally admitted. "That wasn't included in the mission."

"But the mission was to kill them?" Taft said.

John turned his head to look at Taft. "Yes."

"Could this mission have come from Freeman?" Taft said. "If the mission was highly classified and you ran amok afterward, that would explain his desire to find you. Of course, that only explains the tip of the iceberg, so to speak."

"I can't remember," John said. "My first memory of seeing Freeman is at the . . ."

"Where, John?"

"It's all a blur," John admitted. "Old memories meshed together with new ones. Newspaper stories of what happened in New York that I don't remember, but that I read about. It all forms one big blur in my mind. No, wait. I think it was at the church in Texas. He chased me. I remember now. He said he was my old friend Ben Freeman, something like that, but who the hell is he?"

"He's tried to kill you numerous times, shot me and left me for dead. That's some friend," Taft said. "Whoever he is."

"The thing is, it's hard for me to put together what I remember with what I've read about," John said. The strain of the headache coupled with lack of sleep suddenly hit him like a brick in the face. "I'm tired," he said.

"Let's go back to the motel and sleep this off," Taft suggested. "If there is one thing I learned from years of police work, it's that a rested mind is a sharp mind."

"Does that count if you don't have one?" John remarked as he stood up.

James Farris stopped just short of seething, allowing himself the luxury of anger before pulling it back to outward irritation at the situation at hand. From behind his desk, Farris looked across at Freeman and Cone. Both men appeared bleary-eyed and exhausted from working sixty out of the past seventy-two hours. Farris was short on sympathy. Not that he advocated killing an FBI agent to accomplish a goal, but they had Tibbets in their sights and allowed him to slip away through careless execution of a plan. The only saving grace for Freeman in the debacle was that the men who screwed up were FBI and not his own. Blame, if there were some to go around, ran downhill like everything else inside the Beltway.

"Progress?" Farris said.

"He's gone under, Jim," Freeman said. "Way under. Our computers and the FBI are searching the country for any tidbit of information that might give us a clue. So far, nothing."

"What about your department?" Farris said to Cone.

"Short of putting Tibbets on the terrorist watch list and distributing an APB to local law enforcement around the country, we're doing everything that we can," Cone said.

"Which appears to be nothing," Farris said.

"Jim, in defense of what happened out there, the FBI couldn't have allowed John to kill Agent Cone," Freeman said.

"Oh, cut the crap, Ben," Farris said. "They sent inexperienced men who fucked up, and that's the end of it. If either of you see this differently, tell me where I'm wrong."

Neither Freeman nor Cone argued the point. Nearly thirty

seconds passed before Farris looked at his watch. "Monroe should be here any minute," he said.

John and Taft left the tiny airport and walked along the dark road back to the motel. John suddenly paused to look around.

"What?" Taft said.

"My head keeps going back and forth with what I remember and when," John said. "Like a movie where they keep cutting back and forth from scene to scene. This is where I woke up."

"Woke up?"

"The first memory I have is walking on this road," John said. "I have no idea how I arrived here or where I was coming from, but it can only be the airport we just left."

"Question is, how did you get to the airport and who transported you?" Taft said. "My guess is, whoever is responsible for your mission."

"That has to be Freeman."

"Yeah, but like you said, who the hell is Freeman?" Taft said.

John shrugged and they continued walking.

Farris, Freeman and Cone looked at Monroe with anticipation as he fiddled with his notebooks and pen. At the conference table, Farris, short on patience, snapped, "Doctor, please."

Monroe glanced up at Farris, and the quick movement displaced his reading glasses. He adjusted them with his finger, then flipped a notebook to the page he was searching for. "Here it is," he said.

Farris, Freeman and Cone waited. After several seconds passed, Farris said, "Doctor, time is critical here."

"I realize that," Monroe said. "After testing several subjects under the same conditions as John Tibbets, I can clearly state that he is in meltdown status. As the influence of the mind-altering drugs grows weaker in his system, his memory is conflicting with the mental block installed through various brainwashing techniques. In that, I was able to induce amnesia through organic means by damaging the hippocampus, which inhibits the ability to imagine the future. The hippocampus is the . . ."

"Would you speak fucking English for God's sake," Freeman snapped.

There was an awkward moment of silence in the room as Monroe looked at Freeman. Finally, Monroe cleared his throat and said, "John could be controlled because I removed his ability to imagine the future. Without being able to see or imagine future events, he had no compass to past events. Right now, as his hippocampus reverts to normal, past and present are about to collide head on."

"Resulting in?" Freeman said.

"Meltdown," Monroe said.

"Followed by?" Freeman said.

"Slow recapturing of past memories, followed by ability to live in the present and finally the ability to plan the future. When that happens, John Tibbets will be completely restored and fully functional."

Freeman looked at Farris, then turned back to Monroe. "Well, that's just fucking great," he said.

John sat with his back against the headboard of his bed in their motel room. Taft sat at the desk against the wall and smoked a cigar near the open window. John took small sips from a can of soda and reached for his pack of cigarettes on the nightstand. Taft studied the athletic build and taut muscle of John's shirtless torso, lit by the lamp. The man must be close to fifty, Taft thought, but had the build of an athlete in his prime. A great deal of training and work went into constructing the physical specimen that was John Tibbets, so why destroy that work? Why go to all the trouble of developing a man like John just to turn around and kill him? Did Shakespeare burn a play after writing one? It didn't make sense, not to Taft, not without a great deal more facts.

As John lit a cigarette, Taft studied the scars on John's chest and abdomen. The star-shaped abdomen scar was from a bullet wound. Taft remembered seeing it for the first time in the hospital after John saved Gary's life a year ago. The knife scar on John's shoulder was thick and deep. It must have been caused by a long knife thrust in a downward motion. Other, smaller scars seemed to be everywhere on his torso and spoke of a lifetime spent in the thick of it, whatever it was.

"John, do you have any idea how you acquired so many body scars?" Taft said.

John blew a smoke ring and watched it rise to the ceiling and dissipate. He touched the bullet wound on his stomach. "This one, and only because I read about it, not because I remember the events."

"That's all?"

John nodded his head.

"I suppose it really doesn't matter at this point," Taft said.

John took a sip from the soda can. "No."

"What about your training?" Taft said.

"My training?"

"Yes," Taft said. "If we knew what you were trained for, it might tell us something about your mission."

"Policeman's logic?" John said with a slight grin.

"So to speak."

"I don't know," John said. "An hour ago, the mission was on the tip of my tongue. Now I can't remember a thing. It's all . . . fuzzy."

Taft puffed on the cigar and blew smoke toward the window. "You must have thought this through, John," he said. "Why else

228

would we be here? We could have hidden my family anywhere, yet you chose to return to New Mexico. There must be a reason."

"We talked about it," John said.

"Yes, but do you remember what it is?"

John stared at Taft for many long, silent seconds.

"You said it's the one place Freeman wouldn't look for you," Taft said. "Do you remember saying that?"

"No," John said. "Wait . . . I do. I said that in the car, the Crown Vic."

"Yes, that's right," Taft said. "But why did you say it?"

"Freeman probably thinks we're running for our lives," John said. "Would you go back to the beginning to hide?"

"No, I wouldn't," Taft said. "But will Freeman? It seems to me that if you two worked together, you trained together and that might lead you to think alike."

"True," John said as he crushed out the cigarette in a tin ashtray on the nightstand. "Except that right now I can't remember, much less think, so I have no idea what Freeman will do."

"Let's grab some sleep," Taft said. "Morning has a way of clearing the air."

"How much time do we have?" Freeman asked Monroe.

Monroe glanced at Farris.

"Doctor?" Farris said.

"Two or three days, maybe less," Monroe finally admitted.

"And John will be John again?" Freeman said.

"Yes."

Freeman looked at Farris. "Suggestions?"

"Find him," Farris said. "Stop him before it's too late."

"That's not exactly a game plan, James," Freeman said.

Cone, a silent observer throughout the entire meeting, cleared his throat to give advance warning he was about to speak. Farris caught on and looked at the FBI agent. "You have something to add, Agent Cone?"

"I was wondering something," Cone said and looked at Free-man. "You and Tibbets trained together and worked together for quite a while, isn't that right?"

"Almost eighteen years," Freeman said. "What's on your mind?"

"Same training, same missions, over a long period of time two men can come to think and reason almost exactly the same," Cone said. "I've seen it at the Bureau with agents part-nered for their entire careers."

"Interesting," Farris said. "Where are you going with this?"

"If John and Freeman were trained to act and think alike, I was wondering if Ben put himself in John's shoes, could you figure out where he would go if you were him," Cone said. "If Doctor Monroe is correct and he is running on instinct, where would that instinct take him to escape pursuit?"

"Minus his memory?" Freeman said. He looked at Monroe. "What would you say his status was three days ago?"

"Vague recall of recent events," Monroe said. "No long-term memory to speak of, while at the same time his instincts would be intact."

"And now?"

"Right this moment?" Monroe said, and paused to think. "It's all coming together in his mind like a blender mixing a shake. It will be quite painful and very disorienting, but when that passes, he will be whole again."

"Exactly what will he remember?" Farris said.

"Pretty much his whole life."

"His capture and treatment?" Farris said. "The mission in the Bowery?"

"My guess is he will remember all of it."

Farris turned to Freeman. "Ben?"

Freeman closed his eyes for a moment and when he opened them, he snorted a soft laugh. "I think Agent Cone may have something here," he said. "If the situation was reversed and I was running from John, and Monroe is correct in his theory, the place I would hide would be at the beginning."

"New Mexico?" Farris said.

Freeman looked at Cone and nodded a tiny salute. "Back to his first memory of waking up," Freeman said. "The last place we would look for him. I'll have four men on patrol around that airport within the hour."

"It's been three days," Farris said. "If Monroe's correct and John has regained partial or full memory, he's not going to stay put."

"My guess is he'll run," Freeman said.

"You know him better than anybody, where will he run to?" Farris said.

Freeman looked Farris directly in the eye. "Here, James," Freeman said. "John will come here to Washington."

"For the credit," were the last words Julie said before she died. Before he killed her.

"Orders, John," Freeman said just before he pulled the trigger and assassinated a high-ranking Japanese official.

"Whose?"

"Farris, who else."

"Why? This is an important mission."

"Not for our government, John. Farris looks the other way when you take a private contract inside the country, provided it's not political," Freeman said.

"So what are you going to do, scold me? Take me to Farris for my punishment?" John said. "Or just execute me right here and now?"

"I'm afraid the boss has other ideas for you, John," Freeman said. "There's a new program he wants to put you in."

Al Lamanda

"Fuck you, Ben," John snarled. "And that pencil-pushing desk asshole."

Freeman smiled. "Well, John, that pencil-pushing desk asshole is about to rock your world and make your planets twirl."

Before John could pull the trigger, Julie came up behind him with the stun gun she'd taken from Taft's pocket and stuck it against his back. As John jerked and gasped, the pistol fell from his grasp, but he didn't go down.

"Jesus Christ," Julie said and hit him again with the stun gun, which sent him reeling to the ground. Still conscious, he went into spasms until Julie placed the stun gun against his neck and juiced him a third time. He went under then and Julie stared at him as if she were admiring a great work of art.

"For the credit," Julie said before she died. Before he killed her.

"You're a great deal more than a homeless Bowery bum, I'm afraid," Freeman said. "You might be the greatest assassin this country has ever produced."

John lowered the pistol and stared at Freeman. "What . . . what are you talking about? Assassin?"

"I'm talking about you, John," Freeman said. "Special Forces captain recruited by the CIA back in the late hostilities to handle their dirty laundry. After things cooled off, you went freelance, which is where we come in. The agency, that's us . . . well, we take care of certain inequities for Uncle Sam that nobody else will even acknowledge, much less touch."

John slowly stood up and placed his hands on his head. "You'd do this to me?" he said. "After all we've been through."

Freeman took John's right arm, bent it behind his back, and cuffed it. "This isn't about what we've been through, John." He took

232

John's left arm and placed it into the remaining cuff. "You crossed the line when you started contracting jobs against America's interest. We can't allow that."

John felt beads of sweat on his forehead. "You're government?"

"Private, so to speak," Freeman admitted. "So private we don't exist on paper or in any computer in the world. We're ghosts who operate in a world of goblins."

John felt sweat trickle down his forehead into his eyes. The salt stung and he wiped his face with his left hand. "And I work for you?"

John opened his eyes and peered through the darkness at the faint outline of Taft on the second bed. As was the case with most career cops, Taft was a light sleeper. At the sound of John removing the covers, Taft stirred, sat up and looked at John.

"What?" Taft said in a sleep-filled voice.

John clicked on the lamp on the nightstand between the two beds and reached for his cigarettes. He lit one and looked at Taft. "We were partners," John said as he blew smoke.

"Freeman?" Taft said.

John nodded his head. "More than that," he said. "We were friends, close friends."

"You had a dream?" Taft said. "You saw things?"

"More like remembered things," John said.

"What did you remember?"

"A mission," John said. "Something went wrong. Ghosts."

"Ghosts?" Taft said. "What do you mean, ghosts?"

John blew a smoke ring toward the ceiling and watched it float away before he looked at Taft. "I think I mean me," he finally said.

"You?"

"Listen, you were right about Freeman," John said. "He'll

come here looking for me and if he finds me, he'll find you and your family. I don't know what that means, but until I do, they can't be found and neither can we."

"Agreed," Taft said. "The sonofabitch shot me once in cold blood. I'll not have him doing it again."

"I remember," John said. "At least, I think I do. She . . . Julie, I mean. She tazed me. She said, 'Jesus Christ.' "

"Why?"

John shrugged. "For the credit."

"For the . . . what does that mean?"

"I don't know."

"Maybe she was passed over and thought capturing you somehow would make her bosses take notice?" Taft suggested.

"That could be." John looked at his watch. "Be light in less than an hour. Call your boys and tell them we're coming for the car."

"And then?"

"We'll go for breakfast."

TWENTY

John waited beside the Crown Vic while Taft spoke with his sons outside the mobile home. Several dozen mobile homes occupied the trailer park, but it was early and no one was awake yet to witness the good-byes.

Taft placed his hands on Howard Junior's shoulders. "You boys are the finest sons a man could ask for," he said. "But, right now I need you to be men and take care of your mother. I wish there was time to take you somewhere else, but there isn't. Stay inside unless you need food and then take turns walking to the store. And for God's sake, talk to no one unless it's a grocery clerk."

John leaned against the door of the Crown Vic and lit a cigarette.

"What if our sister should call?" Howard Junior said.

"She won't," John said from the background. "We'll call her first. Mom and Dad are taking a spur of the moment cruise for a week. Call you when we get back."

Howard Junior glared at John. "You have it all figured out, don't you?" he said. "If something happens to my . . ."

"Nothing is going to happen if you do as I say," Taft said. "Starting with I need you and your brother to be men. Am I clear?"

Howard nodded yes.

"You?" Taft said to Michael.

"Don't worry, Dad," Michael said. "We won't let you down."

"I'll have a word with your mother," Taft said, turned and opened the door to the trailer.

Joan was at the tiny round table against the window of the living room. She was about to sip from a cup of tea when Taft walked in and closed the door behind him. She took her sip and held the teacup in both hands.

"Have you time for a cup?" she said. "It will only take a moment."

"I've only got a moment," Taft said.

"So you'll get yourself killed to protect a stranger?" Joan said.

"No, but I would die to protect my wife and my family, which is exactly what I'm doing," Taft said.

Joan took another sip of tea and looked at Taft over the rim of the cup. "You need this, don't you?" she said. "The excitement of being a cop. The chase and the thrill of it all. Well, go on then and get yourself killed."

"Joan, this is not about me," Taft said. "This is about keeping our family alive and in one piece. These people are after something and I'm in the way now. They won't stop and they won't hesitate to hurt you or the boys to get what they want. I won't allow that. I can't allow that, and that is all there is to it."

Joan stood up and wrapped her arms around Taft. "Go on and get yourself killed then," she said into his chest. "I'll be waiting for you when you get back."

Taft kissed her on the forehead. "I know," he said softly.

John and Taft ordered half the breakfast menu in the Egg Muffin Diner on Main Street of the small town near the airport. They had a window table where they could watch the Omelet House Diner across the street. Taft's massive Crown Vic was parked there in a back row, where it could easily be spotted from a passing car.

"What if Freeman hasn't sent any men?" Taft said. "We can't

sit in this diner all day waiting?"

"He sent men," John said. "It's what I would have done in his position to cover all the bases."

"Meaning he thinks you might turn up somewhere else as well?" Taft said as he ate some eggs.

"There could be some city or safe house he knows about that I don't remember," John said. "He could be banking on my remembering it and going there. No, he'll cover all the bases and hope to net me in one of them."

"But you don't remember?"

"Not yet," John said. "Bits and pieces of fractured information keep rolling around upstairs, but nothing with any continuity."

Taft cut into a sausage link and ate half. "My instincts as an old cop say let's look at the facts," he said. "A powerful but unknown government agency wants you killed or captured badly enough to kill innocent bystanders to get their hands on you. You don't know or can't remember why. If we were talking about organized crime, I would say it's because you know where the bodies are buried and there is the possibility you might talk about it."

"Secrets," John said. "You're talking about secrets."

"Many a man died because he couldn't keep his mouth shut," Taft said as he ate the other half of the sausage link.

John sipped coffee as he looked out the window. "He said I crossed the line and he couldn't allow that."

"Freeman?"

"In my dream," John said.

"What does that mean?"

"I don't know. But that's the third time I've seen the same black sedan circle this block."

Taft watched as the black sedan crept by the Omelet House Diner to the end of the block, where it made a left turn.

"They've spotted the Vic," he said.

"I counted four men in the sedan," John said.

"Any backup?"

"Not that I've seen," John said. "But that doesn't mean they aren't there."

John and Taft continued to watch the street. After two minutes, the black sedan appeared again. It slowed and entered the parking lot of the Omelet House, where it found a spot several cars behind the Crown Vic.

"Now what?" Taft said.

"The lights have dimmed and the orchestra is warming up," John said.

"Meaning?" Taft said.

Four men exited the sedan.

"The curtain is about to go up," John said. He tossed a twenty and two fives on the table and stood up. "Wait for me to cross the street, then walk out and turn right. Don't stop until I pick you up."

Taft watched as two of the four men walked around to the rear of the diner. The other two walked to the front door of the diner just as John appeared in the window and crossed the street.

Taft stood up and walked to the door.

John watched as the two men entered the Omelet House. He waited a moment, then pulled the Leatherman Tool from his pocket and extended the razor-sharp knife. He went to the Crown Vic, knelt beside the left-rear tire and jammed the knife into the rubber up to the handle. The tire immediately went flat.

John stood and walked to the dark sedan. He found it unlocked, but without the keys in the ignition. He slid behind the wheel and used the Leatherman Tool to break off the ignition cap and start the engine with a soft push of the exposed button.

He backed out of the spot and exited the parking lot, turned left and spotted Taft halfway down the block. He slowed, pulled alongside the curb and opened the door for Taft, who got right in.

"The Vic?" Taft said as he closed the door.

"Sadly, it has a flat," John said as he feathered the gas. "But not to worry. These government cars have everything."

"Well, while I fiddle with the radio, I suggest we put some distance between the owners of this fine automobile and us," Taft said.

Driving south on Interstate 85, John lit a cigarette as he watched roadside signs. He glanced at Taft, who was removing the wrapper from a fresh cigar. "Ever been to Texas?" John said.

"Not as I recall," Taft said. He struck a paper match to light the cigar. "But it won't be long before an APB is out on this car."

"Probably is already," John said.

"So we need to ditch it pretty soon," Taft said as he puffed great clouds of gray smoke.

"El Paso, two miles," John said as they passed a roadside sign. "Rest stop one thousand feet. Feel like a cup of coffee?"

Freeman and Cone walked from their rented sedan to Freeman's four agents, who were standing beside Taft's Crown Victoria.

"The cop's car, sir," an agent said to Freeman.

Freeman stuck a cigarette between his lips and touched it with the flame of his lighter. He more sighed than exhaled smoke. "No kidding," he said.

"We don't know what happened, sir," another agent said.

"Really?" Freeman said as he looked across the street at

another diner. "Suppose you tell me what you four did."

"Well, sir," the first agent said. "We located the car parked right where it is. Two of us went in the back, the other two in front. They weren't inside the diner. When we returned to the parking lot, our car was gone and the Crown Vic had a flat."

"You can't possibly be this stupid," Freeman said.

"I don't understand, sir," the first agent said.

"I'll explain it to you over breakfast," Freeman said and walked toward the front door of the diner.

John and Taft occupied one of two dozen picnic tables on the lawn area of the rest-stop parking lot. As John sipped coffee, he stared into the lot at eighty or so parked cars.

"I've been here before," John said. "Recently."

Sipping coffee, Taft looked at John. "How recently? You mean after the airport incident?"

"A woman . . . helped me," John said. He sipped coffee and looked at an old sedan as it pulled into a vacant spot in the rear of the lot. "Gloria. Her name was Gloria."

"Who is she?" Taft said. "Why did she help you?"

John looked at Taft. "She's a waitress back in that town. The diner where we left the Vic. I asked her for a ride to El Paso. I paid her for her time. She . . ." He set his coffee container on the table and rubbed his temples with both hands. "My head feels like it's caught in a vise," he said.

"John, just relax," Taft said. "Things will come when they come. I'm going inside and get you something from the gift shop for your headache. I'll be right back."

John nodded and looked at the old sedan. Four teenage boys exited and walked toward the rest-stop main building. He waited until they were inside, then he stood up and walked into the parking lot, randomly checking cars. He settled on a car with

Arizona plates, parked in the rear.

"You're aware that the interior of this twenty-year-old piece of crap smells like wet dog?" Taft said.

"Sick wet dog, actually," John said with a grin from behind the wheel.

"And the sedan?"

"I removed the plates and put them on the car I took the Arizona plates from, and put the Arizona plates on this hunk of rusting metal," John said.

"You did all that in the ten minutes I was gone?" Taft said. "What else you gonna do, pull a rabbit out of your hat?"

"What I'm gonna do is put some distance between us and New Mexico," John said. "We'll take turns driving until tomorrow morning and nap in the car."

"Any particular direction?"

"North."

"Any particular reason?"

"South we'll run out of room pretty damn quick."

"And my family?"

"My guess is Freeman knows we're on the road by now," John said. "He'll have to decide between us and them. If he chooses them, he'll waste valuable time looking for us with no guarantee he'll find them. When he calls . . ."

"Calls?" Taft said, jerking his head to look at John.

"With the resources he and that FBI agent have at their disposal, how much trouble do you think it will be for them to track your cell phone number?" John said.

"What do you suggest?"

"How are you at breaking balls?"

"I was a cop over thirty years, what do you think?"

"Call your son and tell him to ditch all cell phones," John said. "Tell him to buy a couple of disposable cell phones in town after dark and call you with the numbers. After Freeman calls, we'll buy a few disposables of our own."

"You're sure he'll call?" Taft said.

"I would," John said. "So will he."

The four agents stood beside the Crown Vic while Freeman spoke on his cell phone. Standing next to Freeman, Cone watched the main road and sipped coffee from a container.

Freeman looked at his four agents. "Hold on a second, Jim," he said, turned and walked to the Crown Vic. "Change the tire and follow us."

"Change the tire, sir?" an agent said.

"Man's a lifelong cop," Freeman said. "Check the trunk. You'll see he has a full tire and not a donut. It's a cop car, for Christ sake."

Freeman returned to Cone and said into the phone, "Boys, Jim. You sent me boys. How long will it take to get Taft's cell number?"

Twenty miles south of Dodge City, Kansas, Taft's cell phone rang just as he set fire to a fresh cigar. He glanced at John behind the wheel.

"I'll take pissed off government agents for two hundred dollars, Alex," John said.

"I'll see your pissed off and raise you livid," Taft said as he pulled his cell and hit talk. "Captain Howard Taft, NYPD retired, speaking," Taft said. "To whom am I conversing?"

"I think you know who this is," Freeman said.

"As I live and breathe, no thanks to you, if it isn't the man who shot me and left me for dead," Taft said.

"I won't bullshit you and tell you I can track your cell phone," Freeman said. "I'm sure right after this call you'll toss it and buy some disposables. So let me say this. You have one minute to agree to surrender yourself and John to me, or we go after your family. That's it. Simple. Clean. They won't suffer. You will."

"I don't need a minute, since my family is with me right now," Taft said. "And as for John, we parted ways soon after he borrowed your nicely equipped government sedan."

"You're bluffing," Freeman said.

"Am I now?" Taft said. "Tell me, how do you like my Crown Vic? It handles well for such a big car, doesn't it?"

"I'll give you one last opportunity to surrender," Freeman said. "If you don't, I will make it a personal quest to find you and John and execute the both of you in such a way that you'll beg for death. Am I being clear, retired police captain Taft?"

"Hold on a moment, my wife wants to tell me something," Taft said and covered the phone. "Man says surrender or he'll kill us, blah, blah, blah."

"He'll kill us no matter what," John said. "What we need is time and distance."

Taft nodded, uncovered the phone and said, "My bride of nearly forty years says for you to get fucked."

Taft could hear Freeman light a cigarette, inhale and then blow smoke before he said, "You have no idea what you're fucking with, Captain Taft, but you're going to find out and regret it."

"Well, I guess we have nothing more to discuss," Taft said.

"Give John my best, fucker," Freeman said.

Taft lowered the window and was about to toss the cell phone when John said, "Wait. Hold onto that. We might need the stored number later on down the road."

Freeman pushed the disconnect speaker button on the radio, then pocketed his cell phone. "Tough old bastard, I'll give him that," he said and blew cigarette smoke.

Behind the wheel of the sedan, Cone said, "You shot him and left him for dead. Did you really think he'd give himself up to you?"

"Of course not," Freeman said. "But I needed to know if he was alone, with John or with his family, on the road and fill in the blanks."

"And?"

"His family's stashed and he's traveling alone with John."

"To?"

"North."

"Why north?"

"It's where I would go."

"What's north?"

"Washington."

"So you think John's memory is returning?"

Freeman pulled his cell phone out and pushed the speaker button on the radio. "Let's find out," he said.

Seated at his desk, James Farris swung his chair around and looked at the base of the Washington Monument as he spoke on the speakerphone. "I'll call Doctor Monroe immediately, Ben, but he's working with some subjects to try to determine how quickly John's memory will return, so I don't know when he'll call me back."

"Send somebody over there," Freeman said. "Drag him out if you have to, but time is running short, too short to fuck around with the good doctor."

"You really think he's on his way here?" Farris said. "I mean, right now?"

"Do you want to fiddle fuck around and take that chance?"

"No," Farris said. "I don't."

"Call me back after you talk to Monroe," Freeman said. "And have a jet ready to pick us up."

"Where are you?"

"Nowhere at the moment," Freeman said. "But in about four hours, we'll be at the small jetport the FBI and marshals use outside of Dodge City."

"I'll have you picked up," Farris said. "In the meantime, I'll see about contacting Monroe."

"Tell him for me his time is just about up," Freeman said and ended the call.

Farris listened to the hum of the open line over the speaker for a moment, then slowly rotated his chair to push the off button. He looked at Monroe in a chair opposite the desk.

"Tell me now, Doctor, will John Tibbets make a full recovery?" Farris said.

"I don't know," Monroe said softly.

"Find out, or when Freeman comes to skin you alive, I'll let him."

"I don't know about you, but I need to stretch my back," Taft said.

"Dodge City exit," John said. "Let's find an out-of-the-way motel and call it a day."

"I couldn't agree more," Taft said. "I suggest a diner first, followed by a tobacco shop for some cigars and possibly a liquor store for a small nightcap."

"We'll need a new car in the morning," John said.

"I'll take care of the cigars and liquor," Taft said. "I'll leave the cars to you."

"James, with all due respect, this isn't my project," Monroe said. "It's yours."

Farris quietly stared at Monroe across his desk. He showed no outward emotion, no sign or hint of anger at Monroe's remark. Silently, he swiveled his chair to face the window and appeared to look at the Monument building.

After a soft breath, Farris said in a soft monotone, "Doctor, I expect you to do your job. If you threaten me again, you, your wife, children, and every living relative you have will disappear from the face of the Earth. Am I being clear?"

"Yes, Jim," Monroe said as he looked at the back of Farris' head. "Perfectly clear."

Farris spun back around and smiled at Monroe. "Good. So what state of mind is John in, right about now?"

John and Taft shared a window table in a small diner off the highway. The neighborhood had seen better days. Some rundown buildings and several abandoned homes occupied the same block as the diner.

"We'll need to find a mall or shopping plaza," Taft said.

"Cigars, nightcap and cell phones," John said.

"I could use a change of underwear as well," Taft said.

A waitress brought their food and drinks. As she set the plates on the table, Taft said, "Would you know of a nearby shopping center?"

"Mile up the road," the waitress said. "It's a bit seedy, like everything in this neighborhood, but it's clean and has some decent stores."

"Thank you," Taft said as he lifted his burger.

While Taft hit several stores in the strip mall, John waited in the car and smoked a cigarette. As he watched Taft exit one store and walk toward another, a noise on his right caught his attention. A man dressed in rags pushed a shopping cart through the parking lot. The cart, filled with junk, had a bad wheel and it squeaked loudly as he pushed it.

Closer to the car, John saw the man was filthy. He wore several layers of even dirtier clothes and a wool cap even though it was a warm afternoon.

The man spotted John and pushed his cart toward the car. John could see a squeegee and a water spray bottle in the cart. He took a hit on his cigarette and stared at the cart as it came closer.

He sat on a milk crate in the shadows of the Brooklyn Bridge entrance ramp. It was a warm summer night, yet he wore heavy wool clothes and a wool cap. The sweat didn't seem to bother him.

A car approached the entrance ramp. He stood up, removed a pump bottle of water and a squeegee from his shopping cart, and stood in the path of the car where the traffic light hung suspended across the street.

The light went red and the car stopped. He washed the windshield and ran the squeegee across it several times until it was dry. Behind the wheel, Captain Howard Taft handed him a dollar.

"Hey, mister, did you hear me?" the homeless man said. "I asked you for a dollar. I'm hungry."

"Sorry," John said. "It's just you remind me of somebody."

"Yeah, I'm actually Brad Pitt undercover for a movie," the man said. "Now how about that dollar?"

John dug out a five-dollar bill and passed it to him through the open window. The man took the bill, looked at it, then sneered at John. "Big fucking shot," he said and pushed his cart away.

John knew what had set the man off. He'd asked for a dollar, the mainstay of panhandling. John gave him five, a signal to the man that John was superior and looked down on him. That feeling of obsequious behavior was oddly familiar. John felt a chill run down his back.

Out of the corner of his eye, John spotted Taft walking back to the car. He held two paper bags in his arms. A spot of pain formed on John's temple and slowly spread like a crown of thorns.

Taft neared the car. John could see the smile on the old cop's lips.

Taft pulled his badge and held it up to Freeman as he walked toward the man. "This is official police business," Taft said.

Freeman pulled his silenced pistol and shot Taft once in the chest. The pistol produced little more than a cough as a large hole appeared to the left of Taft's heart.

"Not anymore," Freeman said.

John shoved open the car door and jumped out as Taft reached him. "He shot you," John said. "Freeman shot you."

"We know that, John," Taft said. "You read about it and I was there."

"No," John said. "What I mean is I remember it. Something . . . that homeless man walking through the parking lot . . . I gave him some money. He got . . ."

"John, take it easy," Taft said at the stress in John's voice.

"No, listen," John said. "I gave him a five when he asked for a dollar. He took offense and that triggered something. I washed your windshield by the Brooklyn Bridge. You gave me a dollar."

Taft stared at John. "By God, I do remember that."

John wiped beads of sweat from his brow as the headache spread and intensified.

"What is it, John?" Taft said. "What's wrong?"

"That night under the bridge," John said. "I was turning myself in. Julie was with me. She helped me. Freeman and his men showed up out of nowhere and he shot you for no reason. Or maybe he thought you knew too much. Then . . ."

John and Taft looked at each other. Sweat poured down John's face. "Are you all right?" Taft said.

"Julie," John said. "She . . . hit me with a stun gun. She wasn't helping me turn myself in. She was . . . setting me up for Freeman."

"She worked for Freeman all along," Taft said. "Right from the beginning."

John shook his head. "Not worked for, worked with. That's what she meant when she said, 'For the credit.' Catch me and she catches the attention of the boss."

"And maybe a promotion?" Taft said.

"Possibly."

"So, who's the boss?" Taft said.

"I don't know," John said. "But I've got a headache like the running of the bulls. Let's find a motel where I can lay down."

Freeman and Cone watched the private jet come in low for a landing against the backdrop of the darkening sky. Freeman lit a cigarette and punched in the numbers for Farris on his cell phone.

Farris answered on the second ring. "Are you at the airport?"

"Jet's landing now," Freeman said. "Should be in DC in three hours."

"Good, because Monroe feels that right about now his cocktail of drugs and mind-altering techniques has worn off enough for John to remember events clearly," Farris said. "Full memory or close to it will follow shortly. I'm sure you understand what that means."

"If I understand the process correctly," Freeman said. "I don't have to look for John anymore because he'll come looking for us."

"So get here as soon as you can, huh," Farris said and clicked off.

TWENTY-ONE

"*You brought this on yourself, John,*" *Farris said.* "*This is by your own doing.*"

"*Fuck you!*" *John snarled.* "*Remove the handcuffs and I'll show you something of my own doing, you fucking weasel.*"

Farris turned to Monroe. "*He's all yours, Doctor.*"

"*Are you sure, James?*" *Monroe said.*

"*This scum betrayed his country,*" *Farris said.* "*Since we can't exactly bring him before the Attorney General on charges, we might as well get some use out of him as your guinea pig for the future.*"

"*You miserable scumbag, what are you afraid of?*" *John said.*

"*I'm afraid of nothing, John,*" *Farris said.* "*Can you say the same, you traitor?*"

John stared at Farris. "*What are you talking about? Who did I betray?*"

"*Who, John?*" *Farris said.* "*More like what, and that what is your country.*" *Farris turned to Monroe.* "*I'll expect complete progress reports daily.*"

Handcuffed behind his back in a wooden chair, John rattled the cuffs and rocked the chair. "*What are you talking about?*" *he shouted.* "*I'm no traitor! What are you talking about?*"

Naked on a cold cement floor.

Obtaining information from a suspect is fairly easy if you have the skill and knowledge in torture techniques required to get results and not lies. Pain is not very effective in that a suspect will say anything to make the pain stop. Like Dustin Hoffman in the film Marathon Man. *Laurence Olivier used a dental pick to scrape at Hoffman's cavity, and Hoffman agreed to anything Olivier said. Is it safe, Olivier said, and stuck in the pick. It's safe, so safe you wouldn't believe it, Hoffman agreed, to make the pain stop. Is it safe, Olivier said, and stuck the pick in again. No, it's not safe, Hoffman said, to make the pain stop. Stay away, it's not safe.*

Fear is much more effective than pain. Find out what a man is afraid of and you own that man.

Afraid of bugs, things that crawl in the night . . . take away your clothes, lock you in a room with two scorpions, and turn the lights off. Information will flow like water over Niagara Falls.

Indoctrination is an entirely different ballgame. To indoctrinate a subject who has exceptionally strong will, that subject needs to be completely broken down until all that remains is an empty shell. Then you fill that shell with the ideology of your choice. It takes a special talent to achieve results. Hitler did it on a grand scale. Charles Manson did it on a small scale. Both men possessed the strong personality needed to bend others to their will and make them believe what they believed.

Sounds easy.

It's not.

In John's case, it proved to be nearly impossible.

Lock him in a cement room without a bed or toilet, remove all his clothing and leave the lights on twenty four hours a day. Feed him one slice of bread and one cup of water three times a day to weaken his body and dull his mind. Fatigue him to the brink with sleep deprivation by sounding a loud horn every time he nods off. Make it worse by turning off the light for ten minutes, then turning it back on along with the blaring horn.

Wear him down.

Wear him out.

Turn his brain to mush.

251

When he is so weak that the horn and light fail to keep him awake, have two men rush in and beat him awake with clubs.

The average slob walking around would last two days before cracking. A highly trained operative can last for weeks. John held out for six months, losing sixty pounds in the process.

Even then, exhausted and undernourished, he was extraordinary.

Holding a walkie-talkie in his right hand, Farris keyed it to his mouth and said, "He's had enough. Send a team in to remove him to the lab."

Farris departed, leaving the door open. A minute later, two burly men entered and looked at John.

"Poor bastard," one man said. "He looks like shit."

"Who gives a fuck what he looks like," the other man said. "Grab his legs and let's get him out of here."

One man took hold of John's legs, the other grabbed him by the arms and together they lifted. As they carried John to the open door, he suddenly came to life and twisted his body as if wringing out a towel. His legs broke free. Before the empty-handed, very surprised man could react, John delivered a ferocious kick to his groin. As the man fell holding his testicles, John broke his arms free from the second man, jumped to his feet and slammed him into the wall. Grabbing the man by the hair, John slammed his head into the concrete wall a half dozen times. The man fell to the floor a bloody mess.

John turned to the first man, who was whimpering on the floor, cradling his testicles in both hands. "Do you give a fuck now?" John said and kicked him in the side of the head.

As John stepped outside to breathe fresh air for the first time in a month, he noticed that the entire garden was protected by a twelve-foot-high, electrified barbed-wire fence. Situated on posts were surveillance cameras.

The door of the red-brick building opened, and Farris and two more men stepped outside. Farris smiled at John.

"*I underestimated you, John,*" *Farris said. "I won't do it again.*"
He turned to the two men and they approached John with stun guns
in their hands.

But every man, even a John Tibbets, has his breaking point.

One day he awoke on a table in a room painted completely white. It
was an examination table, with clean, white paper running the length
of it. A counter with instruments rested against the wall. A lone chair
adjacent to the table was the only other furnishing in the room.

He tried to move, but his arms and legs were shackled to the table.
A door behind him opened and a man walked in. He didn't recognize
the man's face, but when he spoke, he recognized his voice. It was the
voice from the speaker, the voice that had spoken to him for countless
thousands of hours.

The man spoke to him for a while in that soothing tone John was
so familiar with. After a time, the man said, "What is your name?"

"*John,*" *John said. "John Tibbets.*"

"*And who are you, John?*" *the man said.*

"*I . . . I don't know,*" *John said, his mind a complete blank.*

Farris entered the room and stood next to the man. The man
looked at Farris. "He's ready," the man said. "Do you want him
back?"

"*Are you sure he's ready?*" *Farris said.*

"*For what you want, completely,*" *the man said.*

"*I would never have thought it would take a year,*" *Farris said.*

"*Yes,*" *the man said. "He was quite the subject.*"

"*Amazing,*" *Farris replied.*

John opened his eyes and looked across the motel room to where
Taft was drinking coffee at a small table by the window. The
curtains were drawn, but enough light filtered through to illuminate the room above shadows.

Taft turned his head to look at John. "It's morning," he said. "Noon, actually. Want some coffee? They supply a pot and coffee, but the cream is powdered."

John tossed the covers off and stood up wearing shorts and a T-shirt. He walked to the small table, poured coffee into a cup and sat. His cigarettes were on the table and he lit one with a match. "How long did I sleep?"

"Eleven hours," Taft said. "And you're a better conversationalist asleep than awake."

"I had dreams," John said.

"I gathered."

"No, not dreams." John sipped coffee and thought a moment. "Memories. A lot of memories."

"Tell me."

"Over some lunch," John said. "I'm starving."

Monroe, Freeman and Cone met Farris for breakfast in his office. They ate at the round conference table centered in the room. The somber atmosphere kept the focus on business.

"Ben, Doctor Monroe has concluded through his study of other subjects that by today, possibly tomorrow, John will regain a great deal or most of his memory," Farris said.

"Most?" Freeman said.

"Some things people forget naturally and some things people choose not to remember," Monroe said.

"If I want a fortune cookie, I'll send out for Chinese," Freeman said. "Quit the philosophy bullshit and spell it out plain."

Monroe dabbed his lips with a napkin and looked at Freeman. "John might regain his entire memory, including his capture and treatment," he said, and set the napkin aside. "He might regain as little as fifty percent and it might be fractured."

"Fractured?" Cone said.

"Pieces of a memory missing or out of sequence," Monroe

said. "In that case, John will be more confused than ever."

"And that much more dangerous," Freeman said. "Because he'll be scared."

"Recommendations, Doctor?" Farris said.

"Find him in the next twenty-four hours," Monroe said.

"Or?" Cone said.

Freeman sighed and pulled out his cigarettes. He lit one, blew smoke and said, "He'll find us. Isn't that right, Doctor?"

"Yes," Monroe said.

At a table in the same diner they'd visited the night before, John and Taft ate lunch while John did his best to explain his dreams. "I'm not sure of the sequence of events—the when, the where—but I'm sure of one thing. Freeman and the man he answers to are behind my amnesia."

"From what little I learned from the doctors a year ago, amnesia can be caused by blunt force trauma," Taft said. "A hit on the head."

"No, this was different," John said. "This was . . . more like torture."

"Torture?" Taft said. "To what end?"

"Brainwashing," John said as he sipped coffee.

Taft stared at John.

"To turn me into a homeless amnesia victim," John said.

"Why?"

"Here's where things get a little fuzzy," John said. "Jim said I . . ."

"Who?"

"James Farris, my boss," John said. "He . . ." John paused to stare at Taft. "Farris. I remember James Farris. He's the man in my dreams. He orchestrated my . . . the brainwashing and treatments under the care of . . . Monroe."

"Why, John?" Taft said.

"Cone, he said I was a top-level assassin for Farris," John said. "He said . . . I went rogue."

"Rogue?"

"Off on my own."

"Why?"

John shook his head. "I was . . . salvaged."

"And they took your memory?" Taft said.

"Yes."

"But they kept you alive," Taft said. "Why?"

John rubbed his chin as he thought back upon his conversation with Cone. "Reactivation," he finally said.

"The desert in New Mexico," Taft said. "You were reactivated for an assignment."

"And programmed to forget," John said. "Because . . ."

"It's easier to control a mindless zombie," Taft said.

"Apparently," John said as he sipped more coffee. "But why control me at all?"

Taft sipped coffee as he thought for a moment. "Know what a packrat is?"

"Someone who never throws something away."

"Because they might one day find a use for it," Taft said. "All your skills, all your training, properly controlled, can be very useful, especially to men like Farris and Freeman."

John nodded. "I think I need to hit the road."

"Can we order some dessert first?" Taft said. "I saw a lovely apple pie in the counter on the way in."

A peaceful village nestled in the mountains of Japan. From his vantage point high in the hills, he could see all roads leading into and out of the village, even without binoculars. With his battery-powered, twelve-by-fifty binoculars, he could read the lips of people sipping coffee on the front porch of the only hotel in the village.

Teams of international security men were posted at various spots around the tree-lined hotel grounds as they waited for the dignitaries to appear from their summit. A three-day affair held in the hotel's conference room, the meeting focused on the international monetary trading between European countries. For two days, John had tracked their movements from the hills. His escape route by motorcycle to a car hidden at the base of the hills guaranteed his safety upon completion of the task. His objective was the assassination of the Israeli foreign affairs minister, which guaranteed the start of an all-out war between Israel and the Palestinians. That would neutralize the European currency, threaten stability in the region and allow his employer to profit from the sale of arms to countries forced to take sides.

He knew nothing would happen during the day, so he settled in for an afternoon nap in the shade, setting his watch alarm for four that afternoon. He awoke when Freeman and five of his men surrounded him and removed his weapons.

"You've been decommissioned, John," Freeman said.

"Why? This is a sanctioned mission."

Freeman was dressed in full field gear, as were his men. "We're taking over, John. You're going back to the States."

"Why?"

"The boss wants to see you."

"Farris?"

"Yeah."

John stared at Freeman, trying to read the man. They had worked together off and on for fifteen years, and Freeman was every bit as good as he was. But something wasn't right. Farris would never send in replacements during a mission unless the primary was taken out or the mission went bad. In this case, it was neither.

"Why?" John said.

"I don't ask why, John," Freeman said. "And neither do you. We just follow orders."

"Yeah, what's the digits?" John said. Farris never issued a field

order without a coded series of numbers to prove the order came from him.

Freeman hesitated. At that moment, John knew Freeman had been bought off by a third party. They made eye contact, and John could see movement behind him, but before he could react, one of Freeman's men hit him in the back with a stun gun.

Taft walked out of the motel-room bathroom to find John seated in the wooden chair at the desk, staring into space with a lit cigarette burning between his fingers. "John?" Taft said.

John didn't bat an eye or move a muscle.

Taft gently placed a hand on his shoulder. "John?"

John blinked and looked at Taft. "We need to talk."

"The long or the short of it?"

"Long."

Taft turned and looked at the coffeemaker on the counter outside the bathroom. "Then I'll make us some coffee."

Seated on the bench outside their motel room, John and Taft sipped coffee as they lit cigarette and cigar.

"So," Taft said as he puffed on his cigar. "I gather you've remembered more of your past."

"Remember that movie where the Marine colonel says, 'You want me on that wall. You need me on that wall'?" John said.

"I gather you're not talking about Humpty Dumpty and there are no eggs involved?" Taft said as he blew a thick ring of cigar smoke.

"No, no eggs," John said with a slight grin. He paused to sip coffee and hit on the cigarette. "The agency . . . what I do for them is kill. Threats to our country are dealt with using extreme prejudice if no other solution is at hand. I'm what they call an operative, a ghost inside an agency that doesn't exist. Since I have no official employer, supplementing my income by selling my services is overlooked provided it's discreet and doesn't involve or compromise American interests."

"Overlooked how?"

"Nobody cares if a drug lord is killed by another drug lord or organized crime starts to wipe itself out with a little help," John said. "But that blind eye does a one-eighty when American interests are at stake."

Taft took a small sip of coffee, puffed up great hazy clouds of cigar smoke and looked at John. "You've remembered something important. What is it?"

"Listen to me very carefully now," John said. "There isn't a lot of time. I want you to take the car, pick up your family, and go somewhere safe for a while. I can give you a bit more than three thousand dollars to go with what you already have. It's best to . . ."

"What are you talking about?" Taft said.

"Stay on the move," John said. "No more than overnight at any one place. If . . ."

"I'm not going anywhere unless you give me one hell of a good reason," Taft said. "You owe me at least that much."

John took a final hit off his cigarette and tossed it underfoot. "Okay," he said and sipped coffee. "I guess I owe you a lot more than that. In Japan . . . and I don't know when. There was an international conference of dignitaries. I hired out to kill the Israeli foreign minister and blame the Palestinians in order to start an all-out war in the Middle East. You see . . . the company that hired me stood to make billions in weapons sales."

Taft stared at John for so long an inch of ash fell from his cigar and landed in his coffee mug. "What are you saying, John?" he said as he tossed the remains of his coffee.

"That night a year ago," John said. "I remember saying to Freeman right before Julie Warner tazed me . . . I said, I'm the bad guy. I said it as a question because I remembered the incident in Japan, and I couldn't believe I could betray my country."

"Don't believe it, then," Taft said.

"I wish it was that simple."

"You know, one thing I've learned during three decades of police work is character," Taft said. "And it strikes me you're a man of strong character and principles. Now, I don't know what this is all about, I won't pretend that I do, but one thing I am sure of is you're no more a traitor than I am."

John looked at Taft.

"They may have stolen your memory, but they can't steal your basic character," Taft said. "Like a subject under hypnosis, they won't do what goes against their character no matter what the command."

John lit a fresh cigarette and thought for a moment. "I'm going to Washington."

"I know."

"I have to know the truth, no matter what that is."

"I know."

"I might need some help."

Taft blew a cloud of cigar smoke, then stood up. "I thought you'd never ask."

Twenty-Two

From behind the wheel of a fifteen-year-old Honda that may or may not have been safe to drive, Taft cocked an eye at John. "I do miss that government car," he said.

"If you're wondering, this car is safe," John said. "It will get us where we're going."

"DC is fourteen hundred miles, John," Taft said.

"The kid I traded the sedan for took good care of this piece of junk," John said. "And if they have a Lo-Jack system, by the time they locate him, Freeman's car will look pretty much like this one."

Taft grinned as he lit a cigar. "At least they haven't stolen your sense of humor," he said, puffing clouds of smoke.

"That's about the only thing they haven't stolen," John said. He lit a cigarette and thought for a moment. "If we take turns driving all night, we can reach Little Rock by ten tomorrow morning."

"And then?"

"We'll sleep," John said. "Who knows, I might remember something useful in my sleep."

Freeman stared out the window of Farris' office and appeared not to move for a minute or longer. At his desk, Farris glanced at Monroe, and the doctor gave Farris a tiny shoulder shrug.

"Ben?" Farris finally said softly.

"It's getting dark," Freeman said. "I always liked the Mall at night, especially this time of year."

"I hate to rush things, Ben, but time seems to be running short," Farris said.

Freeman turned away from the window and took the empty chair beside Monroe. "Just the opposite, Jim," he said. "Time is on our side."

"I hate to disagree with you, Ben, but John is regaining more of his memory with each passing hour," Monroe said.

"I know that," Freeman said. "But even if he recalls everything, there's still a good forty-eight hours, maybe more, before he reaches Washington."

"How are you so sure this is where he'll come?" Monroe said.

"It's what I would do," Freeman said.

"I agree," Farris said. "But how does that put time on our side?"

"We have forty-eight hours to plan for John's surprise attack," Freeman said.

As John sliced into a mound of pancakes, Taft stretched his back and stifled a yawn. Outside the diner window, morning sun shone brightly across the cars and trucks in the parking lot.

"Where are we?" Taft said as he dug into his scrambled eggs.

"Benton, off Interstate thirty," John said. "Maybe forty-five minutes south of Little Rock."

"Last thing I remember before you woke me is I turned over the wheel to you around midnight," Taft said. "And I feel like I could go another eight."

"We'll find a motel to hole up in and grab some rest," John said. "It's probably safer to travel at night from here out anyway."

"You think Freeman is expecting you?" Taft said.

"I would be in his place," John said. "But it's the only way to get to the truth."

"So he or they or whomever will probably be prepared for us . . . you . . . and that seems to me to be one hell of a stumbling block," Taft said.

"Or a way in," John said.

Taft picked at his eggs. "How?"

"Let's find a motel and grab some sleep," John said. "I think better at night."

While James Farris napped on the sofa in his office, Freeman sat behind the desk and worked the phones. "I want a four-man crew . . . no, make it a six-man crew in my office for a briefing at noon today. I want ten-year veterans and people I've worked with before. No rookies and no one who will question orders. That's all."

Freeman set the phone down and reached for his package of cigarettes on the desk. He lit one, thought for a moment and picked the phone up again. He punched in one number, waited and said, "What's the most discreet, yet most armored vehicle you have?"

Freeman paused, listened, blew a smoke ring and said, "Have it ready and parked in my parking spot in the garage. No, no driver. Just the keys."

He hung up the phone again, sat and smoked in silence for a moment until he heard Farris roll over and sit up. "You awake, Jim?"

Farris stretched his back. "I am now. Any coffee?"

Freeman stood up from behind the desk and turned toward the counter to his left, where a fresh pot rested in a coffee-maker. He filled two mugs and carried them to Farris.

"Jim, what's your most secret, most secure location?" he said as he handed Farris a mug.

"I assume you mean one that John isn't aware of?" Farris said.

"Or me."

"You, Ben?"

"I've assembled a team to take you into hiding," Freeman said. "I'd rather not know the location."

"You seriously believe John can penetrate our resources all by himself?" Farris said. "With resources of his own?"

"Have you ever been in the field with John?" Freeman said.

"I haven't had that privilege."

"John is his own resource," Freeman said. "He is all that he needs."

"Circle the block one more time," John said.

Taft made a left turn at the intersection and circled the block. The Little Rock neighborhood was drab, lined with discount stores, liquor outlets and rundown hotels. Wedged between two hotels, a mission advertised hot meals with prayer services for all. It reminded Taft of Manhattan's Bowery, especially after dark.

"Not many about," Taft said.

"At one in the morning even the drunks are sleeping it off," John said. "Okay, slow down behind the clinic."

Taft slowed the car to a stop behind the Public Health Free Clinic. An eight-foot-high chain-link fence protected a forty-foot-square backyard. What lawn there was appeared brown and dry, even at night.

"Are you sure about this, John?" Taft said.

"Remember where the Denny's is we checked out?"

"Ten blocks from here, yes."

"I'll meet you there in thirty minutes," John said. "Leave the trunk cracked."

"If you . . ."

"I'm in the mood for a burger," John said as he reached for

the black backpack on the rear seat. "But don't order without me."

John exited the car and stood in the shadows of a squat building until Taft turned the corner. Then he crossed the street and stood in front of the chain-link fence. He scanned the block as he slipped the backpack over his shoulders.

Confident he was alone on the block, John scaled the eight-foot-high fence in one quick motion and landed silently on the dry grass in darkness. Walking at a normal pace, he went to the rear of the clinic where the only door was located. It was heavy steel and alarmed. Earlier, in daylight and from the car, he'd inspected the exterior walls with binoculars for motion detectors. There weren't any.

He removed the backpack and set it on the ground. He unzipped the pouch and dug out the twenty-foot-long rope he'd purchased at a local hardware store. At a rock-climbing store, he'd purchased a grappling hook, the kind used for scaling cliffs. He secured it to one end of the rope.

The building was fifteen feet high with a walled, flat roof. John tossed the hook up and over the roof and yanked on the rope to secure it in place. He replaced the backpack over his shoulders, grabbed the rope and scaled the building in less than thirty seconds.

Over the wall, he stood motionless for a few seconds to get his bearings. A glass dome sat centered on top to allow access from inside the building. He pulled up the rope and carried it to the dome. He slung off the backpack, removed a flashlight from inside and inspected the square dome. It was held in place by its own weight. As best he could see, there were no magnetic alarm contacts.

He slowly lifted the eighty-pound dome from its grooves and set it aside. He set the grappling hook in place and lowered the rope, then glanced at his watch. At best, he would have three minutes to get in and out and another minute to get off the roof before a police cruiser or private security car arrived.

He took a deep breath, took hold of the rope and lowered himself over the side.

Taft took a sip from his third cup of coffee in twenty-seven minutes. He resisted the urge to call Joan, knowing that would only serve to expose her and their sons to even greater danger.

The only play was to see this through to the end. He knew this to be true, yet he felt a twinge of guilt at feeling alive and useful after a year of mowing the lawn and eating lunches in the backyard with Joan.

Meals.

That's what retirement amounted to, in his opinion.

What to have for breakfast, a thirty-minute conversation to decide upon lunch, a decision to eat in or go out for dinner.

In between, not much else.

When this was over . . . if this was over, he would return to work. Not on the job, of course. He had no illusions he could return to full-time police work, but something where he felt useful, where it mattered if he showed or not.

His mind was wandering as a defense mechanism against worry. He realized the worry was not for himself, but for John. He checked his watch. Thirty-one minutes since he'd left John at the clinic.

He shouldn't have left him. He should have stayed with . . .

The front door of the Denny's opened and John strolled in minus the backpack. He spotted Taft, walked to the booth and sat opposite him. "How are the burgers in this place?" John said.

Freeman closed his eyes for a moment on the sofa in Farris' office shortly after his boss was escorted out surrounded by six top agents. They were tested men, veterans in the field. They wouldn't be rattled if the need to draw their weapons arose.

He hoped it wouldn't come to that.

John was on his way, of that he was sure. What condition he would be in was anybody's guess. If Monroe was right, and Freeman had no reason to doubt him, John should have enough of his memory intact to want answers.

Answers Freeman couldn't provide. The agency didn't exist. Funding was funneled through routed budgets from Congress. It had worked that way for six decades. Pensions were siphoned through the FBI, CIA and Justice Department. Farris had the President's ear, but they never met in the Oval Office. If something went wrong, the President, Congress and everybody else in government never heard of James Farris and his department. The cardinal rule, the unbreakable and unspoken law of the agency, was no publicity at all costs.

Freeman opened his eyes and sat up. He stood, went to the coffee pot and filled a mug, then sat behind the desk. He lit a cigarette and smoked in silence. He'd never questioned what he did for a living. He loved his country and had sworn an oath to protect and serve it to the best of his ability. If need be, he would give his life for it.

If need be, he would break every law on the books to protect it. He would lie, cheat and kill in cold blood to stop its enemies cold. What he would not do was betray it.

So why did John?

They came in together as young men after tours of military service, each with a set of values and ideals suited to the department. They trained together, at times lived together, served on missions together and sometimes killed together. John could have had the number-two position behind Farris years ago, except that he enjoyed fieldwork too much to sit behind a desk.

So what turned him?

After 9/11, John was ready to take on the world by himself. He dug in and fought trench warfare for years in the mountains and caves of the Middle East, killing bad guys by the score and relinquishing credit to the military or CIA. When things calmed down, he globetrotted at Farris' request, cherry-picking and whittling down the enemies list.

In between assignments, John spent time at his modest home in Maryland where he trained around the clock. His fitness and ability were unparalleled and matched only by his dedication.

So what turned him?

Money?

Not hardly. After twenty years of fieldwork, John had bank accounts around the world and could easily have afforded to retire and live in luxury. Instead, he chose to live in a modest, two-bedroom home in a middle-class suburb. He drove a nine-year-old car and didn't own a suit or a pair of dress shoes.

Politics?

Freeman wasn't sure if John even knew who occupied the White House during the decades they worked together, that's how much politics interested him. If John belonged to a party or even voted, he kept things tightly to himself.

Of the big three game changers, that left religion. John was a Christian, but that was as far as Freeman knew. He never spoke of faith or God and kept his beliefs close to the vest, if he even had any. Would he suddenly take up some religious cause that would turn him against his country?

Not likely.

It occurred to Freeman there was a fourth reason a man would compromise his principles. A woman. Freeman didn't know if John had a regular girlfriend or not. Their lifestyle was unfit for marriage and family, but most agents found the time to keep steady women in their lives, if only for short bursts. Could John have found a woman he loved so deeply that she'd turned him against his country? Freeman saw that as about the same odds as winning Power Ball.

He sipped coffee and lit a fresh cigarette off the spent one. He couldn't think of one thing that would turn him, so for John to turn must be for reasons foreign to him.

No matter. John was coming. When he arrived, Freeman would ask him face to face and hoped he lived long enough to receive an answer.

At a picnic table at a rest stop on I-95 North, John sipped coffee and lit a cigarette. Opposite him, Taft also sipped coffee and held an unlit cigar in his left hand.

John glanced at his watch. "Now," he said.

"It's one in the morning," Taft said.

"Means nothing to him," John said. "They'll be on lockdown and alert."

Taft nodded, picked up his cell phone and dialed in the call-back number for Ben Freeman's cell phone.

It rang twice.

Freeman said, "Captain Taft or John Tibbets?"

"In a sense, both," Taft said. "This is Captain Taft, NYPD retired, speaking. Am I addressing the man who shot me and left me for dead?"

"That couldn't be helped," Freeman said. "You posed a threat to national security."

"What about now?" Taft said. "Am I still a threat?"

"Yes."

"Would you kill me?"

"Yes."

"My family?"

"No."

"You're an honest man, I'll give you that much."

"I have no reason to lie," Freeman said. "Now, you sound

like a man with something on his mind."

"I'm bringing in John," Taft said. "In exchange for him, I want my life and my family spared. That's it, that's my deal."

"Captain Taft, it isn't that simple."

"Yeah, it is," Taft said. "John has had a complete meltdown. Agree to my deal or I turn him loose to wander the country as just another homeless bum and good luck finding him."

"What do you mean, meltdown?"

"He started to get his memory back," Taft said. "We talked about a great many things. The more he remembered, the more painful it became. Finally, he just sort of shut down."

"Shut down?"

"I'm no doctor, but it appears to me like some kind of mental breakdown," Taft said. "In and out, a lot of babbling, long periods of coma-like sleep."

"Bring him in," Freeman said. "I'll guarantee your deal."

"One other thing," Taft said. "We . . . that is, John and I spoke about a man named Monroe. I would very much like to meet this man."

"Why?"

"To be honest, before John lost it completely, he felt Monroe was the only man who could save him," Taft said. "He was going to bring himself in, but only to Monroe. When John started losing it, he asked me to do it for him. I gave John my word."

"I'll agree to that," Freeman said. "Where do you want to meet?"

"The Mall at noon," Taft said. "When I see you and Monroe sitting on a bench, I'll approach. John will be stashed in a car nearby, but you won't find him if you pull any stunts."

"I gave you my word," Freeman said.

"Then I'll see you tomorrow at noon," Taft said and hung up.

"He give his word?" John said.

"Indeed."

"Then he'll keep it."

Freeman sipped coffee from a deli container and smoked a cigarette as he sat on a bench in the Mall. To his left, the White House glowed brightly in the distance. On his right, the Monument stood tall and illuminated. From the Capitol steps to the Lincoln Memorial was about two miles. Come morning, a hundred thousand or more tourists would fill the Mall and act as the perfect cover for Taft to wiggle in and out unseen until he wanted to be seen. In his situation, Freeman would do the same.

To try to pinpoint where Taft would park his car prior to their meeting would take a month of surveillance and planning and a thousand agents working around the clock. Even then it would require a great deal of luck.

Not that it mattered much. He gave his word and he would keep it. He pulled his cell phone and dialed the number for Monroe.

"We'll hit DC by four and grab a quick six hours' sleep," John said from behind the wheel.

"How exactly is this going to work?" Taft said.

"I'll explain it in the morning," John said.

"One question," Taft said. "How much do you remember? Exactly?"

"Enough to know I have no answers," John said.

"That is of little comfort," Taft said, and lit a fresh cigar.

Twenty-Three

John closed the trunk of the car and looked at Taft. "The GPS is inside the spare tire and activated," he said. "You can monitor it with the cell phone I picked up yesterday at that electronics store. Set it to GPS function and follow it in the rental car."

"What rental car?" Taft said.

"The one you're going to rent as soon as we have breakfast."

"What if they search the car and me?"

"They'll give the car a quick once-over," John said. "They won't pat you down and we'll leave the cell phone in the rental. We'll park it right up the street where you'll have quick access to it. Let's get some breakfast. I need a full stomach."

"This is madness," Monroe said as he looked around at the growing number of tourists inside the Mall.

"Doctor, sit down and shut up," Freeman said, and took a seat on a vacant bench.

Monroe sat beside him. "This could be a trap, you know. John is highly intelligent, even in his present state of mind."

Freeman held a paper bag with two coffee containers in it. He removed both containers and gave one to Monroe. "Well, if this is a trap, then John has to spring it in front of sixty or seventy thousand witnesses and a few dozen metro police," he said. "That's why he picked this place to meet. Both of us would have witnesses if we pulled a double cross."

"I still don't like it," Monroe said. "John is . . ."

"I know what John is, Doctor," Freeman said. "What I don't know is what he isn't, and that's where you come in."

"I still think Jim needs to be . . ."

"Jim is in protective isolation," Freeman said. "I have no idea where he is. He will call me in seven days for an update. If I'm still alive."

"Don't even joke," Monroe said.

Freeman sipped from his container, lit a cigarette and looked at Monroe. "Drink your coffee, Doctor."

In the passenger seat of the car, John finished the last bit of coffee in his takeout container as he smoked a cigarette. Behind the wheel, Taft puffed on a cigar.

John glanced at his watch. "It's time." From his pocket, he removed a one-inch long penknife and slid it between the cigarettes in his half-full pack. He tucked the pack in his shirt pocket.

"Are you sure you wouldn't like something a bit heavier, like my three-fifty-seven Magnum?" Taft said.

"You hold onto that," John said as he removed the bottle of sodium thiopental and syringe from the glove compartment. He removed the wrapper from the syringe, stuck the needle into the sealed top and filled it with six milligrams. "In about thirty seconds or so, I'll be sound asleep. I'll sleep for about ten minutes and when I wake up, I will appear disoriented and feeling no pain, but to Monroe I'll seem to be in the midst of a breakdown."

"Are you sure you know what you're doing?" Taft said.

"A larger dose and I'll go comatose," John said. "An even larger dose mixed with muscle relaxants results in euthanasia."

"Euthanasia? What the hell is this stuff used for?" Taft said.

John rolled up his left shirtsleeve. "Truth serum."

"And they use this at that clinic for what?"

"Painkiller and to treat certain psychiatric disorders."

"And you know all this how?" Taft said. "Wait, I don't want to know."

John selected a spot high on his left forearm. "Captain Taft, it's been a pleasure knowing you," he said, and gave himself the shot.

Monroe reached to his right and tossed his empty coffee container into a wastebasket. "It's seven past twelve," he said. "Your man is late."

"He's not late," Freeman said as he lit a fresh cigarette. "He's been standing right over there for the past ten minutes."

"What?" Monroe said. "Where?"

"Look to my left about ten benches down," Freeman said. "That man of about sixty smoking a cigar, that's Taft."

"What the hell . . . well, why is he standing there?" Monroe said. "And why are we sitting here?"

"The man's a forty-year cop," Freeman said. "Homicide, special crimes, a captain and in New York City, no less. He's checking to make sure we haven't planted backup."

"By standing there?"

"Doctor, I don't have time to explain it to you," Freeman said. He looked at Taft and gave him a tiny nod.

Puffing on his cigar, Taft walked toward Freeman and Monroe. "I know you, and you must be Doctor Monroe," Taft said when he arrived at the bench.

"John has spoken of me?" Monroe said.

"Let's just say he remembers you with fondness," Taft said.

Freeman stood up from the bench. "I assume John is nearby," he said. "Shall we go?"

Monroe stood up and looked at Freeman. "He could be armed. Aren't you going to check him for weapons?"

"Doctor, if there is one thing I'm sure of, it's that he's

armed," Freeman said. He looked at Taft. "Ready?"

Monroe looked at John through the window of the passenger door of the old car. "Is it locked?" Monroe said.

Taft removed the key from his pocket and opened the door to allow Monroe access. "Careful he doesn't fall out," Taft said.

Freeman stood behind Taft as Monroe gently lifted John's head and opened his eyes. "Glazed over," Monroe said. He turned and looked at Taft. "How long has he been like this?"

"Off and on for several days," Taft said. "There have been some times when he's clear as a bell, then he goes into this. I figured there's nothing more I can do for him, but you can."

Monroe gently lowered John's head back to the headrest. "John, can you hear me?" he said. "It's Doctor Monroe."

John's eyes opened for a moment. He looked at Monroe, then slowly closed them.

"We need to get him to my compound immediately," Monroe said.

Freeman turned to Taft. "This piece of crap run?"

"It got us fourteen hundred miles without so much as a blip," Taft said.

"Then it's good-bye, Captain, and may we never see each other again," Freeman said.

Taft nodded, turned, paused and said, "I'll hold you to your word, Mr. Freeman. You shot me once. I'll not have you doing it again."

"Go," Freeman said.

"For Christ's sake, Doctor," Freeman said as he drove the old car. "How much longer?"

From the backseat where Monroe kept an eye on John, he glanced out the window. "A few blocks up, turn left onto Stalwart and go about three miles into Maryland. My complex isn't far from there."

Freeman lit a cigarette and glanced in the rearview mirror. "How is he?"

"Can't really tell from the backseat of this shitbox," Monroe said. "He'll need a complete physical and psychiatric evaluation before I do anything else."

"Is he awake at least?"

"John, can you hear me?" Monroe said.

John shifted his weight and slowly opened his eyes. "I hear you," he said in a whisper.

"Do you know who I am?" Monroe said.

John cocked his head a bit to look at Monroe. "No."

"Do you know who you are, John?" Monroe said.

"I have a headache," John said.

"Not to worry, John," Monroe said. "We'll be at my clinic in a few minutes. I'll give you something for the pain."

"Okay," John said and closed his eyes.

Taft puffed on a fresh cigar as he followed Freeman using the GPS unit he'd placed on the dashboard of the rental sedan. He shadowed the car from a distance of a half mile, secure Freeman hadn't suspected the tail.

Several miles across the border into Maryland, Freeman made a sudden sharp turn and stopped. Taft slowed the rental, watching the GPS. Freeman didn't move again. They'd arrived and parked. Taft feathered the gas to speed up a bit and then followed the GPS to a small home at the end of a long private road. Surrounded by woods, the home sat isolated on all sides.

Taft backed up to the midpoint of the road, turned off the engine and lit a fresh cigar to kill some time.

Monroe's home was small, maybe twelve hundred square feet total, Freeman observed. While furnishings were sparse, they were comfortable enough. "As you may have guessed," Monroe said when he saw Freeman looking around, "this is not my primary residence."

Freeman placed John on the sofa in the living room, turned and looked at Monroe. "I don't really care where you live, Doctor, but you said we were going to your complex."

"And we have," Monroe said. "John, can you stand and walk on your own?"

"Yes," John said and stood up.

"Then follow me," Monroe said.

John and Freeman walked behind Monroe to the small kitchen where Monroe opened a pantry door and clicked on a light. Canned goods lined several shelves. From his pocket, Monroe removed a small remote and pressed a button. A moment later, the back wall of the pantry slowly swung open to reveal a hidden doorway.

"Hold on a moment while I turn on the lights," Monroe said. He reached in and flicked a switch on the wall. "Go on, John," he said. "We'll follow you."

John looked into the doorway. A long flight of stairs led down to the basement.

"It's okay," Monroe said. "Everything we'll be fine once we go down to my lab."

John took the first step. By the third step, Freeman was behind him, followed by Monroe. As John's left foot touched the fifth step, he pivoted his upper body sharply to the right and jammed Freeman in the stomach with his right elbow. As Freeman doubled over, John took Freeman's left arm and flung him over his shoulder. Freeman tumbled the remaining fifteen steps to the basement floor.

Stunned, Monroe didn't move a muscle as John turned, took three steps in one bound, slashed out with his right hand and chopped Monroe across the left side of his neck.

"Your turn to sleep," John said as he caught Monroe's limp body.

A man smokes enough cigars, he gets so he can use them like a clock. For instance, the seven and a half-inch long Macanudo burned for a good hour. Taft smoked it to the midpoint before looking at his watch. Thirty-one minutes had passed since John entered the house.

A lot can happen in thirty-one minutes.

When Freeman opened his eyes, he was tied with rope to a hardback wooden chair. It took a moment for him to realize he was inside an examination room of some kind. To his left, Monroe was also in a chair, but his hands and feet were free. He was awake, but for some reason didn't move.

That reason was John.

From the chair he sat in, John sipped coffee from a mug, then lit a cigarette and looked at Freeman. "No hard feelings, Ben," he said. "I could have killed you if I wanted, but that's not what I want."

"Thiopental?" Freeman said.

John nodded as he took a hit on his cigarette.

"I figured," Freeman said.

"You knew or suspected?"

"Suspected."

"Why didn't you try to stop me?"

"Curiosity mixed with professional courtesy."

"Do you really think you're going to get away with this?" Monroe said.

"Who's going to stop me?" John said. "You?"

"Doctor, I'd be quiet for the time being," Freeman said.

"We were friends?" John said to Freeman.

"And partners," Freeman said. "For a lot of years."

John sipped coffee, took a puff on the cigarette and said, "Funny thing. I have this memory, well, sort of a memory. I'm in Japan, about to kill some minister and start a war. That's where you picked me up, isn't it?"

"Yes," Freeman said.

"I hired out?"

"That's the intel."

"Who hired me?"

Freeman didn't answer.

"Come on, Ben," John said. "You, the boss, you found out what I did, you must have investigated it before you acted. Who hired me?"

"I don't know."

"How much did I get paid?"

"I don't know."

"How did you get wind of my activity?"

"I don't know," Freeman said. "Farris did. I acted on his orders."

"His orders," John said. "Because, you know, it's a very funny thing. The more I remember, the more things don't make sense to me."

"It's because you're . . . ," Monroe said.

"I didn't ask you a goddamn thing," John snapped.

"John, what doesn't make sense to you?" Freeman said.

"How after a lifetime of service to my country I would sell it out for a quick payday just like that," John said.

"I don't know," Freeman said.

John looked at Monroe. "But he does, don't you, Doctor?"

"I follow orders," Monroe said. "Just like everybody else."

John stood up, set the coffee mug on a nearby examination table, dropped the cigarette into the coffee and walked toward Monroe. "Let's talk about those orders," he said.

"I'm not allowed to . . . ," Monroe said.

John grabbed Monroe by the shirt and yanked him to his feet. "New chain of command," he said. "It starts and ends with me. I want to know why and how I sold out my country."

"I don't know that," Monroe said.

John removed his pack of cigarettes from a pocket, withdrew the one-inch long knife, and held it loosely by his side in his right hand.

Monroe looked at the tiny knife. "What are you going to do with that?"

With lightning fast reflexes, John jutted his right hand up and out and drove the one-inch blade into the left side of Monroe's chest, then withdrew it immediately.

A red stain appeared on Monroe's white shirt. It took a few seconds for him to realize he'd been stabbed. Then he staggered backward and would have fallen into the chair, except that John yanked him back up by the shirt.

"What were your orders?" John said.

"You . . . stabbed me," Monroe said as the blood dripped down his shirt to the floor.

"I would tell him what he wants to know," Freeman said.

"Help me, Agent Freeman," Monroe said.

"My hands are tied, Doctor," Freeman said. "Literally."

"What were your orders?" John said.

"You're crazy," Monroe said.

John shoved the tiny knife into the right side of Monroe's chest. A second stain immediately appeared.

"Your orders?" John said.

"I just run the clinic," Monroe stammered as he fought to stay on his feet.

John stabbed him a third time between the second and third rib. "You do a hell of a lot more than that, Doctor. You brainwashed me, stole my memory. Why?"

Monroe fell to his knees as three wounds dripped blood.

Nearly unconscious from the pain of the third wound, he appeared ready to fall over when John grabbed him by the hair and yanked hard.

"Right now they're three painful holes without much damage," John said. "But I'm going to keep stabbing you," he said, and jammed the knife into Monroe's stomach several times. "And stabbing you until the blood loss drops your blood pressure to the point your heart stops. I figure another dozen holes and you should start to feel light-headed. A few more after that and . . ."

"Stop . . . stop!" Monroe yelled. "For God's sake stop!"

"What do you know?" John said.

"Help me," Monroe sobbed.

John lifted Monroe and placed him in his chair.

"John, listen to me," Freeman said. "As much as I dislike this nitwit, he is vital to our national security."

"Your national security, Ben, not mine," John said. "I'm a traitor, remember?"

"Please," Monroe begged. His white shirt was deep red and blood ran down his pants to the floor.

"Please, what?" John said and jammed the knife into Monroe's stomach one more time.

Freeman tugged at the ropes around his wrists and rocked his chair. "If you kill him, you'll be hunted like a fucking rabid dog for the rest of your life."

"Unlike now?" John said.

Blood pouring down his shirt, Monroe started to sob openly. "Please don't do this," he said.

"I'm not doing this, you are," John said. "You want it to stop, tell me what I want to know."

"Live to fight another day, Doctor," Freeman said.

Monroe nodded. "What do you want to know?"

"Everything." John pulled up his chair, sat and lit a cigarette.

"About ten years ago . . ."

"The short version," John said. "Unless you want to bleed out before you get to the point."

"After nine-eleven, I experimented with certain mind-altering techniques for the military," Monroe said. "The agency became interested after I achieved results with some low-life terrorists captured on the battlefield."

"Results?"

"Brainwashing them into talking rather than using conventional techniques," Monroe said. "A full-scale project was called for and funded by secret budgets. The goal was to turn a dedicated fanatic into a source of information without his knowledge. Set him free to gather information for our purposes without him being aware of his involvement."

"An American Manchurian candidate?" John said.

"But for real, not a movie."

"And I fit into this how?"

"Jim wanted a . . ."

"Farris?"

"Yes. He wanted a full-scale test on the strongest candidate possible," Monroe said. "You."

"Wait," Freeman said. "Are you saying John volunteered for this shit?"

"He volunteered to be the subject when Farris explained the goals of the mission," Monroe said. "John, you were magnificent. A year is how long it took to break you down, erase your memory and break your will."

"That doesn't make sense," Freeman said. "John was selling his services. I picked him up in Japan where he was about to assassinate a dignitary and start a war."

"I know nothing of that," Monroe said. "Controlling him once the project concluded was Jim's area."

"Jim wouldn't send him to Japan on a mission like that,"

Freeman said. "You must have failed or instilled in John some secondary program or just plain fucked up."

"I assure you, Ben, that I didn't fuck anything up," Monroe said. "As far as I know, John was under total control at all times."

"Control by who?" Freeman said.

"James, of course," Monroe said.

"But that means . . . ," Freeman said. He looked at John.

"Farris sent me to Japan to start a war," John said.

"That doesn't make sense," Freeman said.

"It does if somebody benefits," John said. "A lot of money to be made supplying weapons to under-gunned countries suddenly in the middle of a war. I'd examine Jim's bank accounts if I were you."

"Doctor, is this possible?" Freeman said. "Could John have been so controlled by Farris he would go to Japan like that?"

"Hey, I'm goddamn bleeding to death here," Monroe said.

John turned and walked to the door, where he paused to set the knife on his chair. He turned and looked back at Monroe. "Your one chance to live is to pick up the knife and cut him loose," John said, opened the door and walked out.

TWENTY-FOUR

John parked the car in front of the mobile home and turned off the engine. It wasn't quite daylight yet, more that time in between dawn and sunrise where everything is shadows with a hint of light in the background.

John lit a cigarette, turned and looked at Taft. "Been a hell of a party, Captain."

"It doesn't have to end just yet," Taft said.

"It does for you," John said.

"I can get you help," Taft said. "The best doctors in New York or Minnesota. Your memory will come back intact. All it takes is time."

"That's the one thing I don't have," John said. "We both know they're not going to stop looking for me."

Taft nodded his head. "Take care, John. One thing I'm sure of is you're not the bad guy in all this."

John extended his right hand and clasped Taft's. "See you around, Captain."

Taft exited the car and walked to the door of the trailer. He knocked loudly several times and didn't turn around when John drove away. He knocked again and the door swung open.

Wearing her bathrobe, Joan looked at Taft.

"I've been thinking we should sell the house and take a nice cruise somewhere," Taft said. "What do you think?"

Midnight. The witching hour. Freeman stood on the long private dock off the southern shore of Maryland. A dense fog blocked his view of anything ten feet in front of him. In the distance, he spotted a small light. It was difficult to judge through the fog and the dark how far away the light was, but what did that matter? He would wait.

He turned his back to light a cigarette, then faced the water with the cigarette cupped to shield the tiny red ember. The light on the ocean grew closer. Somewhere, he couldn't tell the direction, a foghorn blew.

A gull sounded across the water. Waves splashed against the wood posts of the dock.

The light grew larger and stronger.

Freeman smoked the cigarette to the filter and flicked it into the water below. A powerful beam of light suddenly came on from the approaching boat. Freeman placed his hand over his eyes and scanned the fog. A six-sleeper boat slowly came into view. The engines purred softly as it made its approach to the dock.

Voices spoke softly, ropes were thrown, and someone jumped onto the dock to anchor them. Freeman stepped forward to greet the six-man team that materialized in front of him with weapons drawn.

"Hello, sir," an agent said.

"Excellent job, men," Freeman said. "There's a van at the end of the dock with the keys in it. Take a few days and rest up. James down below?"

"Yes, sir," the agent said. "We're to secure the area and escort him topside."

"I'll do that," Freeman said. "You guys take off."

"Thank you, sir," the agent said. "We could sure use the rest."

Freeman watched the six agents walk to the end of the dock, where they vanished in the pea-soup-thick fog. He heard doors open and close, and the engine of the van start. He waited until he heard the van drive away to remove his Glock pistol from its shoulder holster inside his jacket.

From a pocket, Freeman took a four-inch-long black silencer and attached it to the barrel of the Glock. He held the massive pistol by his side as he stepped over the wall of the boat onto the deck.

A staircase led below deck. Only a single bulb was lit on the table. The interior was lavish, with expensive furnishings. Freeman stood centered in the main room between the dining table and galley door. A bedroom door slid open. James Farris stepped out, dressed in a lime-green warm-up suit and white deck shoes.

For a moment, Farris didn't see Freeman standing in the shadows. He seemed startled when his eyes met Freeman's. Then a smile slowly crossed Farris' lips. "You gave me a start, Ben," Farris said. "Why didn't you announce yourself?"

"I was wondering what a boat like this cost," Freeman said.

"What are you . . . ?"

Farris paused when Freeman stepped into the light with the Glock at his side.

"You won't need that, Ben," Farris said. "We're perfectly safe. The team is right outside, waiting for . . ."

"I sent them away," Freeman said.

"Why?"

Freeman flicked his wrist as he fired the Glock, and a red stain immediately appeared in Farris' lower abdomen. Farris staggered backward, hit the table and fell into a chair.

Holding his abdomen, Farris looked at Freeman. "Are you crazy?" he said.

"Three hundred thousand, maybe more," Freeman said. "Where does a government employee get that kind of money, Jim?"

Gasping in pain, his face a twisted mask of agony, Farris looked at Freeman. "I'm gut shot here, you fucking idiot. I need a hospital."

"What you need is to tell me how millions of dollars found their way into private numbered accounts I found in your personal home computer," Freeman said.

"I need a doctor!" Farris shouted.

"You want a doctor?" Freeman said. "Go get one, you son of a bitch."

He aimed the Glock and fired one shot into Farris' left knee, then another shot into the right knee.

Farris fell from the chair to the floor, screaming.

"All you have to do is crawl off the boat to the end of the dock and wave someone down for a ride before you bleed out," Freeman said, turned and put a bullet through the boat's communications system.

"Ben, please?" Farris sobbed.

"I'd quit crying and get moving if I were you," Freeman said, turned and walked up the stairs.

On the dock, Freeman stood and watched a shadow walk toward him through the fog. The shadow walked softly, professionally. Slowly the shadow became FBI Agent Cone. He cradled a high-powered rifle in his right arm.

Freeman lit a cigarette. "Thanks for the backup."

They walked to the end of the dock. "No problem," Cone said. "So, you're top dog now?"

"I need a right-hand man," Freeman said. "You interested?"

Of all the cities in his district, Montreal was by far and away Father Simon's favorite. For many reasons. The beautiful scenery, the rolling hills and old side streets, the rich, diversified culture, magnificent churches and schools, and many more reasons too numerous to mention in a short conversation.

Simon was an accountant, the chief purse-strings puller for the province. If a church or school somewhere needed a new roof, the request went to him for approval. A few weeks ago, a request for roofing shingles and other materials for the homeless shelter came across his desk. The shelter was the largest such facility in his district, and Simon approved the request because a leaky roof going into winter was not an option. Mission director Robert Gibson explained that there was enough manpower between homeless men at the shelter and volunteers to keep labor costs to a minimum.

As Simon and Gibson toured the large facility, Simon was impressed by the work done on the roof and grounds. "How many are volunteers?" he asked as he paused to look up at the flat roof of the mission sleeping quarters.

"Well, let's see now," Gibson said as he did a quick scan. "At least twenty men are mission regulars. About a dozen are volunteers, but that number goes up or down depending on the day. Oh, see that big guy up top who looks like he could play defensive tackle in the CFL?"

Simon shielded his eyes from the sun and looked at the large man on the roof. He was shirtless and carrying an eighty-pound bundle of shingles on his shoulder as if it was a feather pillow.

"He showed up about ten days ago looking for a meal," Gibson said. "Claims to have amnesia."

"Amnesia?" Simon said.

"So he claims."

"Is it true?"

"I had the police check him out and he has no record as far as they can tell," Gibson said. "He speaks five languages and is strong as a bull, as you can see. He's also been quite handy. I've scheduled appointments at the clinic with a psychiatrist early next week."

Simon watched as the man flipped the shingles over his

shoulder and broke open the wrapping. "What's his name?" Simon asked.

"John," Gibson said. "That's all I know for now."

"Well, let me know how it turns out," Simon said. "We can't have our reputation tarnished by scandal."

"I wouldn't worry about that, but I'll keep you advised."

Simon nodded his head. "Let's go inside. It's about lunch time, isn't it?"

ABOUT THE AUTHOR

Al Lamanda is the author of *Dunston Falls* and *Walking Homeless*. A native of New York City, he resides full time in Maine.